On Bittersweet Place

"A tender— and tenderly .... ian emigre undergoing transplantation shock in t .... protagonist never sheds her guileless idealisr .... ier shed its unassuming grace." —Peter Selgin, author of *Drowning Lessons*

"In the pages of Ronna Wineberg's On Bittersweet Place, one finds echoes of Anzia Yezierska and Betty Smith; in the fictional story of Lena Czernitski's immigrant family in the first quarter of the 20th century the reader recovers a piece of our larger American history. Quite impressive." —Erika Dreifus, author of *Quiet Americans*

"A powerful evocation of the complexities of the early 20th-century immigrant experience too often sugar-coated and sentimentalized. Rich with precise period detail and iconic historical references, On Bittersweet Place brings to life the travails and triumphs of one Jewish-American family readers will not easily forget."
—Joan Leegant, author of *Wherever You Go*

"Youth is never all sweet, and On Bittersweet Place's Lena, a Russian-born Jewish teenager in 1920s Chicago, certainly has her share of troubles. The sweetness is there, though, in this heartfelt coming-of-age tale— in the tenderness of Wineberg's beautiful prose and the pluck of its resilient young heroine. A story that stays with you."
—Anne Korkeakivi, author of *An Unexpected Guest*

ALSO BY RONNA WINEBERG
Second Language

"Reading the stories in Second Language is like entering a series of complex, absorbing worlds... This is a beautifully written and deeply satisfying collection."
—Margot Livesey

"The situations of Ronna Wineberg's characters are diverse, but they circle one inescapable theme with flawless emotional accuracy: that few are fulfilled, and even fewer will live out their lives without at least trying, bravely, to make a break for it."
—Rosellen Brown

ON
BITTERSWEET
PLACE

A NOVEL

RONNA
WINEBERG

Relegation Books, USA

ISBN: 978-0-9847648-1-5
Library of Congress Control Number: 2014940559

on
bittersweet place

A NOVEL

RONNA

WINEBERG

RELEGATIONBOOKS

2014

To Daniel, Genia, and Simone,
And also to the memory of my parents

All journeys have secret destinations of which the traveler is unaware.

—Martin Buber

PROLOGUE

September 1922

The first day in the apartment on Bittersweet Place, my father carried two wooden crates to a corner of the living room. He set a wide piece of wood on top. "Desk," he said. "This is your desk, Lena." He gave me three pencils and a square black notebook. Here I began my labors in English. I was ten years old. Each night, I printed words. *Smokestacks in the sky. Rise high. Blue. Like a sea. Der yam.* The noises of the city and the apartment were my companions. The roar of the elevated train. The clatter of cars. The *landsleit* and relatives talking and arguing.

From the open window, I imagined I could see all the way to Maxwell Street, where pushcarts squeezed one next to another like squatters' houses, where the odors of sweet warm breads and foul raw chickens rose in the air. If I walked east from the apartment, I knew I would find the blue waters of Lake Michigan.

In Russia, we lived by a gray-green lake, in a white wooden house in Belilovka. What we saw then was all that we knew: the hilly green land, the smoke that flowed like ribbons from a lumber mill, my father's letters that arrived from America on thin white paper.

At my desk, I willed myself to forget the past. But the memories charged through my mind. My grandfather at the head of the table. His dark beard gleaming like satin. My grandmother next to him. My two uncles and my older brother. I felt safe in that house by the lake. Then, we'd heard drunken laughter from outside. "Cossacks.

The *Petlurias*," my mother had cried. "Go to the forest. Quick." She'd pushed my brother and me to a window in the back. We scrambled out barefoot and ran.

This was what I wanted to forget: the dark, damp forest. My brother's hand clutching mine. The smell of pine, the cold dirt beneath our feet. The scratch of weeds. We hid behind a cluster of trees in terrified silence. And then the crack of a gun and the awful screams. Later that night, I wept when I saw my grandfather slumped on the table, his arm stretched out as if he'd been offering the visitors a glass of wine.

At my desk, I told myself: Lena, stop thinking about this. Instead, I tried to concentrate on schoolwork. Then I printed in my notebook. I prepared a list. At first, I wrote in Russian. Later, as I became better at it, in English. I added and erased until my list felt exact and complete.

My Fears
by Lena Czernitski

September 15, 1922

1. I Will never speak good English
2. Will not have one American friend
3. I will be attacked on the street by an American Petluria
4. I Will lose someone dear to me
5. Will never have a home that is safe
6. Will never grow up
7. I will never ever know happiness again

I wrote my fears to try to pull them out of me. I promised myself I would find a solution for every problem. I would work hard, learn English. I would become like an American so I could have American friendships. When I had banished all my fears from my heart and mind, I would belong in this new country, I was sure. The *Goldene Medina*. This golden land. I would finally be strong and grown up.

Chicago
1925

We had all come from Russia when I was ten. That is what I told everyone I met in Chicago, as if we'd decided to come here and we did, as if we'd planned our journey with excitement, packed our suitcases, and then boarded the ship. I said my old life was in the past. I couldn't bear to tell the truth. That we—my mother and my brother, Simon, my Uncle Maurice and Uncle William—had crawled out of Russia like rats from inside the forest, on the damp dirt and prickly weeds, afraid if we were discovered, we would be shot like my grandfather had been. As if he were cattle being slaughtered by a *shochet*. "Drunken Cossacks. *Petlurias*. Peasants. They murdered him," my mother had cried. "They hate us. Hate Jews." She had dressed me in a red velvet dress and Simon in a red wool jacket a few weeks after my grandfather died, and we marched in a parade to show we believed in the Bolshevik government.

But still we weren't safe. Cossacks roamed the streets. My uncles began to sell flour and sugar in Kiev. They rode on the roof of a train to the city, bought a loaf of bread, dug out the inside, and stuffed the money they earned there. They covered the money with bread, so they wouldn't be robbed. We saved all the money we could, until finally we fled in the darkness, into the forest, leaving our white wooden house by the lake.

We slept during the day and pushed ahead at night, on foot and in a wagon. My mother bribed the guards at the Russian border. The Polish guards demanded money, too. We waited in Poland ten months while she and my uncles worked and saved. Then we sailed on the dirty, crowded ship that brought us to America, where I saw my father again.

I didn't tell anyone that my father had left Belilovka in 1914. I was two years old. After he left, the war began, and we didn't see him for eight years. I didn't mention I had no memory of him. Or that my grandfather had owned a flour mill and a place for fishing on the lake.

He employed three hundred peasants. On New Year's Eve, he gave a party for them all. I didn't explain that he was a learned and respected man, and that after the czar was overthrown, the peasants shouted, "Peace, land, and bread. Kill Jews and save Russia." Our family lost everything. Eighteen relatives of my father's and mother's were killed, too, people I was too young to remember.

Nor did I explain that on our journey to Poland I had dropped my shoe and lost it. I cried so bitterly that the man who drove us in the wagon wanted to leave me in the forest with the wolves. I never told anyone that Uncle William had clamped his hand against my mouth to muffle my cries and convinced the man to let me stay. I didn't mention we had to leave my grandmother and aunt in Belilovka. They came to Chicago on their own difficult journey. And I didn't tell anyone that my parents argued loudly in Yiddish at night now. Or that my mother sometimes wept as she sat at her sewing machine in the small bedroom where she worked on the mending she did for pay.

I never explained this about my family. I never explained the past. I smiled instead.

It was enough that anyone who visited us saw that my parents, my brother and I, and my two uncles lived in a tiny apartment, crammed together like the sardines Uncle Maurice ate for breakfast. My family spoke with raw, choppy accents. In the evening Uncle William sang *Ochi Chyornye* and other sad Russian songs.

Once, and only once, I brought home a friend from school. She had blue eyes and silky blond hair. "This is where you live?" Mary Hall asked as we climbed the stairs in the dusty stairwell. I nodded as we walked into the dim square apartment entry. She gazed at the scratched wooden floor, at the yellowed photograph of my grandfather hanging on the wall, in his black coat and tall black yarmulke, with his long, dark beard. She inhaled the sharp scent of boiled cabbage and onions. She winced.

"Yes," I said uneasily. "We live here."

She glanced at the glass cup with the golden handle and the chipped blue porcelain ballerina. My mother had carried these with her from Russia. They sat displayed on the small wobbly table in our entry. Then

Mary Hall stared down the narrow hallway that led to the bedrooms. Pairs of old shoes stood lined there, like tired brothers, one next to the other. She giggled. "Oh, I'm sorry. I don't know what I'm laughing about. Let's go in."

"No, wait here," I stammered. My face felt hot with shame. I ran to my desk to find the assignment for school she had asked to borrow.

Then I hurried back and handed her the sheet of paper. "I just remembered, my brother is sick," I said. "My mother says you can't stay here. You might get sick, too."

"Oh, no," Mary Hall said. "I'll visit another time."

But I knew she wouldn't. I pulled open the door and watched her leave. I longed to be like her and the other girls at school, with their beautiful blond hair. They were lucky. Blessed to have grown up in one place. They had no problems. But I was nothing like them at all.

Every night, our living room was filled with *landsleit*—countrymen, who also came from Russia—and with my mother's family. The room burst with conversation and noise. It seemed to me that my father had married not only my mother, but her family, too. He had come to Chicago in 1914 because his cousin lived here, but the cousin later moved away. My father's relatives lived in New Jersey, and his parents had died before I was born, but my mother was the oldest of six, with three brothers and two sisters.

Evenings, I sat at my desk, the wide wooden board balanced on two crates. I tried to concentrate on schoolwork. But the noise interrupted me. My father had built Simon a desk, too, in the opposite corner from mine. Simon's desk was usually empty. He was fifteen, two years older than I was, and he came home late every night. He did his school assignments in the bedroom, sitting on the floor. He insisted on being alone, although I begged him to let me join him.

While the *landsleit* talked and smoked cigarettes, I perched in my corner and planned my secret future. I would become a great artist, I vowed to myself, and find a grand love. He and I would run away together and live where it was silent and safe and beautiful. We wouldn't argue like my parents did. We would earn money, and I could help my family. We would never set foot on Bittersweet Place again.

Truthfully, I didn't know where I'd find this grand love. And I didn't know if I could draw. But I was determined to try.

Uncle Abie Rubolsky, my mother's brother, often came to our apartment. He was heavy, with a big belly and narrow eyes like slits. He loved to drink whiskey and *schnapps*. Aunt Ida, his wife, visited, too. Thin, with sunken brown eyes like craters and a small nose, she lounged on our old blue sofa, reciting poetry in a wobbly voice. She always carried a book, written in Russian or English. Aunt Feyga, who had stayed behind in Russia with my grandmother, joined us. She had scraggly gray hair and large uneven breasts that heaved when she laughed. My mother brought sewing into our living room and stitched clothing there and talked.

But my grandmother didn't visit us. She lived with Aunt Feyga now and was old and tired. She never left her apartment at night.

Neighbors stopped by, too, like Mr. Usher Cohen, a short, sour man with an arrogant manner, a man who, my father said, was a great success in business. Mr. Cohen had small green eyes and wide, chapped lips. He was rich, and I envied this. He wore trousers and vests of fine wools and soft cottons. But he had only one hand, the left one. He'd lost the other in an accident in a lumber mill in Russia. Even so, he played cards at our apartment. I tried not to stare at his smooth right stump. He and Uncle Maurice insisted on playing for money. My father refused. Whiskey and *schnapps* and vodka, the snap of pinochle cards, the smells of onions and *shmaltz* rose in the rooms. Uncle William sang in his sweet, mournful voice. He wanted to become a singer. We were his audience.

In our family, each person was so different, one from the other. Sometimes I sat at my desk and looked around the living room. What was each person's true nature? I wondered. What did they think in their hearts? What made Uncle Abie speak in a booming voice and Uncle William sing? Why did Aunt Ida always read a book? All of this made me question what my own true nature was and what kind of journey I'd have to take to find out. I wanted to put everyone and every object on paper. My father's crown of wavy red hair. My mother's sad brown eyes. Simon's confident smile. The tall brass lamp with its bright white pleated shade, like a flapper's skirt.

When I tried to draw Aunt Feyga's plump face or the long, slouching shape of the blue sofa and its round, shadowy arms instead of doing schoolwork, my mother somehow knew. "Stop staring and making useless marks on paper, Lena," she said, standing at my desk.

"They're not useless," I muttered. "They're art."

Uncle William was my mother's youngest brother, and I loved him dearly, not only for putting his hand over my mouth on the wagon that terrible night in Russia, but because of the way he spoke to me and looked at me, with kindness, as though he understood the real me, my true nature, saw what was in my heart. Uncle Maurice had none of William's sweetness.

In Russia, Uncle Maurice had worked in the lumber mill. He drank whiskey with Cossacks. His name had been Moshe Rubolsky there, but now that we lived in America, he insisted the family call him Maurice. "The name is French," he explained. "In America, my name is Maurice Roberts." His voice was deep, as if he were a radio announcer. His coarse brown mustache spilled over his lips. He wore his sandy hair slicked back. Uncle Maurice's smile was wide, his teeth large and uneven. Those on the bottom were stained yellow. He brushed them often to try to polish them.

He went out with one lady friend after another. The women he brought to the apartment had big breasts and wore tight wool sweaters and touched my uncle's hand.

My mother often looked at her brother with impatience. "Be a *mensch*," she told Uncle Maurice when he stumbled into the apartment reeking of the same terrible smells, drinking with women instead of Cossacks. "Be a *mensch* to those women and grow up for God's sake."

But my mother loved her family, especially her brothers. One night she was talking to Uncle Maurice in the living room. I was at my desk. The others were in the kitchen. The living room was drafty, and the radiator clanked and spewed out heat.

"Reesa," Uncle Maurice was saying. "I know how we can make money. You must trust me. I can lift us out of this awful life. I promise you."

I glanced up. His eyes were green, the color of spring leaves, and his smile seemed to charm my mother and sometimes even me.

My mother frowned and shook her head.

"Make her listen to me, Lena," he called out.

"She is listening," I said.

"No. Make her do what I say." He turned to my mother.

I went back to my history book.

"What's the worry?" he said to her. "I'll talk to Chaim. I have a plan. Aren't you my sister, my blood? I want the best for you, for everyone. I want to help the family."

"Stop your dreams, Maurice. Work at the laundry more. That is how you will help the family."

"I'm going to do better things with my life than that."

He worked in the family business, the Granville Laundry. My father and the other relatives worked there, too.

"I do not want to hear your stories, Maurice," my mother said. She placed a hand on top of his. "You, of all of us, are made for this new country. America is like the finest piece of clothing and fits you perfectly. William has a soft soul, and for him, I worry. But you. You are smart. Strong. Brash. Use your luck."

"Not luck. Skill, I have skill. Reesa, Reesa. You don't see the world for what it is."

"I see more than I want to."

"So we have the Prohibition here? I bring you whiskey and vodka and *schnapps* when Chaim cannot get them—things you can't buy in a store."

"You do. And I do not ask where you find these things."

"In America there is always a way to solve a problem. Even so, our father would never want us to live this life. Like beggars. Stinking beggars. He turns over in his grave. I hear him grumble at night. But enough. Let's go to the kitchen for more vodka and *schnapps*."

"Lena," my mother said, as if she'd just realized I was in the room, too. "Go to bed."

I went to the bedroom I shared with Simon and Uncle William. Simon wasn't home yet. Though I often doubted my mother's wisdom and opinions, in this case she was right, I thought. Uncle Maurice was made for this country. He even looked the most American of all of us with the clothing he bought from Goldblatt's, the department store, instead of from a cart on Maxwell Street. He was smart. He'd ridden on the roof of the train to Kiev. He'd guided us out of Belilovka, into the forest, as if we were a band of Cossacks, and he was our leader. He knew how to get along in the world, like Mr. Usher Cohen did.

Voices rose from the kitchen, and I heard the clink of glasses.

I didn't know what my uncle's plan was, but I would listen when he told us, and study him carefully. I would learn from him, I decided, so I would be made for this new country, too.

An Invitation
October 1925

It was a cool fall afternoon. Rain-washed brown and yellow leaves clung to the trees. The storm had shaken some of the branches bare, and the air smelled fresh. My schoolbooks were piled in a canvas satchel slung over my shoulder.

Miss Healy, my teacher this year, had assigned work to complete at home. I was eager to get started. She was a tall, plump woman with bobbed gray hair. She was strict, but not unkind, and she always wore gray—the same steel-gray dress and coat.

Most days, like today, I walked or rode the streetcar by myself and returned from school without my brother. Simon was unhappy to be my escort. He was taller than me and skinny. My mother said he grew taller every day, that he was all arms and legs. Once a week, she peered at his trousers to see if he had outgrown them again. He looked like my father, with wavy red hair and pale blue eyes, the same fair skin dotted with tiny freckles, like dust. I missed being with Simon. After my father left Belilovka, Simon had taken care of me. But Simon didn't seem to miss me now. He usually went to the Jewish Center after school to play basketball with friends. Sometimes he helped Mr. Usher Cohen with his business until late, moving heavy boxes to a car for delivery.

Besides Uncle William, Simon was the one person in our family who could understand me, I thought, and I could understand him. He and I had shared that terrible night in Belilovka. But he didn't want to talk about much of anything now.

"Lena," he'd said this morning. We were in our coats, leaving for school. "You always want to talk about that night in the forest or the family or something."

"I do not," I'd said.

"Well, I've got important things to do. School and work, and I want to be a swell basketball player."

"You do?"

"Yeah. I don't have time to stand around and talk to you."

"We used to talk all the time," I'd said, disappointed. "We did everything together. Don't you remember, Simon?"

"It's true. We did. But those were the old days." He'd grinned and hurried ahead of me, out the door.

The school was six blocks from our apartment, a beige brick building set back from the street. I was the tallest in my class and the oldest. I hated this and felt ashamed. When my parents first enrolled me there, I was just learning English. The principal assigned me to the youngest group. I felt then as if I'd been brought to another new country, with rules and people I didn't understand. But I kept to myself and worked hard. I was surprised to find that English was easy for me. I learned quickly, which was a great relief. I loved the sounds. The words seemed like a song. I repeated them over and over. I read books from school again and again. My father helped Simon and me with assignments. Each year, I'd been promoted, sometimes three grades in one year. I was proud of this. But it wasn't enough. I was in sixth grade now. I should have been in eighth grade. I was determined to be placed with students my own age, and then I wanted to skip beyond them. Even if I hadn't found a grand love or become a great artist, I would finish high school and run away from home.

There were a few other older girls in my class, Mary Hall and Elka Amsall. I didn't know the reason for this. I didn't ask. What happened at school and why was a mystery to me.

Today after school, I walked home along Broadway, a big, commercial street, almost like a village. There was a butcher shop, a fishmonger, a grocery, bakeries, dry goods and hardware stores. I liked to look through the windows into the stores. Women and men with bundles rushed past me along the sidewalk.

After a while Broadway split in two, and I followed the arm that became Clarendon Avenue until I reached our street.

Bittersweet Place was just one long block and narrow like a snake, a street that went nowhere, I thought. It stopped at Clarendon to the west and at what my father called "the street with no name" to the east. Our street had such an odd name, not a beautiful one like others in the neighborhood, Belle Plaine or Cornelia. I wondered how something could be both bitter and sweet, and why we had to end up here at all.

The rain began to pick up, and I hurried home. Tall trees grew on both sides of our street. I hurried past the brick buildings that stood close together like relatives. The red brick building where we lived was in the middle of the block. Weeds grew in the small front yard. Four steps led up to our building. Inside, I climbed the three flights of stairs in the dingy stairwell, opened our apartment door, and stepped in slowly.

Often, like today, no one was at home. I hated arriving alone. I always switched on every light in every room, then sat and tried to calm myself. "You are in the kitchen on Bittersweet Place," I told myself. "In Chicago, Illinois. You are not a little girl; you are not in Russia. You are thirteen years old. Almost grown up. Your mother will be home soon, your father, and your brother. You are safe. Lena, you are *not* alone."

Now I stopped in our long, narrow hallway. On each side of the hallway were doors. First was the bedroom I shared with Simon and Uncle William. Next was my parents' bedroom, then the bathroom. A tiny, closet-like space stood next, barely big enough for the bed where Uncle Maurice slept. The living room stood across the hall from the bedrooms. At the end of the hall was the kitchen. The living room opened onto a sleeping porch. Simon or my uncles spent the night there in mild weather.

The apartment was silent and empty. I tried to banish my fear. I performed my ritual of switching on every light and reminding myself where I was and who I was. Then I realized I loved the silence. The radiator spewed out heat and warmed the rooms. The apartment seemed twice as large as it normally did now that I was the only one there. This silence seemed like a gift from God, as if God were tapping me on the shoulder and whispering, "See, Lena Czernitski, this silence is for you, so you can think whatever you want, decide what and who you want to be. Right now, you don't have to talk to another soul."

I smiled in response to this thought and set my books on my desk. Then I flopped onto the sofa. I pulled off my hat and coat, damp from the rain. Mud covered my brown-strapped shoes. I unbuckled them, slipped them off, and saw that my legs were splattered with mud, too.

Bathing was still a luxury to me. I loved sitting in the white claw-foot tub, the hot water lapping over my skin. I loved the sweet scent of soap, the very act of washing, spreading soap on my body, rubbing it until the suds bubbled on my arms, on my legs.

In the bathroom, I switched on the faucet and filled the tub. Then I peeled off my clothing and stepped in, sinking into the wonderful warm water. I bathed with great patience, scrubbing every inch of myself, pushing my thick brown curls back from my face. I scrubbed my shoulders twice—they were my favorite attribute. I glanced down and studied the swelling on my chest, the two cones of flesh, my breasts. My God, I thought, as I did each time I looked there now. It's really happened. I plunged deep into the water. Then I climbed out of the tub and wrapped myself in a thick white towel.

The towel was the most luxurious one we owned. My mother had purchased it from a store, not from a cart on Maxwell Street; the fabric felt soft, not stiff like the others. It wasn't really mine to use. But I would borrow it, I told myself. After all, I was growing up. I could bathe by myself. I could stay alone in the apartment, enjoy this silence, and not be afraid.

Wrapped in the towel, I strolled out of the bathroom into the long hallway of our apartment, pleased with myself. It was then that I saw Uncle Maurice.

He stood at the other end of the hall, in his black wool tweed overcoat. "Home from school?" he said. He smiled and gazed at me from head to toe.

"Yes." I smiled weakly, startled. I hadn't heard him come into the apartment. "What happened to your work?" I asked. Uncle Maurice hated the laundry. Last week he had threatened to quit again, and I wondered if he finally had. He always complained about the angry customers, the terrible heat, the piles of dirty clothing rancid with sweat.

"Temporary problems, honey. Nothing to worry about. It all comes out in the wash." He laughed, as if he'd told a joke.

"Oh," I said.

We stood looking at one another.

Then he ambled toward me. Coins rattled in his pocket. Suddenly, for no reason I could understand, I became afraid. He was my uncle, I told myself. He was made for this new country. There was no reason to be afraid. I clutched the towel around me tightly.

"C'mere, honey," he said. "God in heaven, you've grown up. Soon boys will be chasing you."

"I don't want boys to chase me," I said. I took a few steps backward. The elevated train roared outside.

"Come here and let me see how you've grown." His voice sounded husky, like a purr, as if he were suddenly an animal, a cat. I imagined he had fur; his large hands and the dark strands of hair there looked like fur. I imagined he wasn't my uncle, just an alley cat.

"I haven't grown," I said. "I'm still a child."

"Still a child." His voice was harsh, not sweet like Uncle William's. He stood so close to me that I could smell his stale breath, the odor of cigarettes and whiskey. He began to hum then, a melody without variation.

I took another step backward. "I have to do my schoolwork now," I said. I turned away from him to go to my room.

But he reached out, gripped my wrist, and wrenched my hand from the towel. The cloth fell from my body.

I stared at him and could not think. My eyes felt as if they might leap from my head. I remembered how Simon and I had fled to the woods the night my grandfather was shot. I didn't think then, either. I had done what I was told.

"That's it," he said. "Stand still." Uncle Maurice was bending toward me. I was frozen to the spot where I stood. His large hands touched me; the hairy fingers slid across my chest, cold fingers, like the barrel of a gun, to my breasts, to my belly, and my legs. I shivered. He began to stick his finger inside me, as if he wanted to poke all the way up to my heart.

I jumped back. "Don't," I screeched, but my voice stuck in my throat. "My God, don't."

"Don't be afraid." He embraced me and pushed me against the wall. His damp overcoat scratched against my skin. His hot breath blew in my ear. His belt buckle was hard and cold. "People are God's language," he murmured. "Nothing to be afraid of, *mama shayna.*"

I couldn't breathe, and I prayed my mother would come home and save me. Uncle Maurice was so much bigger than I was, like a *Petluria*, a Cossack, with his wild mustache and his rough laugh.

"Don't," I shouted in panic. "Stop that." I hit my fist against his back.

He grabbed my arm and squeezed it. With his other hand, he unzipped his pants, jammed my hand inside them, and rubbed my fingers against his hard, bumpy skin.

I gasped and yanked my hand away.

"Nothing to be afraid of," he said, gripping my arm. He bent and kissed the cone of my breast. "We won't tell anyone," he whispered. "It's our secret. Our people need secrets to live." Then he sucked in a breath, bit his lip, and trudged to his bedroom.

I grabbed the towel from the floor, flung it around me, and ran to the bathroom, beginning to sob, but I bit my lip to force myself to be quiet. I slammed the door shut. My God, what had he done? I stared at myself in the mirror, my brown eyes blotched and puffy with tears, my brown curls falling limply to my shoulders, the soft white towel wrapped around my body. What had I been thinking? I had, after all, been in the hallway, in this towel, parading about half-naked, as my uncle might say. Perhaps, to him that was invitation enough.

"You can't know about people from the outside," my mother said three days later. She pointed to herself. Her thick black hair with its gray streaks was pulled into a bun. A yellow flowered apron hung over her drab green housedress, and her large breasts, swollen like bread dough, pushed into the coarse fabric. She had big, solid bones. She and I were in the kitchen. A pile of clothing to mend sat on a chair. "You don't know the diamonds inside the heart. You don't know the *tsuris*," she went on. "Lena, no matter how people look, in their souls everyone has troubles of one kind or another."

I nodded and thought about Uncle Maurice.

My mother held a spool of white thread and a button to sew onto the white cotton blouse I was wearing. She snapped off a long piece of thread and pressed it into my hand. "Chew on this," she ordered. "I don't wish to sew out your brains."

I stuffed the thread into my mouth, but didn't chew it. In the past, I had done what my mother told me to do. She'd warned that if she sewed my clothing while I wore it, she would stitch out my brains unless I chomped on thread. I'd believed this would keep me safe. Now I knew better. Nothing kept you safe.

"That's just a story, a dumb superstition," I said to her. "It's stupid. You can't sew out someone's *brains*." I spit out the thread and threw it onto the table.

My mother stitched in silence. Finally, she broke the thread from the button. "There," she said. "Done."

Then she turned to the wooden board on the countertop and began to slice a yellow onion, as if chopping wood.

I longed to tell her about Uncle Maurice. But I had lost my voice. I had been losing it ever since we left Russia, and now that I'd felt my uncle's cold hands on my skin I could no longer speak from my heart. I could talk, but not about important things. My heart was underground. I was growing up in private, I realized, growing up alone.

My mother scooped a handful of onions and sprinkled them into the frying pan. Grease crackled and splattered. The sharp odor stung my eyes. I blinked hard. You can't know the troubles, I thought. You can't begin to know what's in my heart.

I sat at the round kitchen table and took a sip from my glass of milk. I debated how to begin. I would say in a strong, confident voice: When you weren't home after school, Uncle Maurice looked at me and he—I couldn't bear to say it. No. This would confirm all that had happened—the roar of the elevated train; Uncle Maurice's ugly, hairy fingers touching me; the awful feel of him. I didn't want this to be real.

My mother slapped a slab of raw liver into the frying pan. The meat sizzled. "What is on your mind?" She eyed me with concern. "Why are you sitting, Lena, staring? Don't. Your face is like a herring. Your frown scares me. You looked for a moment like someone who is not well. Who is trying to speak, but cannot." She pointed to her forehead. "Not well in the head."

"I'm trying to say nothing," I replied. Uncle Maurice belonged in a hospital for crazy people. My mother didn't know my thoughts, thank goodness. I forced a smile and hoped that what she said wasn't a curse, an omen of what would happen to me. "I was wondering about people," I said carefully. "What they think about when they do things."

"They think about everything," she said.

"If you do something that makes another person act…" I stopped. "Makes a person act badly. Makes someone do something that's very wrong. Does that make *you* bad?"

"I do not understand." She frowned. "Tell me an example. Can you tell me a story about this?"

"I have no story." I licked a drop of milk from the rim of the glass.

"Open your mouth and speak, Lena. If someone asks you a question, this is an invitation to say what is in your heart. It is difficult to get such an invitation." She rubbed her greasy hands against her apron. "You are too shy. Your head is full of cotton. You must talk to people. I want to help you. How will you live in the world?"

"I talk plenty," I said. "Sometimes people need quiet. To think their thoughts."

She placed another onion on the wooden board.

I wasn't shy, I wanted to tell her. I was only thinking about Uncle Maurice and hoping he would die at the family laundry. The best jobs were in the front, behind the long wooden counter. You could talk to customers there. In the back stood the hot pressing machines, like giant monsters. Heat rose everywhere. The foul smells of sweat on other people's clothing could suffocate you. I wanted Uncle Maurice to suffocate there.

My mother sighed. She faced me. "I will give you tea."

Tea has that sweet orange scent, she often told me, like the tea from the old country.

"*Di'alte haim*," she said now. "How we used to drink tea in the house by the lake. On the long oak table. We had a good life there. Your grandmother was young and strong. In Belilovka, people knew one another. We shared our lives, our souls. Do you remember, Lena?"

She rested her hand on my shoulder. Her skin was rough from her sewing work. I stared at the gray that threaded through her hair and thought about the girls at school who had been born here and lived in one place. They had always been safe. "Sometimes I feel so…not loved," I blurted out.

"Not loved?" My mother's eyes widened. "Never."

The ping of anguish rose in her voice. Her thick black eyebrows arched together, as if she were in terrible pain. She sank into the chair next to mine. "We love you like life itself, Lena. Phhh, phhh," she said and spit, to chase away an evil eye that might make my words come true. "Don't you know? Everything we do, we do for you." She threw her arms around me and pulled me onto her lap. "When you're unhappy, think about another time," she said. "This is what I think: In Belilovka, we had the horses, white linens, and furs. My beautiful black Persian lamb coat. The mill my father owned. The glass cups with the golden handles. It was ours. Do you remember?" She held me so close I was afraid she might never let go.

I opened my mouth to tell her about Uncle Maurice.

"Hush." Her breath smelled of bitter onions and dark tea; her skin was fragrant with the scent of rose soap. "The family is the most important thing," she said. "I thank God every day for them. That's your problem, Lena. You are not grateful enough."

When we were new to America, I wanted her comfort, but as I grew older I hugged her because I longed to please her, so that she might stop weeping by her sewing machine, so that she and my father wouldn't yell their Yiddish words. Now I understood I could only please her with silence.

"I'm too old for hugs. I'm almost grown up," I said. "You don't see me. Look at me, Mama. Take a good look at me."

But on her lap I felt helpless and small, like I'd felt with Uncle Maurice. She just folded her arms around me; her hands pressed against my back and pinched into my skin.

"I hate to let you out in this city," she whispered. Her tears burned my cheek. "Here, with us, you are safe. There, in the world, in the city, you can be swallowed up."

I heard the roar of the elevated train. My mother leaned her head against mine and began to sing softly, *Ochi Chyornye*, the song Uncle William sang. Her voice was sweet and sad like his. Her arms anchored me, as if they were a noose around my body. I vowed to myself I would grow up and leave her—the past and Belilovka—far behind. Erase it from memory. I would never live my mother's life. I hated her life, and I hated mine.

As she hugged me, I felt my own ping of anguish and betrayal. Of shame. Fear shimmied inside me. Even so, I gathered all my strength. "You're wrong, Mama," I cried. "No one is safe here anymore. Just wait. You'll see."

I saw that she couldn't help me. No one in my family could, so I would have to help myself. I pushed away from her arms, jumped from her lap, and ran to my room.

The First American
January–February, 1926

Leah Grace was almost three years old, but she had already become our family's future. She had been born in Chicago. Soft golden curls crowned her head. Where she had gotten that sunny color, I didn't know. Her parents—Aunt Razel, my mother's sister, and Uncle Charlie—like most of our family, had coarse, dark hair, the heavy tangled coils of Russians. Perhaps because Leah Grace had been born here, she looked like an American, with her pale green eyes, a small upturned nose, and golden hair. This country changed you, even at birth.

Sometimes I took care of my cousin when her parents were busy. Aunt Razel gave me candy or invited me to stay for dinner in return. Our family shared everything—food, time, possessions. We often ate dinner with the aunts and uncles. My aunts loaned my mother their clothing. She gave them hers. Everyone worked at the Granville Laundry. We knew no one would take advantage of anyone else. You always helped a relative, and you knew a relative would help you.

I now knew this was not true of Uncle Maurice. After my terrible encounter with him, I despised him. I wouldn't talk to him or look at him when he spoke to me. I wouldn't stay in a room alone with him. I didn't confide to anyone about what he'd done. He hadn't tried to touch me again, and I didn't know if he would, but I was afraid that he might. I'd been lucky, though; these last months my mother had been at home working on her sewing repairs when I returned from school. But she had started to make her deliveries of mending in the afternoons again, leaving me alone in the empty and dangerous apartment.

I felt I had to make a plan to be sure I was safe. So today I told her I didn't want to come home and stay by myself in the apartment.

"You are fourteen years old now," she replied. "You act like a child younger than Leah Grace. I don't understand why you will not come home when no one is here."

It was January and cold outside. My mother was baking a cake filled with raisins and apples. She had baked this same cake on my birthday. It was my only celebration. I had turned fourteen in October, three weeks after my awful experience with Uncle Maurice.

Flour coated her hands. The scent of cinnamon fluttered in the kitchen, and heat from the oven warmed the room.

"I'd rather go to the laundry after school," I said.

My mother's hair was wound into a loose bun. She wore her green cotton housedress, and it billowed around her stocky body. Her brown eyes were large, and her face with its creamy skin and long, narrow nose was pretty, although she rarely smiled. "Explain why to me," she said.

"I want to be with people," I said. "I want to be in the world. It's too lonely here. I can go to Aunt Razel's, too, and help with Leah Grace. Yes, that's exactly what I'll do. You let Simon go wherever he wants."

"I do not understand you, Lena." My mother shook her head and rubbed her hands on her housedress. "You never listen. Not to me. You will not progress in life if you are so full of your own thoughts. Simon is older than you. And if you spend time with Leah Grace, you will go backward. She is a child. The most beautiful I have seen. But a baby."

"Reesa, it's enough," my father said. He walked into the kitchen. The *Chicago Tribune* lay folded beneath his arm. "If she wants to go to the laundry or visit Leah Grace, why not? What's the harm in it?"

"There is plenty of harm," she said.

"I don't think so." He turned to me. "Come, Lena. I have a moment to read with you before dinner."

In the living room, my father pulled Simon's chair next to mine, sat down, and spread the newspaper on my desk. I sat next to him.

"Let's see what we can learn," he said, skimming a page. "It seems America may join the World Court, but we will need to wait to see if this happens. The Senate, in our capitol, will vote on this."

"My teacher told us that, too."

"Good. Then you know." He thumbed through the pages. My father had learned to read and write in English when he first came to Chicago, he often told us.

"Here," he said, tapping a finger on the newspaper. "Here's an article about a book." He read aloud:

> Literary Spotlight by Fanny Butcher. *An American Tragedy.* To me, Theodore Dreiser's books have no beauty. They are always badly written. Mr. Dreiser has no more sense of the beauty of words than he has of...

"But Papa, this sounds like a terrible book," I interrupted.

"This is one opinion, Lena. It's important to learn about books, even ones you will never read. This will help you in school. Now you read to me."

I did, and the few times I stumbled on a word, he corrected me.

Despite my mother's objections, on the days Simon was not available after school, which was almost every day, I rode the streetcar to the Granville Laundry and sat on one of the wooden chairs placed in the front for customers. My father stood behind the long counter and helped people who brought in clothing. I did my schoolwork. Some days I walked home from school and then went a few blocks farther to Belle Plaine Avenue and Leah Grace's apartment.

My aunt and uncle liked this new arrangement. I did, too. So I stopped going to the laundry. Leah Grace ran to the door to greet me. "I want to see the lake," she would say. She laughed and placed her small hand in mine. She always wore a brightly colored cotton dress and a ribbon in her hair. Often, I had so much schoolwork to do that I said no to her suggestion, and I sat in their living room, working on my assignments. It felt cozy in the apartment with my cousin. Leah Grace nestled next to me on the sofa, leaned her head against my arm, and drew lines on a piece of paper.

When she grasped my hand and smiled, she seemed to me like a living *Goldene Medina*. She was the reason we'd fled through the forest and waited in Poland until we could board the ship for America. She would be safe as my grandfather hadn't been. No one in the family said this, but I knew they believed it. Unlike me, she was cleansed of the old. She was lucky, like the girls at school, who were blessed to grow up in one place.

Even her name was part American: Grace. Aunt Razel had read the name in the *Chicago Tribune.*

Leah Grace had been born in our apartment. It was a moment of happiness for our family.

My mother had been excited about a new baby. She'd lost a child in Russia before Simon was born, she told us one afternoon, a baby girl, who died of a fever. I had listened, surprised. My mother's voice had ached with a quiet sadness, as if she still carried that sorrow in her heart.

On a Sunday morning, Aunt Razel and Uncle Charlie had come to the apartment. My aunt's stomach looked so round and large that it seemed the skin might burst. My mother made tea, and Aunt Razel slumped into the sofa, shuddered, and shut her eyes. After awhile, she clutched her stomach and moaned. My mother whispered to my father and Uncle Charlie. She told Simon and me to go outside.

He and I sat on the steps of our building in the breezy March sunshine.

"We'll have a new cousin soon," I said with excitement.

"It will be the first American in the family," he said. "Not fake like us."

"Do you think you're fake, Simon?"

"Lena. Everything I say isn't the law."

He stood up, and I did, too. We went to Broadway and wandered in the stores.

Later, my father was waiting for us at home, outside. "She is a girl," he beamed. "Come, children. There was no time for a hospital."

A stale odor floated in my parents' bedroom, and damp towels were piled on the floor. The shades were pulled shut. Aunt Razel was asleep in the bed. Sweat glistened like tears on her forehead. A baby wrapped in a towel lay sleeping in her arms.

Wisps of golden hair curled on the baby's head. She had rosy, soft skin, a small nose and eyes, and lovely miniature lips. Her toes peeked out from the bottom of the towel like tiny pale peas.

"Let your aunt rest," my mother whispered.

In the living room, the relatives had gathered. My father poured *schnapps* for everyone, even for Simon and me.

"To our first American," my father said, raising his glass. "This is a great event for our family."

"May she always bring us joy," said Uncle Abie. "And have a life of good health."

"A life of adventure," Uncle Maurice said.

Everyone raised their glasses and drank. Simon swallowed his *schnapps* in one gulp, like a man. I drank mine, too, but I sputtered and coughed.

"The Almighty has been good to us," my mother had chimed in. "She is a blessing, this child, to our family, and for Razel and Charlie."

Then we'd heard the baby's cries, and my mother had hurried to help my aunt.

One day, Leah Grace and I were sitting on the sofa. I had to write an essay for school entitled "Five Interesting and Important Facts about the Civil War." I had written only two facts so far.

"Lena, can you draw a tree?" she asked. She was drawing circles on paper.

"I'll try," I said. I set aside the assignment. In my book satchel I found more paper. I drew a wide tree trunk, a pattern of lines for bark, and branches that stretched outward like pairs of thin, bony arms. Since it was winter, I didn't put leaves on the tree. I printed:

TREE. "I'll teach you to spell," I said. "T-R-E-E."

"Tree," she repeated. She scribbled on her paper. "This is a flower. Can you make one?"

Her drawing looked like a wobbly circle, but I said, "That's nice. I'll draw one, too."

I drew on my paper until the lines became shapes and finally two flowers with petals like tear drops. I drew long stems and large leaves that pointed upward. I tried to imagine sunlight brushing against the leaves, and I tapped the pencil against the paper to make dots for shadows. I was happy with the drawing. I printed: FLOWER.

"Oh, that's pretty, Lena. Can you teach my dolls to draw?" She raced to her room and returned with a pile of cloth dolls dressed in white taffeta skirts my mother had sewn. Leah Grace lined up the dolls on the sofa, our companions.

"Do they have names?" I asked.

"No." She shook her head, frowning.

"We'll give them names." And we did. Beatrice and Leonora, Isadora and Lillian. We taught them to spell "flower" and "tree." When I finished my assignment, I helped Leah Grace place the dolls in a single neat row on her bedroom floor.

I ate dinner there that night as I often did, part of my plan to avoid Uncle Maurice.

California

March–May 1926

In our family we relied on our own remedies. We never consulted doctors, except when required by the school. For colds, sore throats, fevers—for everything really—we drank guggle muggle, a concoction of warm milk, raw egg, whiskey, honey, lemon, cinnamon, and other spices my mother added. This had a sharp, tart taste and burned my throat. But our illnesses always passed.

Aunt Razel was a thin, nervous woman with narrow lips. She styled her coarse dark hair into perfect curls. Her red lipstick bled over her lips and into her skin. She said to my mother one March afternoon in our kitchen, "Leah Grace has a frail nature. She is always tired, Reesa. I have decided to have a doctor look at her."

"You will make problems where there are none," my mother said. They sat next to each other at the table, drinking tea. "Leah Grace will be fine. If you worry so much, what you imagine will come true. God help us then."

Aunt Razel spit, to ward off the evil eye, and I plunged my hands into the sink of hot, soapy water. For once, I agreed with my mother. I saw nothing frail about Leah Grace.

At school the next day, during recess, I thought about Aunt Razel's words. A cement yard opened in front of the building. Windows stared out in pairs from the school like sets of eyes. I stood by myself in the yard. Boys and girls mingled nearby. Mary Hall waved me over to her group. I nodded, but took my time joining her.

Aunt Razel *was* making problems where there were none, I thought. For once, my mother was right. But what if Leah Grace needed a doctor? Would my aunt find one who could help? The nurse at school sent students to doctors. I would ask her. She was Irish, but I didn't think this would make a difference. Most of the teachers had Irish names, like Monahan, Farrell, or O'Shaunessey, or

American ones, like Marshall or Grubb.

Today was windy, a true late-winter day. The sun was shining, and the sky was blue, but the air was cold. I dug my hands into my coat pockets and walked toward Mary Hall and the girls who stood with her. She was friendly sometimes, but I remembered how she'd laughed when she saw our apartment. I supposed she could be cruel again.

Three boys strutted past me. One of them stopped in front of me. "Ugly Jew," he sneered. "Russian pig."

I stared at him in fury. I wanted to punch him and his stupid blond hair. My face became hot. "Shut up, you fool," I spat out. "Just shut up." I swung around to join the girls.

The boys laughed behind me.

Just then, Miss Healy clapped her hands. She stood by the building, in her gray dress and gray coat, flanked by serious Miss Marshall and stooped Mr. Bender, the principal.

"Lena Czernitski. Elka Amsall," Miss Healy shouted. "Mary Hall." A long gold chain dangled around her neck. Her glasses were pinned to the chain. She raised the spectacles to her eyes and peered at us. "Are you bothering Philip Schloss and the other boys? Stop it. And boys, stop laughing at the girls. Silence. I want complete silence. It's time to go inside."

Mary Hall rolled her eyes. "That's just swell," she whispered. "We didn't do anything wrong."

I shrugged, but didn't answer. I didn't want to create problems here. I wasn't going to tell anyone what the boy had said to me, either.

Miss Healy led us in two straight lines into the building, to a large dimly lit room for our assembly. Every two weeks the music teacher, Miss Farrell, taught us group singing. We sang songs like "Onward Christian Soldiers" and "Holy, Holy, Holy," or "America the Beautiful."

We took our seats. I sat between Mary Hall and an empty chair. Miss Healy directed the hateful boy with the blond hair to go to the empty seat beside me.

I winced, but said nothing.

"All of you have to learn to get along," she said to us sternly. "I don't want whispering or talking. Fold your hands on your laps. I want to hear everyone singing every word. That means you, Lena Czernitski, and you, Philip Schloss." Miss Healy sat with the other teachers in the row in front of us.

I bit my lip and stared straight ahead.

Miss Farrell walked to the center of the room, graceful like a dancer, in a pink skirt and pink sweater. She waved her small baton. We began with "Rock of Ages."

I didn't know all the words, and we had no written words to follow, but I joined in the singing anyway. Our voices rose together, tinny and uneven.

Philip Schloss stumbled on the words. He didn't know the melody, and this pleased me. He *was* stupid, I thought, a cruel, stupid, ugly fool.

After school that day, Leah Grace and I walked from her apartment toward the lake, her hand in mine. I studied her carefully. She looked strong and she smiled, as she always did. Her face looked rosy and bright. I realized my happiest moments were the ones I spent with her. In those moments, the difficulties in my world disappeared.

I still secretly hoped someday I would find someone who would understand my most private thoughts, and I his. He would be nothing like the hateful boys at school. We would live someplace silent and safe and beautiful, far from Bittersweet Place and Uncle Maurice. Leah Grace would live there, too. My parents had met because of each of their parents; the families had arranged the marriage. My mother and father had spoken on just one occasion, they told me, before they'd become engaged. But things were done differently here. I would live a completely different life from my parents.

But would I find a grand love? I wondered as my cousin and I made our way to the lake. Would I ever live in a place where people didn't hurt other people or call them cruel names? And would anything erase my awful memory of Uncle Maurice? For the length of my life would I think of him?

Leah Grace wore a yellow cotton dress, a bulky black wool coat, and a red wool scarf. I wore a long-sleeved, light blue cotton dress. My mother had sewn it. The dress was one of my favorites and fashionable. A pink cotton sash wound around the dropped waist. I wore her old gray wool coat. The wind blew fiercely. But Leah Grace wanted to be outside. I did, too. We rounded the corner and saw Lake Michigan in the distance. Then we swung our arms back and forth, as if we were one body with four arms. We hummed a melody we made up.

When we reached the sand, we raced to the water. Summers, the lake was lazy, and the breeze felt gentle, like a parent's kiss. But in winter and even now, almost spring, the lake seemed like a great, dangerous sea. Clumps of sticks and pebbles had washed up onto the shore. A chilly March wind slapped our faces. Leah Grace didn't seem bothered by the cold. Waves beat against the sand, like the choppy waves that had slashed the ship when we sailed to America.

"Come and swim, Lena." She pulled me closer to the lake, but Aunt Razel had warned us to go no further than the water's edge.

That night in bed, I lay awake. In the cool darkness of the room, I mulled over Aunt Razel's words again. Leah Grace seemed perfectly fine to me. She didn't need a doctor. I remembered how we'd been questioned by one doctor after another at Ellis Island. They rushed from person to person. Simon and I had roamed the vast halls, holding hands. We ate our meals at a long table, sitting with strangers. We ate foods we'd never eaten before. I chewed on a hardboiled egg, its smooth tasteless white, the grainy dry yolk.

We didn't know where our uncles were. A stern white-haired doctor told us our mother had an infection in her nails, a dangerous fungus, he said. The authorities had taken her to the hospital. They might have to send her back, he warned.

The only doctor I liked there was not a doctor, but my father. He had appeared beside my bed when I was quarantined in the hospital ward for measles. I lay on a hard mattress in a dim, drafty room filled with sick and miserable children. An identification tag dangled on a string around my neck. I was sure this meant I would be sent away, back to the ship, back to Belilovka.

My father wore a neat white doctor's coat, and he smiled his splendid smile that gave him dimples. He was tall and broadly built, and he towered over me with his wavy red hair, bushy blond eyebrows, and blue eyes as clear as jewels. He looked at me kindly, asked in Russian, "How are you feeling today?"

I was feverish and afraid. I didn't know where my mother or Simon were, or my uncles. I shrugged, surprised a doctor spoke my language. He told me how beautiful America was and that when I was healthy, I would see the whole country, from New York all the way to California. Then he said, "Finally, my Lena, it's you."

"I don't know you," I mumbled, frightened.

"I'm your father."

I had stared at him, certain this was a dream.

He told me he had snuck in and stolen a doctor's white coat and stethoscope to surprise me. Then he'd hugged me. "I had to see you," he whispered. "My Lena, my child." A week later, he took us on a crowded train, past farms and cities, to our new home.

On Friday night, a few weeks after Aunt Razel spoke to my mother about Leah Grace, we sat at the kitchen table—my mother, my father, Simon, Uncle William, and I. I was lucky; Uncle Maurice was off with a lady friend. He had begun to stay away from the apartment more and more. Some nights he didn't come home at all.

A white cotton cloth covered the table. My mother had embroidered the edge of the fabric with red and yellow flowers. Silver candlesticks gleamed on the windowsill. The flames of the Sabbath candles sparkled. My old grandmother had hidden the candlesticks beneath a mattress in the house in Belilovka, then had sewed them into the lining of her coat and brought them with her on her journey to Chicago.

We were eating the *challah* my mother and I had baked. My mother insisted on blessings over candles, wine, and bread, although she rarely went to the synagogue. She separated milk from meat, too, like my old grandmother did. My parents usually allowed Simon to do as he pleased, but my mother insisted he eat with us on Friday nights. She insisted I eat at home on Friday nights, too, and not at Leah Grace's apartment. My mother prepared a special meal then, as if each Friday we had something to celebrate.

Uncle William suddenly stood up as if he were going to sing to us.

Instead, he spoke. "Maurice and I have a plan," he said, directing his words to my mother. "We are going to move to California."

"To live?" she said. "Why would you go there?" She set her fork on her plate.

"To become a singer, a great success," he explained with excitement. He opened his arms, as if to embrace all of us and the whole world. "I'll sing in nightclubs, and someday on the radio. Maurice will open a laundry business and a swanky restaurant." William sat down. "We have a fine plan. Maurice will leave before me. I'll meet him there. We need to be on our own. We're grown men. Reesa, it's like a paradise there in California, people say it. There are cities and the countryside. You can fish and walk. There are lakes and horses, just like in Russia. Forests and mountains. Anything you can imagine. Anything you want. And people have money there. They aren't afraid to part with it."

"Oh, I think it is a paradise," I agreed, thrilled that Uncle Maurice would be leaving. "I've read about California in school."

"It's a swell place," Simon offered. "Lena is right about that."

"Don't go, William." My mother leaned toward him, ignoring Simon and me. "It's not safe. No one in the family lives there."

My father shook his head with disapproval. He was a practical man, free with his opinions. Now his wavy red hair glowed in the candlelight. "Don't be foolish," he said to William. "Don't let Maurice tell you what to do. How will you live? Where will the money come from?"

Uncle William smiled. "Let's eat." He pointed to the bowls heaped with stuffed cabbage and roasted potatoes, to the platter of baked chicken. "We have a feast here. The rest we'll speak of another time."

That night, from my bedroom, I heard my father and two uncles talking in the living room. "Don't go to California, William," my father said in a loud, angry whisper. "They'll make shit out of you. And you'll be *shtupping* your *goy* there, too."

Shtupping. My heart almost stopped. I knew what the word meant. It was what Uncle Maurice had wanted to do with me. I glanced at Simon to see if he'd heard. But Simon lay asleep on top of blankets on the bedroom floor. My father spoke softly now. I could barely hear him. So I climbed from bed and tiptoed to the living room in my long white nightgown. I peeked into the room.

My uncles huddled in the corner, near my desk. They faced my father. His hands sliced the air as he spoke. His back was toward me.

Uncle William's shoulders tensed. My father spit out the word *goy* again. Then *shiksa*.

William jerked his head back. I was afraid he might hit my father.

In a low murmur, William said, "Where I go and who I have for a companion is none of your business."

Uncle Maurice frowned; his ugly, evil mustache twitched. "Do you think we'd live here if we had a choice, Chaim? You won't even help us buy bigger machines for the laundry. We could wash clothing for laundries on Clark and Addison and for the big hotels. We'd grow the business and become rich."

"I told you, I won't do it," my father declared. "And you hardly live here anymore. So you finally decided to come home tonight."

"Look at you," Uncle Maurice sneered. "How you behave. You and your secrets. *Gey in d'rerd arayn.* Go to hell."

What secrets? I thought. How dare he say this to my father?

My father took a step back. His shoulders sagged. "Then let it be," he said to William. "May God grant you all you wish for yourself."

The elevated train roared.

Then he muttered, "*A beyze tsung iz erger fun a shlechter hant.*" An angry tongue is worse than an evil hand. "I'm surprised, William. You're becoming like *him*." My father swung around to leave and saw me. "Go to sleep, Lena," he commanded wearily. "This isn't for your ears."

I hurried to the bedroom, wanting to hear more.

I hated the arguments in our apartment. Besides, Uncle William was my favorite uncle. He looked just like what I thought a man should be: tall and thin, with dark curly hair and a long, masculine nose. His brown eyes were like my mother's. He was her youngest brother, the youngest in her family.

I loved his voice. My mother said he had a perfect voice, like an angel. And he did. I could lose myself in it. He often sang after dinner, a cappella, and would burst out with Russian songs, like *Ochi Chyornye*. He would stand, as if performing in a concert hall. When he thrust back his head and sang one note for as long as he could, I knew in my heart, in every fiber of my being, that someday he would go to California and become famous, sing on the radio and in movies. I would have the pleasure of knowing he was William, my uncle, my mother's youngest brother, with eyes like hers. He would, I was sure, return home and rescue us from the fat black rats that scampered on Bittersweet Place at night, from the piles of clothing my mother took in to mend. From the awful taunts at school, "Jew girl. Ugly. Stupid."

Uncle William said I was his favorite, too. I felt beautiful when he spoke to me, and I imagined that he would scoop me into his arms and take me to California. I wasn't afraid of him. I knew he wasn't like Uncle Maurice. The school I would go to there would be clean and new. The students would be friendly and kind. I imagined my clothing, silk and fine cottons, and the food, sweet butter and thick jam bought from a store, and chunks of tender meat, not the limp vegetables my mother prepared, or the tough liver. We would listen to the radio and the Victrola, go to the theater. I would never smell fried onions again. I would sleep in my own bed in my own room. Uncle Maurice would live far away, in another state or another country.

A week after William announced his plans, when I came home from school, my mother told me Uncle Maurice had left on a train for

California that morning.

"When is he coming back?" I asked.

"This I don't know." Sadness tinged her voice. "He had no time to say goodbye to you or Simon. He is too busy with his plans. Oh, Lena, I don't understand why he left us."

My heart trilled with happiness and relief—if there was a God, He had answered my prayers. Uncle Maurice was gone. I felt as if the stone in my heart had been pulled out.

Then two weeks later, on a Saturday, we accompanied Uncle William to the street—Simon, my parents, and I. Uncle Abie and Aunt Ida were there, too. Mr. Usher Cohen, our neighbor, joined us. Leah Grace felt too tired to be with us, my mother said.

Earlier that morning, I'd overheard my father tell my mother that Uncle William had bought an automobile, a black Chevrolet, in a complicated arrangement with money William claimed he'd saved from his work at the laundry. "How could William save such money?" my father had said. "I'm sure he hasn't told us everything. He's gotten the car some other way. Maurice must have been part of it, that thief. He's rotten, no good."

I knew he was worse than that.

William planned to drive to California with his girlfriend—the woman, the *shiksa* my father had spoken of. He was leaving us now to pick her up. But first he would stop at Aunt Feyga's apartment to say another goodbye to his mother, my old grandmother.

He placed his suitcase in the back seat of the Chevrolet, slammed the door, and stood beside the car. The black metal gleamed. "The car salesman taught me to drive," William told us proudly.

I gazed at my uncle's smile. I couldn't imagine how he and Maurice would manage in California. I longed to warn him about Uncle Maurice. But I couldn't find the words.

In the bright morning sunlight, William kissed each of us goodbye. His skin was luminous with a sweet jasmine scent. He wore a gray suit jacket, gray trousers, and a vest, as if he were going to the synagogue on the holiest day. A handsome black fedora perched on his head. He hugged my father and my mother, then Simon, and then me. He hugged bulky Uncle Abie and thin Aunt Ida. He even embraced short, one-handed Mr. Usher Cohen.

My mother kissed one side of William's face, then the other. She kissed his fingers. "Don't leave us for long," she whispered to her youngest brother. "Go in health. And please, come back to us in health, too."

One afternoon in the middle of May, my mother asked me to help her write a letter. When she was growing up, the tutors had spent most of their time teaching the boys. She often told me she wanted to study English but she hadn't begun yet. Though she could write some Yiddish and Russian, she preferred that I write for her in English.

I plopped on the bed in her bedroom. She sat facing the sewing machine. Above it, a window looked out at a brick building. A few slats of sunlight slunk into the room.

I thought of Uncle Maurice, as I did almost every day. I wished he were dead or that he would never come back home. Perhaps every person in the world could make one wish a day, and some of those billions of wishes would be granted. Maybe mine would be, too. Even if it wasn't, there was pleasure in just wishing. At first, I had been happy when he left, but I soon discovered the fist of fear in me hadn't disappeared.

"Let me think my thoughts," my mother said. She seemed somber today. I had learned to mimic her moods and was quiet, too.

I began thinking about Leah Grace. I hadn't seen her in several days. After Uncle Maurice moved to California, I didn't need to avoid the empty apartment anymore. Instead I came home and worked at my desk. I could concentrate in the silence now that he was gone. I'd stopped going to visit Leah Grace every afternoon.

Sometimes Aunt Razel and Uncle Charlie had brought Leah Grace to the laundry or our apartment, but they soon stopped. My mother told me they'd decided to hire someone to watch Leah Grace. When this proved expensive, Aunt Razel stayed home with her.

The school year was almost over, and I didn't have much time to visit anyone. Miss Healy had started to give us long and difficult assignments to do at home. She could be unfair, but she wasn't mean. I had to please her so she would promote me two or even three grades, and then I would finally be with students my own age. Afternoons and evenings, I sat at my desk or in my bedroom, working hard on the assignments.

It had been four days ago that I'd gone with my mother to my cousin's apartment. I'd been shocked. Leah Grace sat huddled on the sofa in a red taffeta dress. She was pale and thin, like a bleached prune. I promised I would take her to the beach when the weather was warmer. It was still windy and damp then, even though it was May.

She didn't smile. "I'm too tired, Leeeeena," she whispered.

My mother handed Aunt Razel a large pot of guggle muggle, and the two of them went to talk in the kitchen. I sat on the sofa and scooted close to Leah Grace. She had leaned against me, shut her eyes, and fallen asleep. What had the doctor done to her? I'd wondered uneasily.

Now, I wanted to ask if the guggle muggle or the doctor had helped Leah Grace. But I said nothing, afraid of my mother's answer. What if my cousin were terribly sick? What if they had to put her in a miserable hospital ward like the one I'd been in at Ellis Island? Why didn't the doctor *do* something for her? I realized I'd never asked the nurse at school for a doctor's name, and I felt badly about this, and resolved to ask her tomorrow. And I would visit Leah Grace this afternoon, I decided, after I finished my mother's letter. I didn't care how much schoolwork I had to do. Today was warmer. The sun was shining. She and I could walk to the lake and sit in the breeze. If Leah Grace was too tired, I would lift her into my arms and carry her. I would draw a picture of her; maybe this would make her smile. And when school was over for the year, I'd visit her every day again.

I tapped my pencil against the piece of paper, impatient for my mother to finish her thoughts and begin her letter. She swayed to the click-clack rhythm of the sewing machine. Her foot pressed back and forth on the treadle as she mended the seam of a dress.

I decided to begin a letter of my own:

Dear Uncle William,

How are you and the rest? Please do not tell Uncle Maurice that I wrote to you. He will be insulted that I didn't write to him. I am helping Mother with her letter. We all want you to come home. I enclose a poem I composed for school.

My name is Lena
I have a dimple,
My smile is charming, I've got a brain.
Oh yes, and as you can see,
I dabble in poetry.

Please write us a letter. Don't forget us, Uncle William. Sing a song just for me!

Lena

The sewing machine stopped. My mother slid the white silk dress from beneath the needle and laid it on top of the clothing piled next to me on the bed. She took a breath. "Now I am ready," she said, bending over the machine to mend a pair of trousers. "Listen carefully, Lena. I must tell William news, important news."

I wrote as she dictated:

Dear William,

I write a few lines to let you know we received your last letter and are glad you are getting along. We still want you to come home. How is Maurice? I hope he is staying out of trouble.

I sent you a letter at the Paul Street number, but I do not believe you received it.

William, four weeks ago, Leah Grace took sick with pneumonia. She got well after three weeks,

but her tumor had come back in a child form of
cancer. She could not… This morning, Tuesday, at
9:30, she left us for a world that

I dropped the paper and stared at my mother. Tears filled her eyes.
"No," I finally shouted. "No! Why didn't you tell me she was so sick?
She can't be gone."

My mother swiveled to face me. "I did not know how to tell you."
Her skin was pale. "I did not want it to be true. I wish I could have
told you before. Now you know." She reached out her hand to me.
"Oh, Lena."

I hurled the pencil to the floor. "I didn't spend enough time with
her. How could you let this happen? I never even said goodbye to
her. I won't write another word for you."

But my mother continued to dictate, as if she expected all emotion
to bend to her will.

"Oh, William," she went on sorrowfully.

Finally, I picked up the pencil, gulped my tears, and slowly wrote
her words:

> Oh, William. Leah Grace suffered so. And
> Charlie and Razel—we don't know what to do with
> them.
>
> Goodbye, William. Write to us soon. I know
> you will excuse my unclear thoughts. I did not
> know how to tell you our news. Lena has helped
> me with writing this. She is very sad, too.
>
> Your loving sister,
> Reesa

"There," I said. "Your letter is finished." I threw the paper on the
bed. "You knew the doctor couldn't help her, and you never told me.
I won't write a word for you again."

A *Shiva* in Chicago
May 1926

Simon and I went to school the day of the funeral and the burial.
"You are too young to go to a cemetery," my mother said.

But in the evening we accompanied my parents. For seven days
and nights, the family sat *shiva* for Leah Grace.

Platters of food lay on the kitchen table in Uncle Charlie's and
Aunt Razel's apartment, plates of gefilte fish, fresh breads, stewed
chicken, a cherry pie, meatballs drowning in thick brown sauce.
Relatives, friends, neighbors, and people I didn't know crowded in.
The apartment was stuffy. The summer heat had arrived early, but the
windows were closed. The door to Leah Grace's room was shut like
the lid of a coffin.

On the first day of *shiva*, I wandered around, afraid to talk to Aunt
Razel or Uncle Charlie. White sheets hung over the mirrors. Uncle
Charlie sank into the sofa, staring at his lap. Aunt Razel sat on a low
stool in the living room. Her dress hung on her like a loose black
shroud. Her lipstick was smeared. Her eyes—dull, flat, like paint
on paper—frightened me. My mother served food and somberly
greeted the guests. Aunt Feyga pushed her scraggly gray hair back
from her face and gazed forlornly at Razel. Feyga usually collected
coins for the poor, though it seemed to me that we all needed our
coins just to live, but tonight she didn't bring out her *pushke* box or
ask for donations.

Simon sat on the sofa, too, sullen and glum, eyeing the floor. I
wanted to talk to him about Leah Grace. If only he could be a friend
to me like she might have been. But he didn't want to talk to anyone
now.

In the early evening, before the sun set, the men gathered in the
living room. My father stood with them and Simon did, too. They all
looked to the east and prayed for Leah Grace and her soul. I sat with

the women and watched. The backs of the standing mourners faced us, a wall of men. Uncle Abie led the service. They sang the Hebrew prayers like one voice rising.

After awhile, when the men had finished, my father walked over to me. "Come," he said. He guided me to Uncle Charlie's and Aunt Razel's bedroom. The space was just big enough for the mattress. A green blanket was draped over the bed. Blue curtains hid the window. My father switched on the floor lamp that stood wedged between the mattress and the wall. He sat on the edge of the bed. I perched next to him.

His red hair was wildly coiled as if he had forgotten to comb it. The lamp cast a halo of light on his lap. "So, when this happens, this with Leah Grace, we can't find answers," he said. "Now, again, we learn what it means to have no answers."

I didn't reply. I realized I had questions I didn't know how to ask him. Why did Leah Grace have to suffer? Would I suffer like that someday, too?

"I believe God loaned Leah Grace to Aunt Razel and Uncle Charlie," my father went on, as if he could read my mind. He seemed so sad, his face pale.

I struggled to concentrate.

"He gave them a beautiful jewel and told them, 'Here, enjoy for awhile.'" My father clapped his hands. "Then it was time to snatch her back."

I shuddered and imagined God's giant hands grabbing Leah Grace's golden hair and yanking her up to the sky.

"But why now?" I asked. "Why did he have to take her away so soon?"

My father shrugged. His shoulders drooped. "Every day that you live, you find more questions than answers, my Lena. Only God knows. And I don't have a way to ask him."

Just then my mother came in. "Chaim," she said. She began to cry.

A look of uncharacteristic tenderness rose on his face. He stood up and then turned to me. "Remember, my Lena, the whole wide world is a narrow bridge. The most important thing is not to be afraid." He kissed the top of my head and then put his arm around my mother.

I left them and stood in the gloomy hallway, straining to hear the low tones of their whispered words. For a while, I sat in an armchair in the living room. Simon had gone home. More people walked in. Soon the din of conversation filled the small space. Aunt Razel sat on her low stool, murmuring to Uncle Charlie. It seemed as if my aunt were moaning, in terrible physical pain. I gazed at the black-and-white photograph of Leah Grace on the mantel. She was smiling and looking out at us. I leaned into the armchair and pretended to sleep. I imagined her room, her bed covered by a white-flowered blanket. Her dolls with their white taffeta skirts sat lined in a row on the floor there, one next to the other, like brides.

Then I hurried from the living room and ran into Aunt Razel's and Uncle Charlie's bedroom. No one was there. I flung myself onto the bed and squeezed shut my eyes. How dare anyone make a home when life could change so quickly? I thought. How dare people believe they were safe, that anything in this world would last?

My whole life unfolded in my mind: the house by the lake, the dark, damp forest, my grandfather slumped and dead. The long, terrible journey to our new home. Finally, the *Goldene Medina* and my father. Uncle Maurice's awful hands on my skin. Leah Grace's smile.

I tried to understand my father's words. *The world is a narrow bridge.* What did he mean? It seemed to me he had been talking not only about Leah Grace but also about the future, what we could hope for in our adopted land. But look what had happened here, I thought. What kind of golden land was this?

Tears streaked my face. Then I heard footsteps. Suddenly my father stood beside me, just as he had appeared at Ellis Island to rescue us, take us home. "There you are, my Lena," he said.

"I don't understand why she had to die," I cried to him.

He sighed and stroked my hair. "If only we could write the future as we want. We can't. We have to live and watch each day unfold.

But the rabbis tell us that even a moment in paradise can be enough."

"What can be enough?" I said. "I don't understand."

"Paradise. A moment that makes you happy," he said quietly. "That makes you feel grateful. This is all we can really ask for in life."

I knew my father was trying to soothe me, and I wanted to believe his words. But I didn't know how I could feel grateful now. "Papa," I finally said. "The rabbis are wrong."

"Ah," he whispered. He sat next to me on the bed. "Poor Leah Grace. Remember how sweet it felt to hold her small hand? The touch of her will always be in your mind. What are we, after all? Just people. This you have seen. And for everyone—nothing lasts. Even the life of someone we love." He stopped, and then went on. "*Di toi'ern fun treren zeinen kain mol nit farshlossen.* Wherever you live, the gates of tears, they say, are never shut."

Then my father was silent and I was, too. I wanted to slam shut the gates of tears. For my whole life, I would think about Leah Grace. I would draw a picture of her so I could remember everything about her. But the days would pass, I knew, and she would never grow up. She would always be three years old in my mind.

The Slap

September 1926

Although my mother made the day-to-day decisions in our apartment, my father seemed to me to be the most essential person in our family. Night after night when we first arrived in Chicago he had sat patiently with Simon and me in the living room. He pointed to objects and taught us the English words for them.

He had learned English from old books, he told us, when he came to America. He had lived in a rooming house then, for years, and a neighbor, a teacher of English, helped him. He had become a citizen of America in 1921, seven years after he came to Chicago. "One day, you will become citizens, too," he'd said.

My father had read the *Chicago Tribune* aloud to us and helped with schoolwork. He supplied us with pencils and notebooks from the family laundry, sharpening the pencils with a kitchen knife. He told us the president of the United States was Mr. Warren G. Harding. A president was nothing like a czar, he assured us. "In America," my father said to us, "you can be happy and free, go where you wish. There are gangsters, but they aren't like the Cossacks. They won't come to our apartment. They're interested in other gangsters. You don't have to be afraid."

He told us about movies and the Yiddish theater. He explained to Simon about basketball, baseball, and Jack Dempsey, who was a very famous boxer, he said. My father told us there had been a great fire in Chicago many years ago, before he was even born. Most of the city had been destroyed and then was rebuilt.

Simon and I had nodded and listened. But I wondered how I would remember it all.

"You can read about all of life in the *Chicago Tribune*," my father had said. "Or there's a newspaper your mother will like—two of them, the *Daily Jewish Courier* and the *Jewish Daily Forward*. In Yiddish.

There's a section in one, the 'Bintel Brief,' that gives advice about personal problems. But my advice is to rely on your own thoughts, and talk to your mother or me or your teacher about a problem. I strongly advise you to read only a newspaper written in English words. And read the books your teachers tell you about in school."

He taught us about the elevated train and the streetcar, and he took us downtown to see the stores, arcades, theaters, and the Chicago River that snaked along the edge of downtown. Automobiles chugged noisily on the wide streets and spewed smoke and the smell of gasoline. Men and women rushed past each other, frowning. We stopped to look up at a tall building on Michigan Avenue. "This," my father said, "is the London Guarantee Building. It is built from a special stone. The stone of lime. I have read that Chicago itself was founded at this very place. Once, an Indian fort stood right here. A fort, my children, is like a village."

At the river, boats glided on the water. My father pointed to a bridge that spanned the water. "Here is a drawbridge," he said. "The bridge opens in the middle, so that the tallest boats can pass beneath it." He guided us to two gleaming white buildings near the river, like castles. "These are skyscrapers," he said. "They are owned by a Mr. Wrigley. He is a very rich and important man."

My father had showed us Maxwell Street, where pushcarts sat jammed with merchandise. Fruits, vegetables, meats, flowers, rags, towels, and clothing sat piled in heaps on carts. Peddlers shouted and cursed. Men stood in front of stores, yelling for customers to come in. The smells of raw chicken, whiskey, and apples swirled in the air. You could buy anything you wanted as long as you had money to pay for it. People crowded into the street, speaking a jumble of languages I couldn't understand, as if all the countries of the world converged here.

My mother never joined us on these excursions. She forbid Simon and me from going to these places alone.

My father looked Irish, my friend Elka Amsall told me. Just last week, when Elka had seen him outside the school building, she'd said, "He looks a little like my father, except your dad's nose is bigger.

His hair is so red. My father is Polish but everyone thinks he's Irish. Does your father drink a lot? Mine does."

"Not a lot," I answered. I had never seen my father drink too much, but he loved *schnapps* and red wine and vodka, especially when he played pinochle. His face became rosy then, and his laugh was loud and loose. "What does your father do when he drinks?" I asked. "Mine plays cards."

Elka dug her heel into the cement of the schoolyard. "Oh, mine yells. Slaps my brother. My mother. Me."

"That's awful."

She nodded.

There had been no slapping in our apartment, but the sharp sounds of yelling spilled into the rooms. My parents' arguing had grown louder now that my uncles lived in California.

My father often worked late at the Granville Laundry, as if he had to finish my uncles' jobs there, too. He came home sweaty and tired, sometimes too tired to look at the *Chicago Tribune* or read with me. My mother did her sewing repairs, cooked, and took care of mail and correspondence with my help. She didn't seem interested in the newspaper or the world. Each day, she lamented that we hadn't received a response to the letter we'd sent to Uncle William four months ago about Leah Grace's death.

The uncles seemed to have disappeared, which was a great relief to me. Still, I missed Uncle William. I had to become accustomed to his absence, just as I was struggling to get used to the absence of Leah Grace. Now, instead of visiting the lake with her, I wandered there by myself, bringing along a pad of paper for company. Afternoons when school was finished for the day, I sat on a patch of grass beneath a tree and watched the waves melt into the sand. And then, because I was bored and lonely and missed Leah Grace terribly, I drew what I saw. I discovered I could do this. I could stare at a tree or person and sketch lines on paper so they resembled objects and people. I found I could draw happily for hours. If I was going to become a great artist, I needed to practice, I decided. The more time I spent doing this, the more lifelike my drawings were, and the better they seemed to me. I forgot about the past and Uncle Maurice when I drew. I loved moving the pencil across the paper and creating shapes. I sketched the slope of a nose, the wide arch of an eyebrow, a forehead with a fan of wrinkles. I sketched people who strolled along the sand, and I tried to capture the way the light and shadows crept across their faces. I couldn't figure out exactly how to draw a hand or lips. I even tried to draw a picture of Leah Grace from memory. But I couldn't duplicate her smile.

Sometimes if it was raining, I went to the library and drew pictures there.

I hid the sketches beneath my bed. Uncle William had saved papers in a square wooden box, and when he left for California, he'd taken the papers with him. After Leah Grace's death I started putting my drawings in the box. I kept two spare pencils there, too. My father had given them to me. I didn't worry that anyone would find the box; I was the only one who cleaned and swept the bedroom. I never drew at our apartment anymore, and I wasn't sure why I hid my drawings from my family. I assumed my mother would again tell me drawing was a waste of time and that it took me away from chores and schoolwork. "Stop making useless marks on paper," she would tell me, as she had before. And I wanted to keep my pictures a secret between Leah Grace and me, make them just for her. Maybe she would return to earth some day, I imagined; maybe my sketches could help bring her back. I knew this was a foolish wish, yet I couldn't help wishing it.

"William will come home," my mother told us one night at dinner. "You will see. He'll surprise us. That is why there are no letters. Maurice will come home, too. They know we all ache for Leah Grace. They know they belong here, with us, their family."

"When you help a person, this is what happens." My father shook his head. "They spit on your hand, can't look you in the eyes. Remember my words. We helped William and Maurice. We won't see either one of them again."

"You are wrong, Chaim," she said. "Always wrong."

I sat in my parents' bedroom, my schoolbooks spread on their bed. It was the middle of September. Miss Healy had promoted me, but just one grade. I was in seventh grade now. Simon was in high school this year, in a different school from mine. Now I'd never see him, I thought with disappointment. My teacher this year, Miss Marshall, was strict and exacting. She gave complicated assignments to be done at home each night. I preferred to do work for school at my desk. But the people in the living room distracted me, so I'd retreated to my parents' room.

The clink of glasses and clamor of voices pushed into the bedroom. When I finished the assignment to write an essay on a favorite landscape, I went to see who was here.

Three card tables stood in the living room. Aunt Ida had wrapped herself in a piece of black silk fabric with a pattern of red roses, as if it were a shawl. A book lay in her lap, *The Mysterious Rider* by Zane Grey. She sat at a table with my father, reciting a poem to him. Aunt Razel sat listlessly on the sofa. She had become thinner since Leah Grace's death, and her hair had turned completely white.

The windows were open to let in the evening air, but the September heat, as warm as a summer day, had settled in the room.

Now that Uncle Maurice had gone away, my father or Uncle Abie brought *schnapps* and vodka to our apartment. Sometimes Mr. Usher Cohen brought bottles of whiskey or wine as a gift for us, too.

My father stood up and climbed onto his chair. My mother was carrying a glass pitcher of hot tea into the room. She glanced at him in horror, set the pitcher on a table, and yanked his arm.

"Chaim, what is this?" she said. "Get down from there."

"I wish to make an announcement," he replied sharply. "Can all of you hear?"

Heads nodded. I nodded, too.

"I am now forming a family club," he said.

Uncle Abie, Uncle Charlie, and Mr. Mort Seligman sat at the second table, playing pinochle. Mr. Seligman was hard of hearing. My mother had told me he'd pushed an ice pick in his ears to escape going to the army in Russia. At the third table, Uncle Myron—Aunt Feyga's husband—was talking with Mr. Usher Cohen and his wife, Mrs. Gerta Cohen. Aunt Feyga huddled on the sofa, waiting for my mother to join her. Her gray hair coiled outward like weeds, and she smiled crookedly. A blue metal *pushke* box sat on her lap. I slid onto the sofa next to her.

Everyone looked up at my father.

"I wish to make known the official formation of the Czernitski family club," he said, beaming. His face was flushed, a shade lighter than his hair. "We will have rules, like the Lodges do. Like the Masons."

"A club," said Uncle Abie. His stomach bulged beneath his white shirt. His dark bushy eyebrows grew in almost one long line across his forehead. "With special *schnapps*? A handshake? Drinks?" He squinted. "Are there more drinks, Reesa? More than wine and tea?"

"What about money?" Uncle Charlie interrupted. He rarely spoke since Leah Grace's death. "Do we have to pay for this, this—honor?"

I didn't see how my father could ask people for money to come to our apartment. This was my world, too, I thought, and now he was starting a club. I didn't know what this meant. Would the relatives and friends come here even more often, bringing more noise and conversation? Would it be a club of the old country or the new world?

"There is no club." My mother frowned. "No money will be collected. Chaim, get down from that chair."

I looked up at my father again.

He didn't move.

"What about the others?" Aunt Ida clutched her book to her chest. "Do you have to be a blood relation?"

Mrs. Gerta Cohen's thin brows were penciled over with thick marks. They formed two wide arches above her eyes like the span of a bridge. An eyebrow lifted upward. "We may not be family," she said, "but you can't ask us to leave before we finish this game of cards."

My father smiled; his dimples spread into his cheeks. He was enjoying himself, despite my mother's displeasure. He jumped down from the chair. "You are just like family. We can include anyone who we decide is acceptable."

Uncle Myron shook his bald head and slid his smudged spectacles off his nose. "What's 'acceptable'? And who will judge?"

"Will God Almighty be the judge?" boomed Mr. Usher Cohen. He had escaped from Russia after he lost his right hand. He didn't have the proper papers to come to America, so he snuck onto a ship. He knew how to get along in the world, my father always said with admiration. I watched Mr. Cohen now, wondering if he understood things about life that I should learn.

"Do you have to *prove* you're a Jew to be a member of this club?" Mr. Cohen pushed on. "And do the ladies stay in the room or not?"

Mrs. Cohen blushed, and I did, too. Then I thought about Uncle Maurice.

"Nonsense. You don't have to prove anything." My father laughed and his pale eyes glowed. "You are the first non-family members allowed in this club. You and the Seligmans are as close as blood. And we will include the children, Lena and Simon."

I didn't know if I wanted to be a member. I would have to wait and see.

"Money." Mr. Cohen thrust his stump in the air. "You never told us, Chaim. Must we pay for this privilege?"

"This I haven't considered," my father said, sitting next to Aunt Ida.

"You will not consider it." My mother sat at the table, too.

"If William were here, he would sing," Uncle Charlie said. "We need music, a special song for our club." He began to hum.

"Stop, Charlie." Abie gulped his glass of red wine. His huge belly heaved. "I want to remind you. In Russia, we had our beautiful baby grand piano, near the kitchen. Do you remember, Reesa? And when the revolution came..." He spit into his glass. "The peasants sat on the piano, pulled it out of the house. Destroyed it. Destroyed everything. And our father...we couldn't bury him for three days, couldn't get out of the stinking village to go to the city. It's gone. Everything gone." His eyes welled with tears.

"Enough of this talk," my mother said.

"Where you stood then was where you ran from," he whispered hoarsely.

"Too much talk kills the soul, Abie." My mother stood up and planted her hands on her hips. "Too much *schnapps*. It's *meshuggeneh*, a club. A crazy dream. You're a dreamer, Chaim. We will never have the life again that we had there."

"We may not have that life," my father countered. "But we will have this club. We'll have a better future here. For all of us, for Lena and Simon."

I bolted up from the sofa, certain my mother would tell me it was rude to leave the room. But I couldn't bear to hear one more word about revolution or peasants or sadness or clubs.

"Lena," she said simply, without admonishment. "Come, go to bed."

My mother was always wrong, I thought the next morning. Her words about my father and the family club made me angry. It wasn't a dream or make-believe. When relatives and *landsleit* gathered, we were more than a club. We were a country whose borders had snapped shut, a separate continent with our own citizens and customs. Not Belilovka, but not America either. My father was simply recognizing what had already come to be.

I felt out of place there, yet so at home. I didn't want my mother's future. She would be pushing the treadle of the old sewing machine forever; the needle would never stop.

My mother was bursting with sadness and complaints, and I was bursting with *wanting*. In school that day, as Miss Marshall talked on and on about grammar, I sat in the drab beige classroom and wrote my list of wants in my notebook, on a separate page from my list of fears:

What I WANT by Lena Czernitski

1. To speak perfect English
2. Have a happy life
3. Become a woman (grow up)
4. Be very completely in love
5. Leave this apartment and Bittersweet Place forever
6. Give my mother money so she does not have to take in sewing
7. Have Uncle William come home
8. Never see Uncle Maurice again
9. Draw beautiful pictures
10. Be safe
11. Be strong

I considered the last point. Strength was a matter of will, I decided. I didn't have enough strength in me, and the next week I learned there was no strength in our apartment either. I would have to make myself strong.

On Monday night, the week after my father formed his club, I lay in bed awake. Simon was asleep on blankets on the floor, his red hair pressed into the pillow, and he curled beneath a sheet. His breath burst out in noisy spurts. I stared at him, wishing he and I could talk about our family and the past, and that he would understand without explanation or apology. Maybe someday this would happen, I thought. Aunt Razel was asleep in Uncle William's old bed. She was staying at our apartment while Uncle Charlie drove to Michigan to help his sick cousin. My aunt's mouth opened into an "O." Her breathing sounded like the scratching of sandpaper.

The noises kept me awake, so I decided to go to the kitchen. In the hall, I heard my parents' voices. The door to their room was open a crack. I tiptoed there and peeked in. The room was dark except for a ribbon of moonlight. My mother stood at the foot of the bed in her nightgown. Her large breasts pushed against the white fabric, her thick hair uncoiled wildly to the middle of her back.

"Listen to me, Chaim. For once, just listen." Her voice sounded strained.

I couldn't see my father.

I was sure she was complaining about the family club. Nothing pleased her. She complained about everything. As I turned to go to the kitchen, she said, "I didn't come to the *Goldene Medina* for you to be *shtupping* that *goyisha* woman. That dog. The *choleria*. Get her out of our lives."

I glanced at the empty hall. It was dark, like a cave, like a tomb.

"Eight years, you and I were apart. What can you expect? We're together now," my father said. "With the children, the family. We can live. It's in the past, Reesa."

"There is no past."

"She's no one. She's a customer at the store, like many customers."

"You. You stole our lives." My mother raised her arms in a choppy motion, pointing to the heavens. "You make my insides sick. Go to hell, go and rot. You couldn't convince William to stay at home. You're a nothing." She dropped her arms to her sides. "You aren't a man."

There was silence. I shut my eyes, afraid to hear more, but afraid to move, that they might notice me.

"We are no longer man and wife." Her voice wobbled, as if it were an instrument with a broken string. "You brought me from one hell to another. Here is where I will die."

"Reesa," he whispered, like a plea. "Stop."

"I hate you," she shouted. "Do not touch me. Never touch me again."

My father's feet thudded on the wooden floor, and my mother disappeared from my view. I heard the unmistakable crack of a slap. And my father's gasp. "You've hurt me. Reesa."

I imagined he was bleeding. I took a step closer to the doorway.

The floorboards creaked in their room. I inched back to the side, out of view. Then the bedroom door slammed shut with a shudder.

I ran to the living room and yanked on the heavy door that led to the rickety fire escape. I hated my mother. She had lied about my father. It was *her* fault, everything wrong with our life was her fault. Didn't she understand? The world was a narrow bridge; the most important thing was not to be afraid. Not to be angry. My father had appeared like a god at Ellis Island and saved me, saved all of us. Nothing would change that.

I swung open the fire escape door, rushed outside, and sat on the highest step. The half moon floated behind a cloud, which blocked all light. The night air washed over me.

You've hurt me. Reesa.

Then the tears came.

An Inspection
September 1926, the next day

No one spoke about the argument, as if it had been part of my imagination. But the next morning my mother accidentally dropped a glass of milk. It shattered on the floor. My father watched helplessly as she knelt and in sullen silence wiped a rag around and around in the oozing white liquid. He looked tense and tired. When Simon raced into the kitchen and said, "Pa, I've got to leave early for school," my father didn't look at him.

I couldn't wait to go to school, to get away from home. As I made my way there alone, all I could think about were my mother's words last night and the sound of the terrible slap.

In the schoolyard, I stood by myself and brooded about my parents. Soon the bell rang and the teachers marched out. Every morning, they lined up each class according to height.

We scrambled to our places in silence. Miss Marshall had warned us not to talk. I went to my spot at the end of the line. I hated being at the end, and I slouched, but this didn't help. Mary Hall stood in front of me. I stared at the back of her head, at her silky blond hair.

Miss Marshall led us into the building. She stopped in the lobby and informed us we would have to pass inspection today. A few students groaned, but I didn't mind, happy for the distraction.

The nurse, Miss Grubb, waited at the first landing on the stairs. She had brown hair that curled to her shoulders. She wore a white dress and smelled of ammonia. A box of tongue depressors sat on a table beside her. She eyed us fiercely. Then she began to check for nits.

The moment of inspection was humiliating. I watched as each student stopped in front of her. First, she inspected the person's clothing with her eyes. Then she lifted two wooden sticks from the box and used them to root around in the student's hair.

Student after student passed before the nurse. She squinted and inspected Sylvia Glassman. Miss Grubb prodded two sticks into Sylvia's greasy brown hair. Then the nurse frowned and broke the sticks with a flourish. She scribbled in a notebook and loudly ordered pale, nervous Sylvia to step aside. It was no secret who had nits.

When my turn came, the woman rummaged in my hair with the sticks. She poked them hard into my head, but she sent me on my way.

All day, I sat glumly in the classroom. Miss Marshall talked on and on about our "forefathers." Elka Amsall whispered to me, but I didn't answer. I usually loved to learn about history, but today I listlessly drew on the corner of a page in my notebook, thinking about the slap.

In the afternoon, I went to the lake. I could see the tall brick buildings of downtown Chicago from there, even Mr. Wrigley's white buildings that gleamed like candles in the sky. I plopped on the grass, looked away from the city, at the lake, and pressed my pencil against a piece of paper. I drew: a tree, a boat sailing on the water, a quick sketch of a mother and child walking. Each time I put pencil to paper, I thanked God that He allowed the sights of my eyes to travel to my fingers. This act of drawing took so much concentration that it blotted out all of my other thoughts. I had to pay close attention to the shape and thickness of my pencil strokes, as if I were capturing a great burst of myself and imprinting this on paper.

The rest of that week I still reeled from the terrible slap. My parents hardly spoke to one another when I was home. I'd handed in the English assignment Miss Marshall had asked for. Along with the essay about a favorite landscape, she'd instructed us to draw the landscape and a portrait as well. I decided to hand in a drawing I'd made of the Montrose Avenue Beach, and I drew a portrait of Leah Grace from memory.

"Miss Czernitski," Miss Marshall said one afternoon. "I need to speak to you after school."

At the end of the day, I stood in the front of the classroom next to her large wooden desk. It was covered with objects she had warned us not to touch—shiny metal pen points, paper clips, brass fasteners, a fountain pen, a pile of papers.

Miss Marshall did not smile. Her bright red lips puffed out as if swollen. This and her narrow, pointy nose made her look like an owl. An angry owl. I was afraid of her. Her brown hair was knotted into a bun so tightly that the skin of her face looked stretched. She wore a blue dress with a wide red sash, and a long necklace of pale blue glass beads with a tassel on the end.

"We have rules about fabricating work," she began, leaning so close to me that I could smell mint on her breath.

"Oh," I replied, not sure what she meant.

"Perhaps you don't understand," she said. "Fabricating. That means giving me a drawing that does not belong to you, that you did not do yourself." She sat straighter, rapped her hand against the desk, and waved my landscape drawing in the air. "Do you understand me now?"

"No," I said, confused.

"You traced this picture. I inspected it carefully. The assignment was to draw *on your own* a landscape that reflected the theme of your English essay. You traced from a book."

"I didn't," I corrected her eagerly. "I sat at the beach, the Montrose Avenue Beach, and made many drawings before this one. That boat. The trees. The woman. I saw them and drew them."

She glared at me with her cold brown eyes. "My dear girl, I will not tolerate lies. You're a child. You're very smart, but you have no training. A child your age couldn't draw this. The perspective. The detail and lines. Impossible. Some of the lines wobble, it's true; but it's too perfect. You traced it, and you're lying to me, Lena Czernitski." She dropped the picture on her desk.

I looked at my drawing, shocked by her words. I felt proud of the picture. I'd thought I'd almost mastered drawing at a distance. I had tried to draw from different angles. The lake was far away; trees, sand, and grass stood in different parts of the paper. I'd tried to capture the way the light brushed against the lake. I drew the mother and child larger because they had been closer to me than the rest.

I had labored to be sure that a person who looked at the drawing would feel as if he or she were right there, inside the picture. That's what I wanted to do. And I had done this.

"Answer me," she snapped.

"I wanted," I said quickly, "to draw the details just right. That's what I tried to do." I wasn't sure what she meant by perspective. I was afraid to ask. "I worked very hard on this. I did it myself."

"You wanted the detail, and you got it by tracing the picture, as you did with the portrait." She slapped her hand against her desk. This made a loud thud. The pen points scattered. "I won't have you lie. Your mother barely speaks English. You're struggling yourself. You write with the wrong hand, your left one. I will fail you for this assignment, and if you don't admit the truth and apologize, I will fail you again and again." She seemed to gloat with pleasure as she spoke. "I plan to talk to your parents about this incident. I don't know what they allow, but I do not tolerate dishonesty. Dishonesty means lying. Do you understand me? We expel students who lie. You people must know what a lie is. You people lie all the time."

I nodded and opened my mouth, but all I could say was, "Oh."

"I am waiting. Say something, please."

"I didn't lie." I stumbled on the words. "This is my own drawing. You have to believe me. I drew the portrait myself, too." I began to rummage frantically in my book bag for a piece of paper. I'd never drawn for anyone except Leah Grace. I would force myself to do this now. "Here, I can show you how I draw."

"I don't have time for this," she fumed. "Are you questioning my judgment? You people won't listen. You're never satisfied. I've made my decision. Our conversation is finished. It may be your drawing, but it is not your own work."

She flung the drawing across the desk. I grabbed it and ran out. At least none of my classmates were there. But this was hardly comfort.

At the apartment, I burst into my parents' bedroom. My mother sat bent over the sewing machine.

"Mama," I cried. "Something awful has happened."

She pressed her foot back and forth against the treadle. The needle fled noisily across a piece of gray cloth. She didn't look at me. "What happens shouldn't happen. Everything can be fixed, except your father," she said dully. "Before he married, he liked to dance. Now he will not dance anymore."

"What are you talking about?" I said.

She yanked a strand of her hair behind her ear. "He tricked me, your father. Before we married he liked to dance. Now he does not. He doesn't care."

"You're not making sense."

"He does not want relations with me." She swung around to face me. "No matter what he says. And I no longer want them with him. Why are you staring, Lena? Don't you want to know the truth?"

"Reesa." Aunt Razel hurried into the room. "She's not feeling well, Lena. Let her rest."

My mother rose shakily. "I am not ill." She gripped the side of the machine. It seemed to me that if she didn't lean on the sewing machine, she would fall over.

"What about me?" I demanded. "I have a problem. A terrible problem. The teacher is going to talk to you. She wants to fail me."

"What can a teacher tell me that I do not know? A mother knows her child. Tell Aunt Razel. The problems become worse as you grow older." My mother sighed. "If it is not one problem, it is another. Every Monday and Thursday there is a new problem. This you will learn all your life."

"I'm not going to learn that." I stared at her. She looked ugly and old and bitter. "I hate you," I cried. "All you do is complain and remember. Why won't you listen to me? I need you to listen." I was shouting. My face grew hot with anger. "It's gone. The life we had in Belilovka is dead and gone. It will never come back. I'm going to leave this awful apartment."

My heart was thumping. I had screamed with all my power.

Tears filled her eyes.

"And I will never come back," I yelled. "Simon never comes home. Papa will leave you alone, too."

Her face sagged as if I'd slapped her. "You don't mean what you say."

"I mean everything. You. The house by the lake. The horses. Your stupid fur coat. It's all dead. No one cares. No one cares what Papa does or doesn't do."

"Lena, please, stop," Aunt Razel said. She watched helplessly; her face scrunched into a frown.

My mother took a gulp of air. "All those people, your grandfather, are still inside you. The way your father was after he went to America. Your insides are crowded with what we left behind."

"Your body may be crowded," I shouted and stormed from the room. "But my insides are fine."

I threw the drawing and my bag of books onto my bed, grabbed my notebook and a pencil, and charged out of the apartment. To soothe myself I ran to the lake. I didn't care what Miss Marshall or anyone said. I would do as I pleased. I sat against a wide oak tree; its long branches stretched outward like arms. The leaves glimmered in the sunlight like a fringed garment. I imagined the branches were strong, kind arms that would protect me. A warm autumn breeze brushed against me. The waves in the lake made a soft rhythmic shushing sound, like the whispering sounds a mother might make to calm a daughter.

I took deep breaths, to stop the shaking in my heart. I felt most myself, I realized, when I was alone, when I sat here and pretended the lake was a great sea. Or when I put pencil to paper and drew and didn't think about the world or other people. This was most important, I decided, not to think about my mother or Leah Grace or Uncle Maurice. Or the awful teacher or our life before we came here. I would create a basket in my mind, a large woven brown basket, and drop each of these worries into it, and in this way, drop away all my troubles. Then I would fling the basket into the sky, to the heavens. And do the same with my fears. I would find a solution for every fear and problem.

I opened my notebook to my list of fears. In bold letters I printed now: "WILL FAIL IN SCHOOL—and no one will help me." I would toss away that fear, too. I would find a way to show Miss Marshall that she was wrong about me. Then I ripped out a fresh page and began to draw the lake.

I drew furiously, all my anger at my mother and Miss Marshall pouring into my hands.

The land around the lake was flat, and the air was as sweet as the air at sea I remembered from our journey here. Birds swooped to the water and back to the sky, as if they couldn't decide where home was. I drew how the grass met the sand and the sand met the water, how the pale blue of the sky met the deep blue of the lake. The sand looked grainy and was littered with white and brown pebbles. People walked past. Shadows wove through the sunlight. I tried to capture all this on paper, just as I had tried to do in the drawing I'd given to Miss Marshall.

I studied my picture, pleased with what I'd done. I felt strong and certain when I drew. I would become a great artist someday, I promised myself again. Miss Marshall would apologize to me. When I grew up, people would gather to see my pictures, amazed, and would admire them. I would meet other artists, too, and I would learn from them. I wanted to put on paper all that I saw in the world. I would draw all the happiness and sadness, the troubles and hope, the faces of people I didn't know and of people I loved. I wanted to capture every person's true nature, the secrets inside, and draw the lake and the sand, and this city with its buildings that stretched into the sky.

I lay on the grass, on my back, happy with this thought. I placed the pencil, my notebook, and my drawing beside me. The last rays of late afternoon sunshine wrapped me in light.

"Hello."

I opened my eyes and looked up.

A boy, older, perhaps Simon's age, stood next to me. He looked familiar. He wore a brown tweed coat, a blue shirt, and gray trousers. He had sandy brown hair and wide, shining green-blue eyes. He smiled at me.

"Hello," he said again.

"Hello," I said cautiously and sat up.

"I'm Maxwell Slovansky. Max. I've seen you before. Walking with a little girl here. Last spring maybe."

Leah Grace, I thought. I nodded. "Yes. That might have been me. I'm Lena." I hesitated. "Lena Czernitski."

"We rhyme."

"Almost."

"Itsky. Ansky." He laughed. "Like a song." He knelt. "Now I know you. You're Simon's sister, aren't you?"

I nodded again.

"He and I play basketball together. He's a great player."

"He is?" I said, surprised.

"Oh, yeah. You should watch him play sometime." He must have seen something in my face because he said, "I don't mean to scare you. If you don't want company, say so."

"No, it's fine," I said. "I like company." Though I didn't know if I wanted to talk to him or not. I felt a little uneasy with Max Slovansky sitting next to me. I glanced at his lanky arms, his sandy hair, at his nose, which was long and graceful.

"What are you doing?" he said. "Schoolwork?"

"Thinking," I said.

He peered at my drawing. "That's pretty good. You can draw. That's great."

I turned the paper over. "That's nice of you to say. What are you doing here?"

"Just walking." He shrugged. "I like being at Lake Michigan. Do you know about the lake? The name is from an Algonquin word. *Michigami*. It means 'great water.' Chicago is from an Indian name, too, from the Illinois tribe and the Miami tribe. It means 'striped skunk.' That's what they called wild leeks. Lots of leeks and onions used to grow here. And really, the lake *is* a great water, it's like an ocean, if you look at it, it's…" He stopped, as if he were embarrassed.

"Oh," I said, impressed.

"I don't know," he stammered. "No good reason for being here. It's a swell day outside, I guess."

"Do you live around here?"

"Near Independence Boulevard."

That was far from our apartment and in a nicer part of the city, where wealthy families lived. "I've never been there," I said.

"Really? The boulevard is huge with big trees and flowers. It's pretty nice." He stood up. "I've got to get home now, but if you want, I'll walk with you. And next time, I'll take you there, to the boulevard, if you like."

"All right." I paused, thinking about this, and then said with great certainty, "I'd like that very much." I wasn't eager to go home, but I suddenly wanted to walk with Max Slovansky. The sun was beginning to sink toward the horizon, and the air was growing colder. I reached for my notebook, the paper and pencil, stood up and shivered. I had run from the apartment so fast that I hadn't brought a sweater or coat.

Max was a few inches taller than me, and thin like Simon. We walked away from the lake, beneath the old stone bridge, and wound west.

"I know the way to your apartment," he said. "I've been there with Simon."

"You have?"

"But you know the way there, too."

We both laughed.

"You live on Bittersweet Place," Max said.

"Yes," I said, embarrassed. "Really, if you think about it, it's an odd name for a street. I mean, how can something be both bitter and sweet? It's not possible."

"Well, it isn't a street. It's a 'place.'"

"But it seems like a street."

"A 'place' is one block long and runs between two streets. That's how they name things in Chicago," he said with authority. "And bittersweet is a wild vine, with berries. The plant is poison for people, but birds can eat it. So it's half happy. The word is an oxymoron, two things that are opposite. It's possible."

"How do you know all this?"

"The library."

"Oh," I said.

"You can find anything you want there."

I nodded. I didn't know what to say to him now, but he didn't seem to mind the silence. As we walked without speaking, I smiled shyly at Max and glanced at his hands, relieved that his were the hands of a boy. His long, thin fingers swung carelessly in the cool fall air. They brushed against mine, and I was startled and pleased, but then they inched away.

A Letter from William
October 1926

My old grandmother had arrived in Chicago a year after we did. She'd traveled with Aunt Feyga, Uncle Myron, and their son in a wagon from Russia to Poland, and then sailed on a ship to New York. It was my grandmother's husband who had been murdered by Cossacks, the *Petlurias*, in the house by the lake in Belilovka. My mother told me that after Simon and I had climbed out of the window and run to the forest, my grandmother dug up the box of money, two jars of gold and the jewelry we kept hidden under the stove beneath a board in the floor. My grandmother gave it all to the intruders. They spared her and the others, but they shattered the windows and shot my grandfather anyway.

Even when my grandmother arrived here, she had been frail. She looked so much older now than she had when we lived in Belilovka; her journey to America had changed her. Aunt Feyga had cared for her since then. My mother warned me not to refer to my grandmother as "the old *bubbe*."

"It's not decent to call her that," my mother said. "Do not call her 'old.' She deserves a name of respect, Lena." But now that I had heard my mother shout at my father and slap him, and Uncle Maurice's hands had crept on my bare skin, I was determined to speak as I wished. There was no respect in our apartment on Bittersweet Place.

Max Slovansky, on the other hand, treated me with great respect. In the two weeks since we had met, he'd found me at the Montrose Avenue Beach on six separate occasions and walked me home. Twice, Simon joined us after basketball practice. He and Max talked about basketball and the games at the Jewish Center, about baseball and Babe Ruth, boxing and Jack Dempsey. Simon ignored me, but Max always drew me into the conversation.

Once, Max invited me to watch them play basketball. I knew

some of the others on the court at the Center, friends of Simon's, too. They all raced across the cement floor, faces flushed, their bodies flying. The room smelled of sweat. Max was right. Simon was a great player. He made basket after basket.

"How's school?" Max asked me today. We were sitting with Simon on the front steps outside our apartment building.

"All right," I said. I didn't want to tell them that Miss Marshall had yelled at me about my drawings and continued to be miserable to me.

"So what did you learn there?" Max said.

Simon rolled his eyes, clearly uninterested.

"History, everything." I stopped. "And we're learning about something very important. We're learning about our 'forefathers.'"

There was silence, and then the three of us laughed.

"Our forefather was the czar," Simon said.

"Exactly," I replied.

"Well, I've got things to do," Simon said. "Swell to see you, Max." He bounded into the building.

"How's the drawing coming along?" Max asked me.

"Good," I said, although now when I thought about drawing, Miss Marshall's ugly face and cruel words crowded into my mind.

"I'll bet it's *great.*" He smiled and stretched out the word as if it were the longest in the dictionary. "I've got to get home, too." We both stood, and he shook my hand vigorously.

I didn't want Max to go. That night, I lay awake in bed and imagined his long fingers, his green-blue eyes, his easy smile.

My old grandmother rarely left Aunt Feyga's apartment or even the bed. Aunt Feyga waddled around her, arranging blankets and feeding her syrupy yellow chicken broth. Aunt Feyga was short and plump, barely five feet tall, and pigeon-toed. Her husband, Uncle Myron, was equally short and sour. They both smelled of cigarettes and worked in the Granville Laundry, but more and more, she stayed home to take care of my grandmother. On my way home from school, I often saw my aunt pacing the sidewalk near her apartment building, clutching her blue *pushke* box, imploring strangers to give coins for the poor. Last week, Max and I had walked past her, and she flung her arms around me, pressed her big, uneven bosom into my body, and then wiggled her box until it touched Max's chin. He stepped back and dropped in a penny.

She and Uncle Myron had one son, Mel, who was already nineteen. Mel rarely attended the family club my father had created or our family's holiday meals. My mother said he was mixed up with gangsters, but what kind and in what manner I didn't know.

My old *bubbe* didn't resemble anyone in the family. She had a thin, bony face and eyes so deeply set they were like open graves in her skin. It seemed to me she was an example of what one could expect and fear in life: You struggled to grow up, got old, grew ugly and sick, then died. She frightened me with her sweaty smell, her puckered skin and bloodshot eyes. But she didn't seem to notice anything was wrong with her. "How is your school? Do you like it?" she mumbled in Yiddish with a toothless smile whenever I visited her.

After school I decided to stop to see her. Max was busy playing basketball. He wouldn't be on the front steps of our apartment like he'd been yesterday, talking to Simon.

Aunt Feyga swung open the door when I knocked. "Are you here to see your *bubbe*?" she asked.

"Yes," I said.

"Come in, come in." She hugged me, and her short, plump body pressed into mine. "Your grandmother has been asking for you."

My aunt ushered me to the living room and left me there. My grandmother's bed was pushed against the living room wall. The smells of garlic and soaps and stale, unpleasant odors I couldn't identify mingled in the air. Furniture crowded the small room—a sofa, the bed, an armchair, and lamp. Six blue *pushke* boxes sat lined up on the fireplace mantel.

My grandmother lay on her back beneath a white wool blanket. Her eyes were shut.

"Hello, *Bubbe*," I whispered. I stood a few feet from the bed. I thought she might be sleeping.

"Step closer, Lena," she croaked. "So I can see you." She opened her eyes.

I tiptoed to the side of the bed. She inched up and leaned against the pillow. Her coarse white hair was pinned into a loose bun. She smiled her toothless smile. We just looked at each other.

Finally, I said, "I wanted to see how you're feeling. Are you feeling all right?"

"You are taller." She eyed me from head to toe. Then she smiled, reached toward me, and placed a trembling hand on my arm. "How happy I am to see you. I kiss you and hug you. My baby, my life," she crooned. The veins on her hand were bumpy beneath her skin.

I jumped back, away from her, afraid her touch would make me frail like she was.

Our family didn't speak about her condition. If she had an illness, I didn't know what it was. My parents and I didn't discuss their argument, either, or the teacher's terrible accusations. On Bittersweet Place, we lived with silence.

I meandered home and performed my chores, reading correspondence aloud and looking for letters in the mail from Uncle William, helping with dinner. But now, after my parents' argument, I did as little to help as I could. If there was no respect between my parents, why should I do what I was asked? My mother didn't speak again about the lack of "relations" with my father or refer to the customer, the *choleria*, who had been part of his past. She didn't talk strangely as she had when I tried to tell her about Miss Marshall. Yet my mother sometimes moved so slowly now, stooped and distracted, her lips pinched. These last weeks a determined sorrow burned in her eyes. She seemed to be living in her mind.

I was filled not only with wanting, but with guilt. My parents worked hard. They did this for Simon and me, I knew. And what did I do? Go to school, draw my pictures, wish Uncle Maurice dead, argue with my mother, and daydream about Max Slovansky. I knew I should be grateful to her, to my father. My greediness for happiness was greater than my gratitude.

Despite my mother's complaints, the family club continued to gather at our apartment three or four nights a week. There didn't seem to be special songs or a secret handshake or rules that I could see, except to drink *schnapps* or vodka or whiskey or hot tea, play pinochle, and talk about the old country, the old life.

"So what kind of club are we really?" Uncle Abie asked my father one night.

I was at my desk writing an essay for school. The topic was "What My Country Means to Me."

"Are we a club to help the world?" Abie went on. He eyed my father. They sat across from each other at a card table. "Tell us already, Chaim."

"The world should help us," my mother said bitterly. She didn't look at my father. She settled on the sofa next to Mrs. Gerta Cohen.

"The purpose of this club is to enjoy life," my father replied. "And to help each other. In time, we'll do more to help the world. But if we are going to help the world, we need to know more about it, about President Coolidge, even Russia. The czar is gone. Stalin and Mr. Trotsky are fighting to lead the country. They call it the Union of Soviet Socialist Republics now. We should all read the *Chicago Tribune*." My father shuffled a deck of cards. Then he dealt them to Uncle Abie, Uncle Myron, Mr. Usher Cohen, and himself. "We must enjoy life for one reason," my father said, "because there are no pockets in a shroud."

A few days later my mother asked me to help at the laundry. Aunt Feyga had to stay with my grandmother, my mother explained, and wouldn't be able to work. None of the other aunts and uncles were able to go to the laundry either. Uncle Abie had a second job at a piano store, and he had to be there every day.

"I need you to help your father," she went on. "Hadie will be pressing clothing in the back, but she cannot talk to customers." Hadie was the kind, quiet Negro woman who worked at the Granville

Laundry, too.

"What about Simon?" I asked. "Why can't he go?"

"He will help another time. I do not have patience to argue. Please do as I say. Go there after school."

That afternoon, I stood at the long wooden counter in the front of the laundry and folded the shirts Hadie had pressed. My father was in the back, taking care of receipts and clothing. I didn't help at the laundry often, but if I had to be there, I liked to work in the front. In the back were the washing machines and giant pressing machines, the piles of soiled clothing, the heat and steam. I liked greeting the customers who arrived at the front door. I liked to pretend that I lived here and that this was a beautiful and quiet house.

The shades in the front window were pulled up. Afternoon sunlight poured in, brightening the dingy gray laundry walls. From where I stood, I could see the large white letters painted on the store's window. They stared at me backward, as if I were looking in a mirror:

GRANVILLE LAUNDRY
CLEANERS & DRYERS
Fine Tailoring Pressing & Repairing
Pants, Suits, Dresses, Shirts

All afternoon, I folded shirts, smoothing the fabrics and straightening the collars, and I helped the few customers who trickled in. Just as I finished the last shirt, about to get ready to leave, the front door opened and a tall, slender, pretty woman strolled in. Her blond hair was swept back behind her ears in a fashionable bob. She had pale skin and pale blue eyes, and she wore a soft brown overcoat. A yellow silk chrysanthemum was pinned to the lapel. She laid two pairs of trousers and a pile of dresses on the counter, and unbuttoned her coat. A long strand of white pearls gleamed against her red dress.

"Hello." She glanced from me toward the back of the store. I was about to greet her, but then she smiled and said, "There you are." She spoke without an accent.

My father approached the counter.

I turned to him. His face opened into a smile. He wasn't looking at me. His expression was radiant. Then his lips settled into a businesslike frown.

"Can I help you?" he said.

The woman's sweet scent filled the front of the laundry, a flutter of lilac perfume.

"Thank you, Henry." She pronounced the word Henry as if it were a melody and part of a song.

I glanced uneasily at my father. I had seen his smile. And I'd never heard anyone call him Henry. Then I gazed at the customer, at her pale skin, the long dark lashes and soft blue eyes.

"I will take care of this, Lena," he said curtly. He began to count the items of clothing and write down the information. "You can go home now."

Aunt Feyga and Aunt Ida were able to work the rest of the week, so the next day I went directly home after school. I retreated into my bedroom and shut the door. My mother called out to me that she was leaving to deliver clothing. I sprawled on the bed, happy for this unexpected silence.

The exchange between my father and the customer had shocked me. She was beautiful, clearly kind to him, the very woman—the customer—my mother had screamed about. *Henry*, the woman had said, like a song. I remembered the words Uncle Maurice had hurled at my father, "Look at how you behave. You and your secrets." Had my father betrayed my mother, betrayed Simon and me, too? Who was my father, after all?

I sat up on the bed, frantic, furious, my heart pounding. How could he do this? I wanted to shout at him, demand an answer. But I told myself: Lena, wait. I couldn't bear to believe my mother or believe what she'd said about my father. Pay attention to your own troubles, I told myself. I felt overwhelmed by troubles. Miss Marshall still accused me of tracing the pictures. She wanted to fail me for the assignment and the whole year, she'd warned me again this week, if I didn't admit my lies. I'd finally told my parents what Miss Marshall had said. They barely listened, intent on their anger with one another.

Now I knelt on the floor and pulled out the square wooden box I kept hidden beneath my bed. I opened the lid and lifted out my drawings. I laid them on the mattress. Sketches of trees, a ship, the lake, the profile of a woman. All in pencil or pen. I wished I had added color to them. The drawings seemed to be crying out for all the bright colors of the rainbow.

I picked up a pencil and drew a line near the woman's nose. I wanted to make the nose longer, more delicate. I sketched her lips to give them more shape. The drawing wasn't quite right, I thought. The lips looked too large. Some of my lines were too thick. I would have to try to draw this again.

Then I heard the tap-tap of knocking and my father's voice. "Lena, I would like to talk to you."

"Now?" I hadn't heard him come home.

I hurriedly began to collect the drawings to hide them, but he turned the knob, opened the door, and peeked in. "Can I join you?"

"Why?" I said angrily.

"I need to talk to you."

I dropped the papers on the bed and frowned. I didn't want to talk to him. Everything distracted and interrupted me—my father, the beautiful customer, my parents' argument, Uncle Maurice, Miss Marshall. I was growing a garden of grudges, I realized, a garden of anger.

His blue tweed overcoat was buttoned, and he carried his gray felt hat. "What are these?" He pointed to the drawings.

"My art."

"Yours?" He bent toward the bed and lifted up a drawing.

"Yes." I nodded.

He looked at me and then spread the pages one next to another across the bed. He opened his eyes wide, studying the pages. "Well. Lena. These are very, very nice. I didn't know you could do this."

"I discovered it," I said. "By accident. When I would sit with Leah Grace and then after."

"A wonderful discovery." He smiled at me. "You can capture beauty."

That was what I longed to do. "Oh, I hope so," I said, thrilled to hear this despite my anger at him.

He smoothed a hand through his wavy red hair. "I wanted to tell you also, I spoke to your teacher this morning. Your mother and I did. We spoke to Miss Marshall."

"You did?" Miss Marshall had been away from the classroom for part of the morning, but she had mentioned nothing to me about my parents. I could imagine the conversation. "You people may tolerate lies," she would say, and my mother would bristle, "What people? You people murdered my father."

"Yes, she telephoned to ask us to meet with her. She told us about the problem with your assignment. She will not reconsider her decision," my father said, interrupting my thoughts. "She will give you a failing grade for the assignment. She's not certain if she will fail you for the year yet. She'll wait to decide. She told us she makes her judgments about students and their work based on her experience. She has given this assignment many times before."

"Every day she's awful to me. She's an old witch."

"I would say she is confused." He nodded. "Confused and unjust. That is how I would describe her."

"If you brought these other drawings to her, maybe she wouldn't be confused." I laid one drawing on top of another. "She would believe me. Yes. That's what you must do, Papa. Bring her the drawings. She'll believe you."

My father was silent. He rubbed a hand against the back of his neck. "She is a person who will not change her mind," he finally said. "This I can see. She will just say you copied or traced these too. We don't want more trouble from her, Lena. Small problems can grow into big ones. We saw that in Russia."

"This is already a big problem. We don't live in Russia. You have to talk to her. You can say anything you want in this country and not be afraid. That's what the teachers tell us. You have to help me." I straightened the drawings into a neat pile and laid them back in the

box. I shut the lid. "Whatever you do, don't tell Mother about these."
If Miss Marshall wasn't going to see these drawings, I didn't want my
mother to have the satisfaction of seeing them, either.

"Remember, be kind to your mother. Even to Miss Marshall."

"I'm not going to be kind to Miss Marshall. People don't listen to
you if you're kind. You have to talk to her again. Please."

"I told you. This I cannot do now. But let me consider it. I didn't
know about these drawings when your mother and I spoke to the
teacher. Let us see what happens with this problem. I still advise you
to be kind. Shall we take a walk?" He pulled a small box from his coat
pocket. "I must bring this to Aunt Feyga."

"Why aren't you at work?"

"I wanted a small vacation. And I had packages to deliver."

Outside, the cool October breeze fluttered against us. The sky
was white, as if a giant shawl were wrapped around it, hiding the
blue and sunlight. Red and golden leaves covered the ground like a
colorful blanket. I kicked one brittle golden leaf along the sidewalk.
The leaf cracked in half.

I didn't know what to say to my father. His argument with my
mother hung between us like a black curtain in a *shiva* house. I had
to tell someone that secret, to tell him. I couldn't bear to think about
it myself any more. I needed to find out the truth.

"I heard you and Mama talking a few weeks ago at night," I finally
said. I gathered my courage. "I was in the hallway. I heard the slap."

"Oh?" His arms swung fiercely as he walked.

"She told you about the customer. The *choleria.*"

He stared ahead. His skin had turned the color of flour. "So she
did," he said.

When we reached Aunt Feyga's building, he sat on the front step.

"I am happy you showed me your art." He patted the step next to
him, and I sat there. Then he rubbed a finger along the smooth felt
of his gray hat and set the hat on his lap. "It is unfortunate you heard
your mother and me. We are Russians, all of us, arguing. Like little
volcanoes." He took a breath. "Sometimes big volcanoes. This I want
you to know: A man is a different creature from a woman. We all live

with a whole world inside our heads, and the heart has its own will. Do you understand what I tell you? The world is a big place, my little Lena. Bigger than you might think."

"Is she *her*, the woman at the store?"

"Your mother exaggerates, tells a *meise*, a story. There is no customer."

"No. That woman in the laundry. She's the one Mama meant. It must be her. She called you Henry."

His jaw tightened. "That one."

"Yes." I waited for him to say more, but he was silent.

"That one," I said. "It was *her*, the customer." I was sure of this now.

He tapped his fingers against his hat brim. Finally, he replied, "She was my good friend. While you were in Russia. She is no longer."

"Why not?"

"How can I explain?" He sighed. "A person makes a decision. You will learn this in life. Maybe some day she will be a friend again." He shrugged. "The future is an unopened book." He gazed away from me, as if he were talking to himself. "Maybe you will meet her. This I don't know."

"I've met her enough," I said. "I know what you're talking about. She's not a friend. You touched her. *Shtupping.*" I spit out the word.

"Lena, stop that," he ordered, shocked. "Watch that tongue."

But I wanted to hurt him. "Uncle Maurice tried to do the same to me."

"Uncle Maurice?"

I stopped, aware we were outside. No one walked past us, but even so, I whispered, "What he did in the hall. At home. You're just like Uncle Maurice."

My father stared at me, squinting. "What am I? I don't understand what you're telling me, Lena."

"Yes." My sudden fury shocked me. "That's what you're like." I burst out with my story.

"No." He clenched his hand into a fist. His left eye twitched, and his face turned red. He put his arm around me, but I pulled away.

"I warned your mother about Maurice," he muttered. "I'll kill that man."

Two weeks later, we received news from Uncle William. On a rainy and gray late-October afternoon, I sat at the kitchen table, looking through our stack of mail.

From the pile, I pulled an envelope and slid out a letter written in his tiny, neat scrawl.

"Finally, from William," my mother said when she saw his handwriting on the letter. "Read it to me, Lena. Please."

I read aloud:

> Dear Lovely Family,
>   I will send more news soon. Too busy to cry anymore about Leah Grace.
>   Your loving brother,
>   William

"This is not right," she said. "How can he be too busy for us?"

I shrugged, crushed by the brevity of his reply.

My mother seemed like her old prickly, sorrowful self again, like the person she had been before her argument with my father. She stood at the kitchen counter and began to chop an onion fiercely, as if she poured her disappointment about the letter into her hands. All these subjects—passion, anger, betrayal, disappointment, affection, and love—were not part of our family's language. They were a part of my language, and mine alone, so I had decided to punish my mother with my silence. I'd begged my father not to say anything to her about Uncle Maurice.

"She'll think it was my fault," I'd said to my father. "I can't speak to her about it. Don't tell her."

"I cannot promise that," he replied.

He and I hadn't talked about Uncle Maurice again. But these last weeks my father sometimes gazed at me with concern. I hadn't forgiven him for the beautiful customer, although I wasn't willing to believe all my mother's accusations. I often mulled over my father's words: A man is a different creature from a woman, he had told me. What did he mean? What did it feel like in your heart to be a man? What was a man's true nature? Were all men dangerous, like Uncle Maurice? I longed to ask someone, but there was no one I could talk to.

My father was right about one point: We all lived with a whole world inside of our heads. My mother lived in her mind, Simon lived in his, and I lived in mine. Everyone in the apartment on Bittersweet Place seemed to be living in his or her separate thoughts. I hadn't seen the beautiful customer again, but at night, in my bed, in the darkness, I could hear the soft musical swish of the way she'd mouthed my father's new name. *Henry.*

Rain splattered against the window. The sky looked as dark as midnight. Thunder bellowed; it was going to storm. I set Uncle William's letter on the kitchen table and fished through the pile of mail. From the bottom, I lifted out another envelope. The address was typewritten: "Mrs. Reesa Czernitski, 245 Bittersweet Place, Chicago Illinois".

My mother finished chopping the onion. She wiped her hands on her blue flowered apron and peered at the envelope. "From who, Lena? Who sent this?"

I read aloud impatiently, "Los Angeles County General Hospital."

"Hospital? Quickly. Open it, read it to me."

I ripped open the envelope very slowly. Why couldn't my mother read these letters herself? Why did I always have to be her eyes? I read to her grudgingly:

> Dear Mrs. Reesa Czernitski:
>
> We wish to inform you that your brother, William, has been admitted as a patient at the Los Angeles County General Hospital. He is currently in the Psychopathic Department, essentially a mental hospital within the larger hospital structure. He has informed us that you are his nearest relation. Please contact us at your earliest opportunity to discuss the situation.
>
> Yours truly,
> Dr. Emanuel Sedgewick

"Oh, no," I said.

My mother swallowed hard. "Mental hospital."

"Are you Uncle William's nearest relation? What about old grandmother?"

"Where is Maurice?" she murmured, then shook her head. "*Bubbe*. You know your grandmother's proper name. She is not 'old' grandmother. She is simply grandmother or *Bubbe*." My mother frowned. "But we must telephone. Do not say a word about William to your grandmother or the relatives. Please. I need your help to find this doctor."

In the living room, on top of an end table, sat our tall black telephone.

My mother kept slugs for the telephone in a glass jar in the kitchen, next to the jar where she kept coins for the streetcar. I carried a handful of slugs to the living room.

"You telephone," she said. "I need time to think about what to say. Use a full, important voice, Lena."

I slid two slugs into the telephone's slot, ashamed of my thoughts about my mother, and suddenly panicked about Uncle William. Of course I would help her. I waited until the operator's nasal voice filtered through.

"I need the Los Angeles County General Hospital," I said.

I imagined the sounds of my voice sweeping through the wires of the telephone until they reached Los Angeles, California, and Uncle William's very room, and I could hear his voice, "Lena, I will sing a song for you."

"Lena." My mother pressed her arms against her chest. "What do they say? Why does so much time pass?"

"I'm waiting."

"May the Almighty help us."

I slid four more slugs into the telephone as the operator instructed.

"Los Angeles County General Hospital," a woman's voice said.

"Yes." I read the man's name on the letter. "I must speak to Dr. Emanuel Sedgewick."

Soon a gruff voice boomed, "May I be of help?"

"Good day," I began. I spoke an octave below my normal tones so I might sound grown up. Heat hissed into the room through the radiator. The elevated train roared. I hoped these sounds didn't reach California. "I am in Chicago, Illinois," I said. My voice sounded brave and certain. "This morning I received a letter regarding Mr. William Czernitski. I wish to discuss this with Dr. Emanuel Sedgewick."

There was a long pause. I heard the rustling of papers, a sigh. "You are Mrs. Reesa Czernitski?"

My mother bent toward the telephone and whispered to me, "Tell him you must find out where William is. We must talk to William."

"Not really," I said to the man. "That's my mother."

"Let me talk to her," he said, "and thank you."

She grasped the receiver, greeted the man, listened, then said, "A nervous collapse?" Her eyes were round and glistening, like glowing full moons, and her lips formed a circle as she spoke. "My brother, Maurice, should be able to help." She listened again.

I imagined Uncle William collapsed, his tall body small enough now to fit into a suitcase.

When my mother hung up, she sank into the sofa and moved her hands together and apart, as if her fingers were knitting needles. "Lena, thank you. You go, do work for school."

"Why is he having a nervous collapse? What upset him?" A chill crept up my arms. Had Uncle Maurice done something terrible to Uncle William and caused this? Would I have a nervous collapse, too?

"William," she repeated, staring past me as if she were gazing directly at the state of California. "He is not well."

"What will happen to him, Mama? We can't leave him there alone."

"I don't know where we will find the money," she murmured, "but we have to bring him home."

Independence Boulevard
November 1926

My father took the train to California. When we left him at the station, my mother grasped my hand as if she might topple over. Her eyes were moist with tears. But after he had been away for two days, she seemed to relax, like a kite floating on a rush of air. She bustled about the apartment with efficiency. She stopped talking about Uncle William. Perhaps she had driven thoughts of him and my father from her mind. I struggled to do this. What if my father returned home with both uncles?

Mr. Usher Cohen had loaned our family money for the trip to California, my father had told us. "But how we will repay Mr. Cohen," he'd said wearily, "I do not know."

I didn't have time to dwell on these worries. School was becoming more and more difficult to bear.

Friday, a few days after my father's departure, Miss Marshall called me to the front of the classroom. I was sure she was going to ask me to recite, which I hated to do. I walked in dread, biting my lower lip. From the front of the room, I stared over rows of students and looked at the white wall behind them.

"Instead of reciting, you are going to help teach a lesson," she said to me.

I sucked in a breath. Children began to giggle. Mary Hall caught my gaze. Her face folded into a frown with what seemed like sympathy. Philip Schloss glared at me, snickering. I stared past them at the wall.

"It is my job to help each student improve." Miss Marshall stood beside me. "I want everyone in class to be quiet. Today Miss Czernitski will be our example. You will learn to write with the proper hand. Follow me." She grasped my forearm, pinching me, and marched me to my desk. Her sweet orange perfume stuck to my skin.

"Please sit down," she ordered. She peered at the class. "Lena holds her pencil with her left hand. No one else here does this. Is this true?"

Some students nodded.

"No one else does," Philip Schloss called out.

Miss Marshall jerked my left hand behind my back, my favorite hand, the one I used for drawing. She laid my other hand on the desktop. Then she lifted a pencil from the desk and positioned my right hand so she could wedge the pencil between my finger and thumb.

"There is a correct, American style of using a pencil," she said. "Complete assignments like this. Practice. Practice. Practice." She rapped her fingers on my desk. Her long red nails clacked against the wood. "The assignment today is to write your name forty times in your best penmanship. Make your push-pulls tidy, your curls even. I want all of you to do this now. In the past, I've had to tie a student's hand behind her back to remind her which hand to use. Do you think that's necessary now, Lena?"

I shook my head no.

When she returned to the front of the room, I pressed pencil to paper, dragging the pencil across it again and again. The writing wobbled miserably, impossible to read, but I refused to cry.

After school, Mary Hall stopped me in the schoolyard. "That was awful, what Miss Marshall did to you," she said.

"Yes." I was startled Mary mentioned this. "I've got to go now." I didn't want to talk to her or anyone about it and hurried out of the yard.

When I arrived home, my mother was sitting in the living room with her sewing. I stood looking at her, my mouth closed tight, as though she had stitched it shut. I couldn't bear to tell her what had happened to me at school. My mother knew nothing of this world; even in her beloved golden land, there were people who tried to murder you, I thought, who were cruel and did not let you breathe.

And like I had done with so many other things, I would wait to tell my father.

My father had embarked on a journey—a charitable, necessary journey, my mother explained—and so she seemed to have granted him a temporary dispensation.

Sunday morning, Simon taught me about dispensation. He and I were standing in the living room. "You want dispensation for taking a nickel from me," he said.

"Dispensation?"

"You want me to forgive you. For stealing."

"I didn't steal," I said. "You gave the nickel to me."

"That's for a judge to decide. Don't argue so much. Or hire a lawyer, like Clarence Darrow. He defended Leopold and Loeb."

"That's awful, Simon. They killed that boy a few years ago. He was only fourteen. Here, in Chicago."

"Everyone knows that. Bobby Franks. Even though it was awful, you need to know about the world."

"No one here thinks about the world, except Papa," I said.

"I do. Coolidge says the United States won't join the World Court. Russia didn't join. Do you even know what the World Court is? Or who Coolidge is?"

"Of course, I do. He's the president, stupid. And the Court is part of the League of Nations. They talk about that at school."

"And Alphonse G. Capone?"

"Everyone knows that. He's a gangster."

"At least you know something. Ma doesn't want to know. I won't live that way. You ought to think about how you want to live, too."

"I live just fine. And I'm not a *gonif*, a thief," I said, appalled by the accusation of stealing. "Besides, you're never home to argue with." I stood on tiptoes, trying to peer into his eyes. "What do you do with those boys, anyway? Izzie Berger and Manny Goldstein? Max told me you go off with them. They aren't nice people, Simon. You'll get in trouble. And Nookie Michaelson is Mel's age. He's a man already. His father is a gangster. You'll have big *tsuris*. You go looking for trouble, you'll find it." I blinked away surprise. My mother's words had burst from my mouth.

He laughed. "Nah. I play basketball with them, and we all work for Mr. Usher Cohen. You know that. You sound like Ma. That's not so bad. She doesn't get angry with me like she does with you."

"You're not home enough for that," I said.

Simon could have stayed home as much as he wanted. He was my mother's prize. She sewed him soft flannel trousers and white cotton shirts. She prepared special meals only for him. Brown bread smothered with butter and sweet apricot jam, strawberries floating in thick cream and coated with blankets of sugar.

"This is not for you, Lena," she'd said last week, and placed a towel over the food until Simon appeared. "Girls are not boys, after all. Simon needs to eat to become a man."

I hated how my mother paid more attention to him than to me. And it seemed the more he ate, the skinnier he became. I wasn't so lucky. I was determined not to add to my pudgy shape so Max Slovansky would think of me as beautiful.

It wasn't fair that Simon could go wherever he wished without telling my mother. It wasn't fair that she loved him more than she loved me.

But I was learning from him. I'd arranged to meet Max at the lake that afternoon. We would ride the streetcar from there to Independence Boulevard and his house.

When my mother asked about my plans for the day, I said, "I'm going to sit at Lake Michigan. To read and walk on the sand. Why do you always ask me? I'm fifteen now." I had turned fifteen last month. My mother had baked a cake filled with raisins and apples for me as she always did on birthdays, but otherwise the day was the same as any other. "If I were Simon, I could do whatever I pleased," I said now. "I would be a man."

"He is not a man yet and you will never be," she said. We were standing in the kitchen. "You sit with your pencils and books too much, Lena. You spend too much time without people." She frowned, her old self again. "You will turn into a person who doesn't know how to speak to other human beings. Remember my words when you are without friends."

"I won't remember anything you say."

"Don't speak to me in such a way. A girl shouldn't speak like that."

"A girl should do whatever she wants." I stormed out of the kitchen. I hated my mother's opinions, but I was thrilled she had believed me, and amazed I could lie with such ease, even pleasure.

I was eager to see Max, and to see where he lived. When I was with him he distracted me from my troubles, from thoughts of the miserable Miss Marshall and the problems at school, from my father and the beautiful customer. How could I become an artist when I had so much to worry about? *There you are…thank you, Henry,* the woman had said to him, her voice tender, as if she were his wife.

Sunday afternoon as planned, Max and I rode the streetcar to the west side of the city, to the stop near Independence Boulevard.

One end of the boulevard opened into a large park, where a few people strolled, dressed in bulky overcoats and scarves. I imagined families picnicked here in warmer weather, but now the park looked a little bleak in the cold November air. Brittle yellow and red leaves clung to trees. The grass was brown and dry. The sun struggled to peek through the clouds; the few rays of light that slithered through warmed my face.

A calm settled inside me as Max and I walked. I rarely felt this in the city, except when I lounged on the sand, drew my pictures, and stared out at the gray-blue waters of Lake Michigan. I used to feel this same calm in Russia, before our terrible troubles.

Max had a long nose and a large space between its tip and his wide lips. I studied his profile. His face was long, too, but not awkwardly so. In a pleasing way, I thought. I wanted to draw him someday. To always remember him. He smiled at me, and his face glowed with warmth.

I returned his smile shyly, then gazed at the boulevard. It was wider than the streets in my neighborhood. Great, tall trees with broad knobby trunks stood like soldiers on both sides, as if this were the grand promenade in Paris I had read about in school.

It was more beautiful here than I imagined, and not at all as Uncle Abie had described it.

"The Jews on Independence and Douglas Boulevards are more German than Jewish," he had told my mother one night before my father left for California. "They don't keep up their property. They have no religious beliefs in Lawndale." Uncle Abie had spit into his creased white handkerchief. "I sat in those houses yesterday on Independence Boulevard like a doctor visiting the sick," he'd said. "I talked to those people who wanted to buy or sell a piano. They aren't like you or me. Some of them even read *Freiheit,* that communist newspaper." Uncle Abie worked three days in the Granville Laundry now, and the rest of the week he worked in the store that sold pianos.

I had listened with great interest.

"I see what I see. I tell you, Reesa," he went on. He lifted a bottle of *schnapps* and poured some into an empty glass. "Those Jews are the new Americans. The future. Soon Simon and Lena and Mel—he's already lost—will be living in Deutschland, too. Worshipping money and *geschlecht.*" He gulped his *schnapps* and burped loudly. "Lust."

"Phhh, phhh, phhh." My mother had spit, to chase away an evil eye—a curse that might make Uncle Abie's words come true.

"To you, life is midnight, darkness, Abie," my father had said. "There's always a complaint."

Aunt Ida had glanced up from her book. Her sunken brown eyes bulged with outrage. "My family in Poland lives a religious life. A good life. Here, you can't live such a life. Oh, I dream of going back there."

But the people I saw on Independence Boulevard didn't seem to be worshipping money or anything else. They seemed like people in my neighborhood, but dressed in more stylish clothing, coats of fine, heavy fabrics.

"Do you know why this is named Independence Boulevard?" Max asked.

"Not because of the Constitution," I said.

We both laughed.

"Declaration of Independence," he said. "Found that in the library, too."

"I thought you did," I said.

Max did not live on the tree-lined boulevard. Halfway down the block, we turned onto another street, and then another. The sign read Millard Avenue.

"This one is ordinary, named after a man who built houses," Max said. "Mr. A. C. Millard. In Chicago, a street that runs north and south is called an 'avenue.'" He paused. "But there are some exceptions."

In the middle of the block, Max stopped. "This is my house," he said.

He pointed to a red brick house. A shining white porch wrapped around the front of it like a ribbon. A white fence rose at the edge of the grass. The house was a grand structure with its own land. The house of a wealthy person. The street wasn't ordinary at all. I glanced at my plain brown coat. My mother had bought the cheap wool from a cart on Maxwell Street. She had sewn this coat, her needle spinning against the cloth.

"You can understand about a person from where they live," Max said.

"Oh?" I smoothed my coat sleeve, trying to flatten the wrinkles. "What do you understand about me?"

"You have a large family. Everyone likes the other."

"They don't," I said.

"To a stranger, that's how it seems."

"You're not a stranger, Max, you're..." I paused. I didn't know what he was. "You're a friend."

"I meant someone who's not in the family. An observer."

I hadn't thought of Max as an observer. Maybe he was. He seemed to carefully regard whatever happened around him.

"Well, this is where *I* live," he informed me again. He walked up the steps to the porch.

"It's beautiful." I drank in the sight of his house. "You must live a happy life here."

"I need to tell you something first." He opened his eyes wide. The green-blue was flecked with brown, a beautiful burst of color. "My mother screams," he said, then he sat down on a step.

I sat beside him. "Screams? I don't understand."

"Just because this house looks big, doesn't mean it's a better place to live than where you live, Lena."

I felt my face grow hot; he knew my thoughts.

"You'll hear her," he said. "But she recovers."

I had seen his mother at the Jewish Center once—pretty, slender Mrs. Slovansky with her wavy brown hair and bright smile, a gold chain with a charm of a heart anchored around her neck. It didn't seem possible she could scream.

But a few minutes later, a screech exploded from the house. And then, "Finish those chores and go get Benny or I will *kill* myself. You make me *meshugge*." A door slammed.

Max stared at his lap.

"Maxwell," his mother yelled again. "Get Benny or it will be the end. Answer me. Are you inside the house or not?"

He was silent.

"Won't you answer her?" I said. "Help her, Max."

He slung one leg over the other. "I will not."

Just then, his younger brother Benny, short and out of breath, bounded up the porch steps. "I'm late," he mumbled.

Max yelled, "Ma, he's coming."

Behind Benny hurried Sophe, Max's older sister. Her short blond curls bounced as she ran and her red coat, wide like a cape, made a swishing sound. She stopped at the steps, and her eyes, like two turquoise stones, met mine. "Hello, Lena," she said. She turned to Max. "I'll talk to her, Maxila." She ran past us, into the house.

A clamor of voices rose from inside. After a few minutes, there was silence.

"My other brother must be working." Max nodded slowly. "That's why my mother is quiet now. Meyer is a writer. When he works, the earth stands still. He's at home, in the room where he writes. He says he can't sleep and write in the same place. I have to share a bedroom with him," Max groaned. "And he has another room, with a desk, just for himself." Max pointed to a window on the second floor. "He has two rooms."

"Well, he must write great words," I said.

"Meyer? Nah. He organizes his papers and sharpens pencils. He likes his papers on the desk to be in the right position. He stares out the window. My father says Meyer won't do anything unless the stars are lined up just right. Ma thinks he's a genius. I think he's a fake. She says he's a real writer. An artist. She says an artist needs silence."

"Oh." I considered this. If Mrs. Slovansky had been my mother, I imagined, she would have talked to Miss Marshall and insisted that artists needed silence and kindness. They could write with whichever hand they pleased.

"I think," Max went on with authority, "to be a writer has different requirements from a person who draws pictures. I don't know for sure. But it's my opinion. Meyer has one poem published in one book, *Illinois Poets*. My mother says this is the beginning of a great future for him."

"Maybe she's correct." I'd never met a writer or an artist. What would I say to such a person? I was thrilled someone so smart and accomplished lived in Max's house.

"Come on," Max said. He started toward the door. "I'll show you."

We entered a large, light-filled parlor, then climbed a long flight of dark wooden steps to the second floor. We tiptoed down the dim hall. A thick rug patterned with blue and red flowers covered the length of the corridor and cushioned our steps. The air was musty. All the doors were closed.

Max knelt by a door at the end of the hall. He peeked through the keyhole. "Here," he whispered.

I knelt next to him. His long, thin fingers positioned my face to the keyhole. His skin felt smooth and warm, and I pressed my eye close to the cold brass opening. At first, all I could see was darkness. I shifted my head. The room and a man came into view. He sat at a desk. I could see his profile. He looked older than Max. In his twenties. The man had green-blue eyes like Max's, and the same-shaped nose. He tapped a hand against the smooth surface of the desk. Then he began to finger pencils, one at a time, as if counting, lifting a pencil and placing it back on the desk. Ten pencils. I pulled away.

"See?" said Max, smiling.

There was a sudden shuffling from inside the room. We dashed down the hall to the stairs.

A door squeaked open. I imagined Meyer was chasing us. Then the door slammed shut with a thud.

"Does everyone need to be completely silent when Meyer sits at his desk?" I said when we were safely on the porch.

"Yes," said Max. "That's the rule of the house. My mother's rule."

"Is it quiet when you do schoolwork?"

"Never." Max sat on the step.

"It seems to me," I said, "that Meyer is your mother's favorite."

"I think, yes." Max paused. "I think he is. He has such a big opinion of himself, too. He thinks he's so smart, and he's convinced my mother."

"That's not right," I said, sitting next to Max. It was still cold outside, I realized, but I'd hardly noticed, so intent was I on conversation with him. I pulled up my coat collar. "It's not right that she screams at you and demands quiet for him."

"Maybe it won't always be like this. One day she'll see that she was wrong. She'll appreciate my best qualities."

"You have many," I teased.

A blush crept across his cheeks. "Thank you. She does confide in me. When she's not screaming. She has a temper."

"You help her, then." I thought about how I now helped my mother as little as I could, doing little more than reading mail and telephoning California for her. She worked hard at her sewing repairs. I knew she did this for Simon and me. My father worked hard, too. Suddenly I felt guilty.

"I try to help her," Max said.

I thought, too, of my mother's weeping fits, how she sometimes pulled into herself, held onto her thoughts tightly. She didn't scream like Mrs. Slovansky, except when she argued with my father. It was as if my mother's eyes and words were a shield for what she hid in her heart. At least a scream held emotion.

"I can't talk to my mother," I said.

"She's a seamstress," Max replied. "So she's learned to sew up life instead of opening life up."

I envisioned my mother frantically stitching up all that was wrong with our life. "Maybe nothing is opened up in our apartment. We don't talk to each other about what's in our hearts."

"Meyer wants to open the world, to understand everything about it." Max stretched his arms upward to the sky, as if his brother could understand the entire universe. "That's the one good thing about him. Because he's a writer. I think this is the best way to live. To speak your thoughts. To say whatever is in your mind. Plainly. Truly."

I hesitated, then said, "Simon is my mother's favorite."

"You don't know that," Max said. "What's a favorite? It can change day to day. That's what I believe. You should, too. At least, now you've met the great writer."

"We didn't meet," I corrected. "But I *saw* him."

"You're very precise."

"Oh, Max," I burst out. "I like you so much." Then I laughed nervously, regretting my words. "I guess I've listened to your advice. To speak my thoughts."

"And I like you. I like that we can sit and talk."

We were silent. Max placed his hand on mine. I stared into his green-blue eyes. Then he leaned in and kissed me. I felt the breath rise in him. I struggled to breathe myself. I didn't freeze like I had done with Uncle Maurice. I had never kissed a boy, but I surrendered everything to Max now, my fears and affection, my modesty and silence; all this, even my soul, seemed to pour from my lips to his. I thought I might faint from the pleasure. It was only a few minutes that we touched, but all seemed to pass from me to him.

I didn't know if the same had occurred for him. He looked so confident. I was afraid to ask, so when our lips parted, I whispered,

"Max, I have a question."

"Let me ask you first." His voice was husky, shaky. "Is it okay with you that we kissed?"

I felt myself blushing. I nodded and stared at the ground. "Do you think we could always be like this?" I said boldly. I looked at him. "Friends. For the length of our lives. I wish so much that this could happen."

He laughed kindly. "Oh, if everything we wish could come true. You and I are friends, but we aren't anywhere near being grown up."

"If you were my..." I stopped and gulped a breath. "Husband. If that were ever to happen...would I be your only wife?" Already, I felt jealous. I knew I shouldn't say this, but I wanted him to kiss only me.

"Of course." He pressed both his hands around mine. "But we're too young for that. And the law doesn't allow a person to have two wives anyway."

"In the Bible, people have two wives."

"They didn't live in Chicago, Illinois."

"I don't think where a person lives has any influence on this kind of thing." I squeezed my lips together, then, realizing this was my fear, I said, "My father may have another wife."

Max raised his eyebrows.

"While we lived in Russia, he had another wife here. Maybe even now."

"Who told you this?"

I described my mother's slap and the beautiful customer. I told Max my father had said the woman was just his "good friend."

"So you don't really know, Lena. If I were you, I'd forget about this. *Choleria* doesn't mean wife. It means a plague, like cholera, or a person who's like a plague. Good friend doesn't mean wife."

I dropped my hands from his, and mine fell into my lap. "No. I disagree. You can never *not* remember, as long as you have eyes and ears."

"But you can't let what you remember blind you." Max's hands encircled mine again. "You could say that what happened in your old home was too terrible to talk about. Or what you think your father did was terrible. But you have to look at the future. Enjoy and celebrate. My mother says that. After she screams." He laughed.

"What about the beautiful customer?" And what about Uncle Maurice? I thought to myself.

Max frowned. He seemed to be searching for an answer. "The rules of the Ten Commandments and the Bible keep order in our lives, I think," he finally said. "But a rule can't change the heart." His voice was strong, as if he were pleased with his words. "I don't think you have a full explanation. If you want an explanation about this beautiful customer, you'll have to ask your father."

"My father?"

"You may not want to hear what he says."

"No." *She was my good friend*, he'd said on the steps of Aunt Feyga's apartment building. *The future is an unopened book.*

"And if you don't want to hear his explanation, well, I wouldn't think about it so much."

I exhaled deeply and felt my shoulders sagging. "You're lucky your family doesn't have these problems."

"Lena Czernitski, if you really knew my family, you would be happier with yours."

I was silent.

"Don't look so sad," he said. "Even if your father has two wives, you don't have to have two husbands."

"No, I don't. I'll have just one." I felt satisfied with Max's answer and his wish to help me. For a moment, I wished I could tell Max about Uncle Maurice, but I couldn't bear to.

"I want you to listen to something. We have a Victrola inside." Max stood up. "Do you know 'Rhapsody in Blue'?"

"Rhapsody?"

"A musical composition. By George Gershwin. Do you know about Louis Armstrong?"

"No." I followed him to the door. "Will your mother mind if we listen? Or will Meyer?"

"We'll listen quietly. Then one day when they aren't home, you'll come back here. I'll play jazz for you on the piano."

"You can play an instrument?"

He nodded with pride and pulled open the door. "I play the piano. Louis Armstrong plays the cornet. He's a Negro who went to live and perform in New York City, but first he was in King Oliver's Creole Jazz Band right here in Chicago. He moved to New York to join Fletcher Henderson's Orchestra. Now he plays trumpet."

I had never heard of these people. "How do you know all this? Not from the library."

"No." He grasped my hand and led me into the house. "Music. It's my second love."

A Hospital Visit
November 1926, the next day

The weather was chilly again. Even though it was still November, I could feel winter's presence, as if the season were a person, pushing against me. My cheeks were rough from the cold. In the hallway of our building after school, I peeled off my green wool hat and jammed it into my canvas book bag. I felt like a woman. I had kissed Max Slovansky. In my heart a sweet sensation swelled—what could only be love. All day I had tried to stop thinking about him, to chase away my feelings, but I couldn't. His lips on mine. His warm skin. His eyes looking at me as if he knew my thoughts.

I felt stronger knowing Max, and began to climb the steps in the musty stairwell.

Now that Uncle Maurice lived in California, I wasn't afraid to come to the apartment alone. I knew my bravery could disappear. My father might return home with both uncles, but I willed myself not to think about this. My mother had told me in the morning that she planned to stay late at the laundry. Simon had disappeared with Nookie Michaelson to play basketball. No one would be home.

I sat on a step in the stairwell, pulled my notebook from my canvas satchel, and opened it. In class, while miserable Miss Marshall talked about Christopher Columbus and how his great discovery had changed humankind, I had studied my list of fears. *Humankind*. The word interrupted me. I'd found it in the dictionary: "Human beings considered collectively." How could Miss Marshall even use that word? She knew nothing about human beings. And how could anyone consider human beings collectively? Each person was so unlike the others, a thread of a different texture and color. Even in my own family. As if God labored at a giant sewing machine.

Each year that we lived in Chicago, I had copied my list of fears to a new notebook. I wanted to remember what I had felt at the moment of arriving here.

My Fears
by Lena Czernitski

September 15, 1922

1. ~~I Will never speak good English~~
2. Will not have one American friend
3. I will be attacked on the street by an American Petluria
4. I Will lose someone dear to me
5. ~~Will never have a home that is safe~~
6. Will never grow up
7. I will never ever know happiness again

My New Fears
8. WILL FAIL IN SCHOOL—and no one will help me

As I sat in the stairwell of our building, I printed another fear on the list. "9. Will never be able to come home alone." Then I crossed it out. My plan was to cross out each fear when I no longer felt afraid. I'd discarded some, only to erase the marks at another time. Nothing was without change, even my fears. I'd added: "WILL FAIL IN SCHOOL—and no one will help me" the day Miss Marshall yelled at me about my drawing. That fear still remained.

Kitchen odors congregated in the hallway near our apartment, a jumble of aromas. Rice. Burnt potatoes. Coffee. Cinnamon cookies. Sour beef *borscht*.

No smells slid from our apartment. I opened the door, and in our entry, I thought about Max again. As I did, I bumped into the small wooden table, my book bag brushing against it. The blue porcelain ballerina and the glass cup with the golden handle, the ones my mother had brought from Russia, fell to the floor. I wasn't quick enough to catch them. I watched helplessly as they hit the wood floor with a loud clatter. These were her favorite possessions. She had wrapped them in sweaters and carried them in her suitcase from Belilovka. I knelt and carefully lifted the broken, cracked pieces from the floor.

Footsteps thudded in the apartment.

Was my father back? Uncle Maurice?

"Is that you, Lena?" my mother yelled.

I charged out of the apartment. I hurriedly slid the broken pieces of the ballerina and glass cup into my book bag and walked back in.

"You said you wouldn't be home today," I answered.

"I left the laundry early," she explained. She stood in the small entryway. "Your grandmother is ill."

I nodded, shut the door, and unbuttoned my coat.

"Do not just stand there, looking into the air." She frowned. "We will have to leave soon for the hospital."

"Hospital?"

My mother planted her hands on her hips. "Your grandmother has been taken to the hospital. She is having trouble breathing. This afternoon, you and I will keep her company."

I was quiet, considering how to reply.

"It is a *mitzvah* to visit the sick," my mother went on, responding to the argument I had not yet made. "The greatest *mitzvah* is when you help someone who cannot help themselves. Your *bubbe* will be unable to return this favor. And it is a *brukhe*, a blessing, to have a family like ours. Today we will go to see her. Tomorrow Aunt Feyga will go. And so on."

"I can't go to the hospital. I have an examination at school tomorrow," I said. "An important examination. I have to do well on it. I'm not going with you."

"If you can stay at the lake yesterday, all day, then you can come with me now," my mother replied. "If your father were home, he would join me. But he is not here. So you and I will go together. And if you do not come with me, you will not go to the lake again."

We rode in the unheated streetcar. My mother and I sat side by side in the drafty air. The car rumbled and clacked along the tracks. We got off in front of a large brick building.

"You will find that you have to do more in this world than you wish to," my mother said to me as we trudged in. "Lena, this is what life is. Doing what you *must*. Unless you put that thought into your head, you will have *tsuris* all your life."

"I have troubles, and I do what people tell me," I said.

"I have not seen a pinch of trouble for you," she said, unbuttoning her coat and lowering her voice. "Not real *tsuris*. Not the trouble we will see in this hospital. Or saw in Russia. *Man muz zayn shtark vie ayzn.* You have to be strong as iron. Remember my words."

"I'm made of blood and skin, not iron," I declared. "Just like my grandmother is."

We walked up four flights of stairs and through a white corridor that smelled of ammonia and sweat. The odor made me a little queasy. It reminded me of the hospital ward at Ellis Island. Even here, I couldn't stop thinking about Max. I loved his skin, his eyes. That he had said music was his second love. Who or what was his first love? I wanted it to be me, only me, only and always.

What a grand house he lived in. And how wonderful to see a real writer, no matter what Max had said. I remembered Max's words: *If you want an explanation...you'll have to ask your father.* I had tried this already, but the discussion with my father about the beautiful customer had turned into my own screams on the steps outside of Aunt Feyga's apartment building. I would have to talk to him again. But I wasn't sure I wanted to know the truth.

My mother entered a room where five beds stood lined in a row. Four of them were empty. My grandmother lay on the fifth bed. Her skin was wrinkled like creased paper. She seemed to be looking at the ceiling, but her eyes were closed. The room was so dreary, it seemed like dusk. The walls must have once been painted white but had turned a dull yellow, like the color of my grandmother's face.

"She is asleep," my mother whispered.

"I know," I said. The sight of my grandmother so still and pale pushed all other thoughts from my head. Except for Leah Grace, who had also been so sick before leaving us. I bit my lip.

"Come," my mother said. "Sit there, Lena." She pointed to the chair.

"No, you can sit on the chair." I sat next to her, on the gray cement floor, leaning my back against the wall.

We sat in silence.

I was not sure what to do. Were we to watch my sleeping old grandmother? To wake her, or try to speak to her? To touch her?

My mother slipped off her black overcoat and laid it carefully on an empty bed. She wore a bulky gray sweater and a blue dress. She pulled off her white gloves, set them on her lap, and folded her hands on top of them. She glanced at my grandmother, then at her lap.

She looked tired, my mother, the skin beneath her eyes puffy, like rising bread dough. I wiggled out of my coat and held it in my arms. Then I shut my eyes and remembered Belilovka. My grandmother used to roll long strips of sticky dough on the wooden table for pies and breads, or sit bent over fabric, sewing with her quick fingers. She baked pies in square pans with ladders of dough pressed on the top. We had lived in her house after my father left Russia, the house by the lake with its rough wooden floors.

I imagined the smoke billowing from the nearby lumber mill, and my grandmother's broad body. Her big breasts like two loaves of round bread, and her wide waist. She used to order Simon and me to do chores. She hugged us when we finished them. She had large, strong hands then, like a man's, with veins that formed bumpy patterns beneath her skin. Now she seemed to have no breasts, and her hands were so thin, even thinner than they were when I saw her at Aunt Feyga's apartment. She had been my mother's best companion after my father left for America. Often when my mother sat staring at a letter from my father, my *bubbe* would rest a veiny hand on my mother's shoulder or kiss her forehead.

My grandmother was a different person now. She looked as if she were two hundred years old. Her breath scratched the air.

I peered around the hospital room and breathed in its sights and smells: the limp curtains, the empty beds, the stinging odor of medicine. The lumpy shape of my grandmother's body, like a sack of grain, hidden beneath the frayed white blanket. My mother's sad stare. This was a place made for sadness. I didn't want to see my *bubbe* here.

From my perch on the floor, I imagined my grandmother lay on a very tall bed, much taller than me. I was standing, I imagined, and my *bubbe* was far away, traveling on the bed to heaven. The ceiling of the room flew off, and then the roof, and I watched as she rose up and out of the building, into the sky, beyond the clouds. Up, up, and as she soared I could see it: The sky was littered with souls. Like billions of tiny glittering stars. Each soul had been a person once. Like Leah Grace had been. And my grandfather. And the other relatives who had been killed in Russia. My grandmother began disappearing into the sky, bed and all, but then she looked back to smile and tell me goodbye.

"Goodbye," I whispered.

"Lena, who are you speaking to?" my mother said. She sighed deeply, and laid her hand on my shoulder. Her moist eyes looked dull and empty.

I glanced around the room. Nothing had changed. My grandmother still lay on the hospital bed.

"This is an awful place," I said. "I don't think *Bubbe* likes it here." I suddenly understood what was happening, and I shivered, though the room was warm. My old grandmother was dying, and in a way, my mother was, too.

"Your *bubbe* is sleeping." My mother kissed my forehead. "But she knows you are here. We will go now."

I followed my mother out of the room and slipped into my coat. I felt moisture in my eyes. Unlike my mother, I didn't believe my grandmother knew we had visited, although I couldn't help hoping that our presence had made a difference.

Uncle William Comes Home
Late November 1926

The hospital had become my grandmother's new home. Each day a different relative visited her. My mother prepared a list: Aunt Feyga, Uncle Charlie, Aunt Razel, Uncle Abie, and so on. Even the Seligmans and Mr. Usher Cohen. My father's name didn't appear.

I had begun to feel his absence. The apartment, which had once been crowded with uncles, with men, was almost empty. Simon came home late every evening. My mother and I were often there alone. Uncle Abie and Aunt Ida stopped by for tea, but without my father, the family club didn't gather, no *landsleit* joined us, there was no laughter, no pinochle, no *schnapps*.

The day after my first visit to the hospital, I came home from school, went to my room, and closed the door. Simon was out, and my mother was in her bedroom. She hadn't mentioned that the cup and ballerina were gone from their place on the table in the entry, but I felt terrible that I'd broken them, especially with my old grandmother so sick. I couldn't bear to tell my mother. I was sure she would be angry with me.

I retrieved the cracked pieces of the glass cup and porcelain ballerina from my book satchel and set them on my bed. In the kitchen, I found an old *Chicago Tribune* and wrapped the pages around the pieces so it made a neat bundle. I wrote in big letters on it: PRIVATE. Then I slid the package beneath my bed, near my box of drawings. I would make this up to my mother, I decided. I'd have to figure out a way to do this in time.

Each night I sat at my desk in the quiet living room with my books, paper, and pencils. I worked on history, arithmetic, and the awful essays Miss Marshall assigned. But it seemed to me this was a sad silence, a nervous, unnatural one.

The silence was only interrupted when, finally, we received word from my father. He was coming home. He sent a telegram with the arrival time, and Uncle Charlie went to meet him at the train station on Sunday morning.

I had planned to see Max on Sunday. His parents would be gone that afternoon. He would play the piano for me, he had told me, and I said I would draw a picture of him. I'd told my mother I was going to the lake, but she insisted I stay home. Because my father was returning, I complied. I wrote Max a note, telling him I couldn't meet him and why. I slid the note into an envelope I took from my mother's supplies. On Friday, Simon gave the sealed envelope to Max at the Center where they played basketball.

On Sunday, the family gathered in our living room. The silence in the apartment disappeared as if it were a caged bird, suddenly freed and out an open window. Relatives waited and talked. Aunt Ida and Uncle Abie sat at a card table. Aunt Razel was there, too, knitting a white wool scarf. She'd started to knit after Leah Grace died. Her stomach had a hint of roundness, like a small dumpling. She was going to have another child. Her knitting needles clicked together loudly. I wondered if these sounds and the swift motion of her hands muted her sadness about Leah Grace.

My mother prepared food in the kitchen. She placed *corshecloffs,* the round poppy seed cookies she baked, in neat circles on a large white plate. Simon sprawled on the living room floor, reading the *Chicago Tribune.* With my father away, Simon had started to buy the newspaper with money he earned from Mr. Usher Cohen. I glanced at a headline: "Capture Giant Negro Moron at Gary, Indiana." My father had told us you could read about all of life in the *Chicago Tribune,* and he was right. What was a "giant Negro moron," anyway? If the person had been Jewish, would the headline be: "Giant Jewish Moron"? Or Irish: "Giant Irish Moron"? I had no answer, but I thought a newspaper didn't need to print the color of a person's skin. I went to my desk and stared out the window. The headlines, this apartment, and our street seemed like another country, so far from

Independence Boulevard and Max.

Heat hissed from the radiator. For a moment, we each thought separate thoughts, as if to speak would confirm the uneasiness we all felt. I knew everyone worried about Uncle William. But I worried about Uncle Maurice as well.

When the front door opened, we all looked up.

"Reesa," my father called out. "We are here."

Finally, my father was home.

Footsteps padded down the hall. Uncle Charlie came into the living room, lifted off his gray felt hat, and set it on an end table. My father followed him, with Uncle William lumbering at his side. Uncle Maurice wasn't with them.

"William," said my mother, as if she were singing. "Chaim." She hurried in from the kitchen. She brushed her lips against my father's lips and then embraced Uncle William.

Uncle William didn't reply. He didn't smile. He wiggled from her arms and gazed at us, as if we were strangers.

The relatives stared in silence.

I wanted to run to my father and hug him, but he was helping Uncle William slip off his bulky overcoat. My father seemed uneasy, as if he had wandered into a *shiva* house. "Sit here, William," he said, pointing to the sofa.

I glanced from him to William and pressed my lips together. Uncle William looked nothing like the man I remembered. His brown trousers were baggy and stained. They bunched beneath his belt. The sleeves of his white shirt were wrinkled and too long. His dark eyes bulged. His skin was chapped. His brownish-black hair fell in clumps onto his forehead. He looked like the men I had seen on Maxwell Street who ate garbage from the sidewalk.

"Where is the talk?" said my father. The journey had exhausted him. Gray half-circles hung beneath his eyes. "Where are the greetings? This isn't a funeral."

"We are so happy to see you both," Uncle Abie said with hesitation.

"Papa," I said.

He walked to my desk, brushed his hand against my cheek, and kissed my forehead. Then he went to Simon, who was still sitting on the floor. He knelt and rubbed Simon's shoulder.

Uncle William sat down stiffly on the sofa. Simon joined him on one side, and I hurried to the other, as if we were bookends holding up our uncle's body. William didn't look to the left or the right. He didn't say, "Hello, Simon. My God, you're almost a man now." Or "Lena, there you are, my special niece, the daughter of my dear sister." He didn't rise, open his arms, and sing *Ochi Chyornye*.

He was silent.

I said, "Hello, Uncle William."

He nodded.

"You had a good journey?" Aunt Razel asked hopefully.

"California is a heaven," my father said. "It is a place to enjoy. The grass is green, even in winter."

"Hello, Uncle William," I said again.

The corners of his mouth quivered into a half-smile. "Hello, Lena." His voice was dull, as if all emotion had been ironed out. Flat. No jazz in his voice, no Louis Armstrong sounds.

The relatives watched us.

"Did you like California?" I asked. My words seemed foolish. "Did you receive our letters?"

"Of course, he did," Simon said.

"California." Uncle William rubbed his cheek. "So far away."

"It's far because it's west," Simon explained. "We live in the middle of the country. Almost the middle."

"Did you sing in California?" I asked. Geography seemed too complicated for Uncle William.

"I don't sing anymore," he said. "She doesn't love me. She has stolen my voice."

"I'm sorry," I said.

"Lena, Simon, it's enough," my mother interrupted sharply. "Come and help me. Let William visit with the others."

In the kitchen, we prepared tea and set the table. I dropped a teaspoon of sugar into each glass and licked the sweet granules from my fingers. When the front door opened again, the voices of Aunt

Feyga, Uncle Myron, and Mr. Usher Cohen rose in the apartment. Simon raced to the door to greet them. My mother moved frantically, lifting a bottle of milk, setting a bowl of strawberry jelly and a loaf of bread on the table, piling more and more *corshecloff* cookies on the large white plate until some tumbled onto the table, then the floor, and crumbled.

I bent to pick up the pieces. "Uncle William isn't well," I said.

"You know that, Lena. He had a collapse. I don't know how long he will be able to stay with us. We will need to look for a special place for him." She spoke in a monotone, dully, as if she had experienced a collapse as well. "Another hospital, such as the one you telephoned." She slumped down into a chair. "We are learning too much about hospitals," she murmured. "Oh, William."

"Is this something Uncle Maurice did? Did he cause the collapse?"

"Why would you think such thoughts?" My mother eyed me. "Where did you get that idea?"

"I don't *think* that," I said. "I was asking a question."

In bed that night, I tried to fasten my memories of Uncle William onto the man who had come home to Bittersweet Place. If only I could make him well again. I remembered him tall and smiling, singing to us, his perfect voice like an angel's. I longed to discuss this with Max: How could a person change so completely? What caused happiness in a person, or sadness? What caused a collapse? Did a person's nature cause it? Did William have a soft soul, like my mother had once said? I was certain Max would know. He would play the piano, kiss me, and tell me why such things happened. Or his brother, Meyer, might have an answer. Meyer wanted to open up the world, Max had said. Someone like that—a writer—would understand this.

Uncle William had saved me when we rode from Belilovka in the darkness through the forest. I remembered the silence of the night. I had slid off one of my brown lace-up shoes to pluck out a clump of dirt. I shook the shoe over the side of the wagon to loosen a stone inside. The ride was bumpy. The shoe slipped from my hand. But the wagon kept moving. My shoe was gone. I knew I had to be quiet, but my body wouldn't obey. I began to cry. I had melted into sobs. My mother held my hand. Uncle William pressed his arm around me.

"Shhh, shh," he whispered. Then he clamped his hand against my mouth until my sobs were trapped in my throat.

But the wagon stopped. The man in front, with the ragged gray mustache, yanked the horses' reins. He climbed down.

"She'll stay here," he grunted. His eyes glowed like fireflies. His lips twitched. "We don't continue unless she's gone, out of the wagon. They'll hear us. Arrest us. Get her out."

Uncle William jumped to the ground and whispered to the man. Urgent whispers. Finally, the man craned his head toward me.

"One more chance," he warned. He squinted and pointed a finger so close to me that his cold skin touched my cheek. I was afraid he would hit me. "If there's a sound from her, she stays behind. Let the wolves eat her."

The man had returned to the front of the wagon. My uncle climbed back in. The clump of the horses' hooves began again. I had rested my head on my mother's shoulder, afraid to move, to make a sound.

But now Uncle William sat on the sofa, curled to one side, an elbow resting on a pillow. He was there when Simon and I left for school in the morning and when I returned in the afternoon. I began to do my school assignments in the kitchen because I couldn't concentrate at my desk while my uncle sat and lamented in the living room. I had to concentrate. I couldn't give Miss Marshall one more reason to fail me.

"She doesn't love me," Uncle William said as he sat there. I heard him from the kitchen. "Why doesn't she love me?"

He was talking about the woman he went to California with, I was sure. Perhaps he felt about her as I did about Max. William loved her, I realized. And I loved Max. This worried me. Love brought so many troubles. For my mother and father, because of the beautiful customer. For all of us, it seemed. I felt badly for Uncle William, and suddenly frightened for Max and me. Would he and I have troubles, too?

During the first week of Uncle William's return, one afternoon I brought him a glass of milk and set it on the end table next to him. He sat on one end of the sofa while I settled into the other.

"Lena," he said, as if he had just recognized me. "Why?"

"I don't know what you're talking about."

"Tell me why she stole my voice."

"That doesn't seem possible, Uncle William." I shrugged with impatience. "No one can take away the voice of another person."

"You're lying. Don't lie." He reached toward me, as if he might grab me, but I sprang up from my seat.

"Be careful," I said. "You could hurt someone."

Frightened, I left to find my mother. She sat at her sewing machine in the bedroom. I walked in and lay on the bed. Dusk had fallen and a gray cloud covered the sky, like a soiled sheet. I was glad to be away from Uncle William. I felt cozy in this room, watching my mother slide a blue silk skirt beneath the needle. The sewing machine purred, and the needle danced slowly across the cloth. Perhaps one day I would bring a pencil and paper here and draw a picture of my mother at work. Then I would bring both the picture and my mother to school. I would stand with her in front of miserable Miss Marshall's desk and wave the picture in the teacher's face. I would prove to Miss Marshall that she was wrong about me.

After a few minutes, my mother said, "Go check on William, Lena. Please." She looked up from her sewing. "You are sitting and doing nothing. Ask if he wants water."

"I already brought him milk."

"Please. Look in on him."

I was a little afraid to go near him. I wasn't afraid he would do something like Uncle Maurice had done, but I worried that if I stood close, William might reach for me. Speak oddly. I was sorry he had lost his voice and his mind, but I wanted no part of this strange new man.

I looked into the living room. It was empty. I glanced around the room twice to be certain, and then I walked in. No one was there.

In the hall, I saw that the door to Uncle Maurice's old bedroom was shut. Suddenly, crying thundered from behind the door.

I knocked. "Uncle William?"

The cries stopped.

I waited, then knocked once more.

"Go away," he said.

"Do you feel ill, Uncle William?"

"Go away."

"Can I help you? Do you want water or food?"

The cries began again.

I went to my mother. "Uncle William is crying," I told her.

She frowned and marched down the hall. "William. Let me help. Come, I will prepare warm milk or guggle muggle."

She placed a hand on the doorknob. The door was locked. She waited, but William said nothing more. After a few minutes she shook her head and trudged back to her bedroom. I followed, as if I were her shadow. I hoped she might tell me what to do, how to help Uncle William. He had collapsed, just as Dr. Sedgewick had said.

She shuffled to the sewing machine. "We don't know what is in William's mind," she said, as if I'd asked. "Let him cry. When he is finished, we will..." She didn't complete her sentence. She mumbled to herself, as if I had disappeared. "*Der kush iz oyberflekhlekh; der bis kumt fun tif'n harts'n.*" The kiss is superficial; the bite comes from deep in the heart.

She brushed her fingers absently across a red cotton dress and began to sew faster and faster. She rocked to the rhythm of the machine as if they were one.

I felt suddenly like an intruder, so I left her alone. I collected my papers from the kitchen table and went to my desk. Uncle William's cries now sounded like long, low moans. My troubles seemed foolish compared to his, compared to what he had become. The woman, that *goy*, the *shiksa*, had bit into his heart. Maybe his mind, too. I would tell Max this: Your mother may scream, but my uncle weeps.

Just as I began my schoolwork, the bedroom door squeaked open. Uncle William emerged and traipsed down the hall of our apartment. He wore no shirt, just a pair of black trousers, ones Simon had outgrown. Dark hairs coiled across his bare chest. The trousers fit tightly and clung to my uncle's calves. His feet were bare, and his toenails were yellow and ragged. I looked away, embarrassed for him, then after a minute, I glanced back. He was no longer there.

My mother's sewing machine clattered loudly.

I jumped out of the chair and peered down the hall. Uncle William stood by the front door. His skin glistened in the dim light. The long arch of his back swayed. His hand fluttered to the doorknob.

"Uncle William," I said. "Why are you standing there?"

He pulled open the door and walked out.

"Mama," I yelled. I dashed to her bedroom. She sat bent over her sewing machine. I pressed my hands on her shoulders. "Come quickly. Uncle William is gone." I took a breath. "He's almost naked."

My mother swung around. "What are you telling me?"

"He left the apartment."

We hurried out after him.

"God in heaven. William," she called to the empty stairwell. "Come back."

I heard the creaking of the door to the roof. Then the door slammed shut.

"I hear him," I said. "Upstairs."

I ran up two steps at a time, four flights in the dingy stairwell, as if I were an athlete or made of iron. My mother climbed behind me. Our footsteps echoed in the narrow space. At the top of the staircase, I pulled open the heavy door to the roof. It scratched against the cement floor. A cold wind blew in my face.

Ours was the tallest building on the street. No trees protected the roof. We were surrounded by the hazy gray sky.

Uncle William hovered near the roof's edge, his back toward me. He stared down into the courtyard below.

"Uncle William," I shouted. "Come inside. You'll be cold out here. It's freezing." I felt chilled without a hat or coat. "Come, I'll help you."

I darted to him and grabbed his hand. His skin was cool and sweaty.

"William," yelled my mother from behind me. "What's happened to you? Come inside. Lena will help you. I will, too."

He shivered and didn't answer. The wind swirled around us fiercely, slapping my face and thumping in my ears.

He wiggled from my grasp and stepped to the side, away from me.

"William!" yelled my mother.

I reached for him again. "Uncle William. Come with us, please," I shouted. "You must."

He stared at me. His mouth opened as if he were about to speak, but he said nothing. Instead, he shoved away my hand, bent forward, and jumped off the edge of the roof.

The Afflicted
December 1926

"I couldn't look, Max," I said. "I couldn't move. When he jumped, I was frozen to the spot on the roof where I stood."

Max and I walked from the lake toward Bittersweet Place. The raw December wind gusted against us. My mind was crowded with thoughts of all that had happened, as if time had not pushed forward. I was still standing in the cold, on the flat black roof, surrounded by the hazy gray sky, shouting, "Uncle William. Come with us, please. You must." Waiting for my uncle to swing around, squeeze my hand and say, "Dear Lena. Of course. Of course, I will come home with you. It's a mistake that I'm on this roof, wearing Simon's old trousers."

"And then?" Max prodded, interrupting my thoughts. Although he knew what had happened, he'd asked me to tell him the events again, in great detail. "I want to see everything as you did," he said.

My breath sped up. I was afraid my heart might leap from my body just as Uncle William had leapt from the roof.

"It's hard to talk about, Max. It was the most terrible moment of my life," I whispered.

"It must have been." He clutched my hand, his woolen glove linked with mine.

"He jumped," I went on. "My mother screamed, 'No!' I was certain she would faint, or I would. But we didn't. Then she was quiet. I thought I would hear Uncle William shouting, or the awful sound of him smashing against the ground. But the wind was blowing, and I couldn't tell if the sounds I heard were the wind or the trees or the fear inside me. I couldn't look, Max." I gulped a breath. "My mother told me to walk away from the edge of the roof, to run to the apartment. 'You come to the apartment, too,' I told her. 'I'll telephone the police.'"

"But he didn't die," Max said with triumph. "Oh, he must have been hurt. But he was lucky. Lena, he was so lucky."

"Maybe not. He has his body, but not his mind." I sighed. "He wouldn't let me save him, but he's alive." Tears gathered in my eyes. It was a relief to talk to Max. Simon wouldn't talk about this. All he'd said was, "Just don't think about it, Lena. Shit. Why did he have to do it?"

Uncle William was alive, but nothing like he'd been.

"He landed in the tree, in the courtyard," I said to Max. "I'll show you."

"My mother would say it was *beshert*," he said. "Just as God meant it to be. But it must have been awful. Oh, you should be a writer, Lena. You could write the story of your uncle and the roof. And the fierce wind."

Tall trees grew next to the sidewalk, towering over Max and me. The branches were stiff and gnarled like claws. They arched over us, as if ready to grab us. My fingers felt numb inside my thin wool gloves. Clouds hid the sunlight, and the air smelled stale.

"It's not a story, Max," I said. "It's real."

"You could write about what happened, so you won't forget."

"I wouldn't want to tell anyone. And I will *never* forget. You can tell Meyer. He can write about it."

"It would take him ten years to compose one paragraph." Max laughed. His coat hung on his body like a flowing cape. His cheeks were flushed from the cold. "Or you could draw a picture of your uncle. Yes. That's what you should do. To pull what happened out of your mind."

"I don't want to draw him," I said.

"Why not?"

"I want to forget about what happened," I said. "I only want to create beautiful things." We rounded the corner onto Bittersweet Place. "The world can be so ugly. I want to freeze beauty as best I can on paper." There was so much beauty in the world, I thought: the lovely length of Max's nose, the wide shape of his forehead. And so many colors: the beautiful dark blue of his coat.

"You don't need to freeze beauty," Max said. "The weather will do it." He stamped his feet, trying to shake warmth into his body. His breath curled like smoke in the air. He began to hum, a marching tune, a pleasing, sweet, triumphant melody.

"That's nice," I said, comforted to be with him. "What's the name of the song?"

"No name. I made it up. I'll name it: 'Lena's Bravery on the Roof.'"

I smiled.

"You *were* brave there," he said.

"I had to be. I felt like I was made of iron."

At my building, we stopped. I wanted Max to kiss me. I reached for his hand.

"Goodbye then," he said, ignoring my hand.

Goodbye? I thought. "Would you like to come in?" I said quickly, ignoring his farewell.

"Yes, if I wouldn't interrupt anything."

"You wouldn't," I assured him, although I didn't know if my mother would be home.

"Will you show me your drawings?" Max asked.

"I could." Then I corrected myself. "Yes, of course I will. I want to show you my drawings."

"That would be swell."

Inside, we climbed the stairs. I was thrilled to have a companion. I wasn't arriving home alone or racing to the roof or dashing to telephone the police. I was on my way to our apartment with Max Slovansky, whom I loved.

I had never asked Max to come to our apartment before. I'd been ashamed of it. He'd been in our apartment once with Simon. After Max told me about his mother and Meyer, I decided someday I might invite him. There was a difference between telling Max about my family and letting him see them and talk to them. Even so, he seemed understanding of other people's oddness, even his own mother's.

Scents of cinnamon cookies drifted from our apartment. I opened the door. As we walked in, I heard voices.

"Is that you, Lena?" called my mother.

"Yes." I turned to Max. "Come this way."

We threaded through the dreary hallway.

In the living room, light from the floor lamp cast a golden glow. The wide white lampshade crowned the top of the metal stand like a gauzy skirt. My mother sat in an armchair next to the lamp. She wore a turquoise dress, the one she wore for special occasions. The long sleeves and slender skirt made her look soft, almost pretty.

On the sofa, across from her, sat a man dressed in a pressed white wool suit. I had never seen him before. Stout with a wide middle, he had small dark eyes and a rosy oval face. A shiny gold ring with a large round red stone shimmered on his pinky.

My mother glanced from me to Max to the man on the sofa. "This is Rabbi Hirschfeld," she said to us. She smiled at the man.

"Good afternoon, children." His voice was deep and loud, as if he were speaking to an entire congregation.

Max and I nodded.

My mother eyed me and frowned. "You have brought a visitor, Lena."

"This is Simon's friend. Max Slovansky."

"Hello." Max shook my mother's hand and the rabbi's.

She squinted, studying him. "I think we have met. At the Center. When you were with Simon there. Please, sit down." She looked at the rabbi. "Rabbi, this is my daughter, Lena, and her friend, Max." Her voice had an unexpected sweetness.

"We were discussing your uncle and the unfortunate event," the rabbi said gravely.

Max and I sat on the sofa a few inches from the man. Max slipped off his coat and laid it on his lap.

"The rabbi has been very kind," my mother said. "We are lucky to know such a man, with such heart." She smiled at the rabbi again.

"Thank you, Mrs. Czernitski," he said. "This is a lesson for you children." The rabbi gazed at Max and me. "Not everything in this world occurs as one wishes."

"Yes," I replied dutifully, unbuttoning my coat.

"Of course, what happens on this earth happens for a reason," he went on. "Although we may not understand why, God the Almighty does. We need to be grateful for that."

I nodded again.

Max folded his hands on his lap.

"Very fortunate, Mrs. Czernitski, that these two children should join us." The rabbi's voice sounded soothing, as if he had recited such words many times.

The rabbi didn't seem like a man of God to me. He smelled of sweet, strong, orange-scented soap, and his gold ring glistened boldly. His thick dark hair with its gray streaks fell in two curly waves onto his forehead. His suit had a fine white weave to it. His smile demanded admiration. He seemed like a man of the world.

"Rabbi Hirschfeld is the new rabbi at the synagogue," my mother explained, as if responding to my thoughts. We attended synagogue only on holidays. My mother said she wanted to attend more often, but my father wasn't interested.

"Yes, I'm the new rabbi." He smiled. His teeth were like white pearls. Those on the top row overlapped the bottom, one tooth stretching crookedly onto the other. "I'm hopeful your mother will convince your father to join us more at the *shul.* I have told her: In life and in the Bible, there are people who are afflicted."

"Yes, Rabbi," said my mother.

"Do you know what it means to be 'afflicted?'" the rabbi asked me.

"Troubled," Max interjected. "You have troubles if you're afflicted."

"A bright young man." The rabbi pressed his hands together. They formed a triangle at his chest. "If you're afflicted," he said to me, "this is your lot in life."

"It is," I agreed, not knowing what else to say.

"Your poor Uncle William is, unfortunately, one of the afflicted ones. We read about them in the Bible. The *anus kasha-ul.* Their hearts are crushed with troubles. For example, King Saul."

I didn't remember the story of King Saul. I stared at the floor.

Wasn't everyone afflicted? My family had been afflicted by so many troubles. I was afflicted by thoughts of Uncle Maurice, by the cruel Miss Marshall, and my worries about the beautiful customer. Even Max was afflicted by his mother's screaming. And the world itself was afflicted by Cossacks and wars, sickness, sadness, and hate. I tried now to understand Uncle William's desperate affliction on the roof.

We had visited him in the hospital three days ago, the same hospital where my grandmother was. His face looked wrinkled and bruised as if he had aged thirty years overnight. His hands trembled. His lips barely moved. My mother had wobbled like a rag doll there, stumbling, as if the strength of blood and bone had been stolen from her. Now her face was rosy, almost youthful, as she sat with the rabbi.

"As you know," the man was saying, "King Saul despaired in the battle with the Philistines. He fell upon his sword, took his own life and—"

"Forgive me, Rabbi, please." My mother stood up abruptly. "I cannot listen to stories about people who do not want to live." She gazed at a photograph of Uncle William that sat on the mantel, one of the few from Russia. He stood tall, a hand pressed on his waist, and he wore a dark suit and yarmulke. His face looked young, sweet, and wise. She sighed, a whistle of sadness. "He is in the hospital. William. Healing from the broken bones. We will bring him to Dunning soon, the special hospital for people with problems of the mind. He will be safe there, I hope."

"Good, good," said the rabbi. "He will receive excellent care."

Max nodded politely as the rabbi spoke. I tapped my fingers on the sofa cushion, disappointed we had become ensnared in this conversation.

"Every week, we will visit him," said my mother. She walked to the doorway. "Rabbi, the children should hear your story. I will go make tea."

"Time will help make this unfortunate event less difficult," he said.

"Make it less," whispered my mother.

"Ah, but there is another story in the Bible," the rabbi said quickly.

"You may know it. The people are wandering in the desert, and the Almighty creates a great cloud in the sky, like a tent, to protect them whenever they stop to rest. But when God lifts the cloud, the people must continue on their journey, even if they are too weary to go on. So it is in life."

"Yes," said my mother. "We could all benefit from a rest and such a cloud. But, please, tell the children your other story."

Max bolted up from his seat. "Excuse me. I need to leave for home. I'm happy to meet you both."

My mother didn't smile. "Thank you."

I waited for her to say she had enjoyed meeting Max, for her to invite him again to our apartment. But she simply swung around and disappeared into the kitchen.

Max slid on his coat.

"I'll walk you to the door," I said.

"I trust," said the rabbi, standing, "that you both learned something important from our conversation. Next time, I will tell you more about King Saul. The *Gemara Shabbat* wisely teaches us: 'When you begin a lesson, you tell a story.'"

"Yes," Max and I replied in unison.

"And every lesson you learn is a *brukhe*, a blessing," the man went on.

We left the rabbi. I peeked back at him after we were in the hall. He was sitting again, rubbing a white handkerchief against his gold ring, polishing it.

I accompanied Max out of our apartment. At the stairs, I said, "I can't show you my drawings now. Another time, I will."

"Another time then."

"Are you sure you can't stay longer?"

"I can stay a little while," he said.

I was about to apologize that my mother hadn't told him how glad she was to meet him, but Max spoke first.

"Come with me to the roof," he said.

"The roof? I couldn't," I said, surprised by his request. "I will never go up there again."

"You must, Lena. You can't be afraid. Do you want to become like your mother and stitch everything up? Or do you want to open up the world?"

"She's not always kind. I don't think she has time for kindness."

"At least she doesn't scream." He glanced at the stairwell that snaked to the roof. "I'm going up. Will you come with me?"

I eyed the steps and hesitated. Max began to climb them. I didn't want to see the roof again or think about Uncle William there. But I wanted to please Max, to be with him. I debated. Finally, I trudged up one step. And another. Max waited and then marched next to me. I didn't feel as if I were made of iron anymore. Our footsteps echoed in the narrow passageway. We didn't talk. This felt like a natural silence, as if he and I were thinking the same thoughts. I could think most clearly away from home, I realized. The words of my family, my mother, crowded out my own thoughts, stretched in my mind and took up all the space. But here, with Max, my mind felt gloriously calm.

Max and I proceeded at a slow, careful pace, up, up the stairs. Now I wasn't so frightened. The most important thing was not to be afraid, I reminded myself. I was merely climbing the steps with Max Slovansky. I *wanted* to be climbing them with him. Uncle William was in the hospital. He was alive. He was safe. I was safe. There was nothing to be afraid of now.

Finally, we reached the heavy wooden door that led to the roof.

"Is this the way?" Max asked.

"Yes."

He placed a hand on the doorknob. The door scratched against the cement floor as he pulled it open. A cold wind blew in our faces.

"This is where we were," I whispered.

On the roof, Max looked to his left, then to his right. "The rabbi should come up here, so he can rethink his simple words about learning a lesson," he said.

I nodded, buttoned my coat, pulled up the collar. "He'd just tell us another story."

When Max reached the center of the roof, he flung his arms

upward, as if he were a rabbi addressing a congregation.

"We're on top of the world. That's our blessing. We don't need rabbis here. We only need each other." He stretched a hand toward me.

I hurried to him, suddenly breathless with longing, as if he could give me something new that I had never known before.

"Look, Lena. It's nice here. Beautiful even." He pointed to the sky. Sunlight burst from beneath clusters of clouds, like shimmering ribbons of light.

"It is beautiful." I shivered from the cold. My eyes focused on the roof's edge where Uncle William had stood. Then I gazed at Max.

"Don't be afraid," he said again. "It's good we're here. You'll see there's nothing to be afraid of. Anyway, I have something to tell you. I might as well tell you now." He linked his long fingers in mine.

"Nothing is wrong, is it?"

"No. But soon I will have a new name. I will no longer be Max Slovansky."

"Who will you be?" I giggled. "The Messiah?"

"I'm not joking, Lena. My father has decided. Slovansky." He puckered his lips in disgust. "The name hurts his business."

Mr. Slovansky sold men's clothing. I had never been to his store. "It's a Jewish name," I said, "so, of course, it wouldn't be good for his business."

"That's right. My father thinks we'll always be judged. Like Negros are judged. Even Meyer. Even if Meyer actually writes a book, who will read one by a writer with a name like that? Slovansky. So soon I will become Max Sloan."

"Sloan," I repeated.

"S-L-O-A-N." Max spelled it. "My father came to America from Lithuania when he was a child. There have been incidents, rocks thrown at his store. Yesterday, someone broke the front window after the store had closed."

"That's terrible. Is everyone all right?"

"Yes. My father said we're lucky no one was hurt. There was glass everywhere. Now his store will become P. Sloan and Son Men's

Manufacturing Company."

"And what does your mother think about it?"

"She doesn't scream at my father." He laughed. "She'll become Mrs. Sloan."

Max slipped his arms around me. He eased his lips to mine. The wind caressed us. The sky around us disappeared. His skin warmed me. I pressed my body against his and imagined that all my afflictions had fallen away, that nothing had happened to Uncle William. Here I was, I thought with amazement, standing on the roof, not at the edge, but in the very center, kissing Max Slovansky. Sloan, I reminded myself.

"Oh, Max," I whispered. "I wish we could bring this moment home with us."

"But we are home, Lena. And we're together. Right here, in Chicago, Illinois."

The Granville Laundry
January 1927

Aside from my father, it was Uncle William and Uncle Maurice who had always spent the most time at the family business. To compensate for my uncles' absence, my father had been working later and later each evening. Aunt Feyga and Uncle Abie could no longer help. My grandmother had come home from the hospital; my aunt needed to care for her again. And Uncle Abie and Aunt Ida worked every day at the piano store now. My old *bubbe* didn't seem any stronger than she had that first day in the hospital. She slept more than she stayed awake. She rarely spoke.

Chanukah and the New Year were behind us, and I felt relieved about that. In school, we had sung Christmas carols, songs that made me feel I would never belong. We sang, "Oh night, when Christ was born, oh night, oh night," and I choked on the words. They were strange to me, forbidden, even seemed dangerous. But Miss Marshall stood like a guard next to my desk, making sure I mouthed every word.

My mother always became wistful this time of year. Winters in Chicago were frigid and bitter, she said, like Russian winters. New Year's Eve reminded her of her father. He had celebrated with the peasants who worked for him, and he gave a party for them all every year. During the holidays, she told Simon and me stories about Belilovka, the lake and the horses, the private tutor, the fine furs and linens. Then the terrible life after the fall of the czar.

I despised these stories. I knew them by heart.

"It's enough, Reesa," my father said.

But my mother insisted on reciting the names of relatives killed by Cossacks, people Simon and I didn't remember; we had been too young. Again this year, she told us, "They murdered eighteen people in our family. And they cut up your grandfather's cousin, Bronick, *alav ha-sholom,* chopped him from ear to toe."

"I hate that story," I groaned. "I won't listen to it again." I had no memory of cousin Bronick and forced myself to push my mother's words out of my mind.

Monday afternoon, after the holidays were over, Simon and I came home from school together. He had skipped playing basketball and didn't have to work for Mr. Usher Cohen. My mother sat hunched in the kitchen, her elbows propped on the table as if she needed them to support her body.

"Lena, Simon," she said. "Do you know where my cup with the golden handle is? And my beautiful porcelain ballerina? The ones I brought from Russia? I have not been able to find them."

"I don't know," Simon said.

"I don't know either," I said. The cracked pieces were still wrapped in the *Chicago Tribune,* hidden beneath my bed.

"I do not understand," she said. "They could not disappear into the air. I have looked everywhere."

There was a silence. I felt a stab of guilt.

"Someday, I hope to find them," she went on. "And if you see them, please tell me. I will ask everyone in the family."

"No, that isn't true. What I said," I told her quietly. "I broke them. I'm sorry."

"Aw, Lena." Simon rolled his eyes. "You did?"

"Broke them?" my mother said.

"That day we went to visit *Bubbe* in the hospital." My voice was a whisper. "It was a mistake. I bumped into the table. They fell to the floor. I was…I was afraid to tell you."

My mother pursed her lips, debating what to do. She eyed me sternly. "The most important is to tell the truth. Thank you, Lena, for telling me. Now I know."

My mother hadn't yelled at me, and I was relieved. I waited for something more, for her to ask why I didn't tell her right away, ask what I'd done with the broken pieces. I'd told a half-truth, I knew, not mentioning where the pieces were.

"Well. You must never be afraid to speak to me," she said. "I am your mother. You have, as you know, just one mother and father." She paused. "The truth is they were important to me, the cup and ballerina. But they are *tchotchkes*, just things. Things come into your life and go out of your life, even people do. You will see this for as long as you live. And we have other problems to worry about now," she said wearily. "Another new change has come to our family."

Simon and I sat down at the kitchen table. I slid into my chair and thought: We have been through enough changes already. Leah Grace's death, the beautiful customer, Uncle William leaping from the roof. And before that, the *Petlurias* storming into Belilovka. Perhaps it was better to be rid of anything that reminded us of Russia and the past.

"We need your help in the laundry," she went on. "Thank the Almighty, this is our only new trouble, except for William. We need both of you. Your father cannot shoulder this burden himself." She reached onto the counter for two bowls, each filled with sliced bananas, a strawberry, and cream. She set one before each of us. I looked at my bowl, annoyed. As usual, Simon's was overflowing; mine was half-filled.

"The aunts and uncles work there," Simon replied.

"We need you there also," she said.

"But I work for Mr. Usher Cohen," he protested.

"And I have to study and do well in school," I said.

"Both of you," she said, "arrange this please with your father."

Her voice was harsh when she said "your father," without the sweetness that had been in her tone when she'd spoken to the rabbi, as if my father had lost his dispensation now that he was home.

"Swell," Simon grunted. He thrust his spoon into his bowl. Puffs of cream splattered on his arm.

But I said yes, I would talk to my father.

The next afternoon, Simon marched into the living room.

"About the laundry," he said to my mother. He flashed a bold smile. "I told you, I've got a job, Ma. Mr. Cohen needs me."

I was at my desk and put down my pencil. Today I had to complete two assignments for school. I had to write an essay: "What Chicago Means to Me." I also had to memorize the Gettysburg Address.

My mother sat on the sofa, sewing a button onto a dress with rapid, nervous stitches, trying to sew up all that was wrong with our life, I imagined.

"Mr. Usher Cohen pays me," Simon pushed on. "We need that money."

"This I know very well," she said.

"What about Mr. Cohen then?"

She continued to sew.

Mr. Usher Cohen lived in a red brick apartment building a few streets from ours. He worked for the Noxzema Company, and had a very important job, my father always said. Simon helped load and unload his trucks, which transported the small blue jars. Mr. Cohen stored boxes crammed with Noxzema jars in the basement of his building.

"I spoke to Mr. Usher Cohen," Simon persisted. "He can't carry the boxes alone, with only one hand. He needs my help." Simon placed a brown paper bag on the sofa. He reached into the bag and slid out a small blue jar and a larger brown jar. He set these on my mother's lap. "For you, Ma. From Mr. Usher Cohen himself."

Greaseless Noxzema Medicated, the jars read. A yellow label with the silhouette of a woman was pasted on the brown one: *Large Hospital Size*.

Her face reddened. She lifted the smaller jar from her lap. "Why does he send these?"

"So you can see how important my work is."

She laid the dress she was mending on the sofa. Then she twisted open the top of the blue jar. A sharp, tingling smell flooded the room. She frowned and handed the jar to Simon.

"You may return these to Mr. Usher Cohen with my blessings. We have no use for them."

I eyed the jars with longing. "I'll use them," I said.

Simon shot a glance at me, then at my mother. "It's a gift, Ma."

"We are not charity," she bristled. "Mr. Usher Cohen is our friend, but we do not need his pity. Give these back to him. For now, you may work for him. I will talk more to your father about this."

I knew Mr. Usher Cohen had loaned the family money for the trip to California. I wondered if my father had been able to repay him or if Mr. Usher Cohen even expected that. Perhaps this was why my mother refused the Noxzema—better not to be beholden to someone like Mr. Usher Cohen.

Unlike Simon, I decided I was happy to cooperate with my mother's request to help at the laundry. Going there would give me the chance to see my father, I thought. Perhaps I'd help for an hour, talk with him, do schoolwork, and then meet Max. I missed my father. He had almost disappeared from my life since his trip to California. I was still angry with him about the beautiful customer, but I couldn't deny my longing to spend time with him again, to talk to him. Although neither he nor my mother had mentioned the beautiful customer again, I felt certain the woman would reappear, like an unwanted ghost, just as I feared Uncle Maurice would walk through our door.

My mother finished her sewing. Simon strolled out of the room, carrying the bag with the Noxzema jars. I tapped my pencil against the desk. I felt like Meyer, the reluctant writer. Instead of working on my essay, I stared out the window. I realized I didn't feel so alone anymore. I had a good friend now, who would help me if I were in trouble. Whenever I thought of Max, comfort settled inside me, just as it did when I was with him.

Even so, our life on Bittersweet Place rocked like a boat on a choppy sea, never finding calm waters.

On Mondays and Wednesdays after school, and on Saturday afternoons, I worked at the laundry. Small dimly lit stores populated Granville Avenue. Automobiles chugged noisily down the street. The shops were jammed with merchandise—food or clothing or hardware. Men and women clutching bundles darted into stores and then spilled onto the sidewalk, dashing in all directions, as if Granville were merely a road that led to a grander, more important street.

Max had told me that a builder, a Mr. Cochran, named the street after Granville, a city in the state of New York.

The back of the laundry was large and gloomy like a cavern. Rows of hanging clothes and stacks of boxes and supplies divided the front of the laundry from the rear as if the two sections were separate stores. In the back, soiled clothing sat in tall piles on two long tables. The washing machines grumbled and whirred, like a chorus of badly tuned musical instruments. The gray cement floor sloped down toward the center, as if the laundry itself might sink into the earth. Next to the rear door was a rusted sewing machine where my mother sometimes did her repairs. Three ironing boards and two pressing machines sat near the adjacent wall, and wedged into the far corner was a large wooden rolltop desk where my father worked on his accounts. A radio, the only one our family owned, stood beside the desk.

Even in winter, the back of the laundry was stuffy and hot. Smells of sweat from other people's clothing, steam, and sour perfume hung in the air. The stench stuck to my clothes and hair. It was hard to breathe unless the rear door was propped open.

I remembered how Uncle Maurice had told my father he wanted to buy bigger machines so we could do the washing for smaller laundries, like the ones on Clark or Addison and for the big hotels.

"We'd grow the business and become rich," he'd boasted.

But my father had refused.

I preferred to stay in the front of the laundry, where I had seen the beautiful customer.

During my first weeks working there, I observed my father more than I spoke with him. At first, this disappointed me. Then I realized I was happy just to be in his presence. His manner of speaking at the laundry was so different from how he spoke at home. He made the customers feel as though he were their friend.

"How's that tooth you're having trouble with?" he asked Mr.

Ernest Frieberg, a small man with bushy gray brows, nervous eyes, and wide lips. Mr. Frieberg always wore baggy beige trousers.

"How's the little one, her fever?" my father asked tall, dour Mrs. Komansky. She described a visit to the doctor, punctuating her words with sighs. My father advised her to prepare guggle muggle for the child. "Ask Reesa for the recipe," he said.

"You must talk to the customers, Lena," he told me one Saturday. "What do we have? A laundry like any other. But the friendships you create bring customers back here. In the same way, you could talk to children at school. You'll find little by little, you gain friends."

"The children at school are mean," I said. "And I have nothing to say to people here."

"Lena, Lena." He laughed. "Not everyone is mean, I'm sure. And you have everything to say. So much bubbles inside your mind. If you begin a conversation, soon you won't be able to stop."

My father, I discovered, could speak to customers in Russian, English, Polish, Yiddish and even a little French. He switched from language to language as easily as switching a pair of shoes. The only person he had difficulty understanding was Hadie, who spoke with a Southern accent.

Hadie had been born in the South. She worked at the laundry, but I couldn't figure out when. Some days she appeared; others, she didn't. She was tall and slender. She pinned her tight black curls away from her face, and she always wore a white dress, like a nurse's uniform, that made her dark skin gleam. She stood at the ironing board near the rear door, her long back bent like a camel, her thin legs supporting her. She pressed shirt after shirt. Long-sleeved. White ones. Putty-colored. Blue-gray. Her dark hand clutched the hot iron and circled the fabric. She placed one shirt on top of another on a single hanger, until twenty hung there. Shirts were difficult to press properly, my father said. Hadie was the only one with the patience to smooth out the collars, the cuffs, and the shoulders correctly.

She didn't talk much, but she had a kind smile. When she laughed, she laid her hands on her face, embarrassed. I was a little afraid of her, but my father trusted her; I knew this, because he had told her where the extra key to the laundry was, something he had not even told me. I had seen her use it. My father had asked me to go to the laundry on a Saturday morning. He told me Hadie would have the key and let me into the laundry. When I'd arrived there, she was outside, entering through the front door, the lock clicking open just ahead of her.

Sometimes my father and I worked together. We stripped the pressed shirts from hangers and folded them. We wrapped them in white paper and string, then wrote the initials of each customer on a small sheet of paper and attached it to the proper package. If the beautiful customer returned here, I would see her initials, I thought. I would know her name.

When I folded clothing by myself, I retreated into thoughts about Max. Sloan. Maybe someday I would change my name, too. Czernitski. Zern. Tern. Hern. A name couldn't change your essential nature, I was sure, but perhaps a new name would change Miss Marshall's treatment of me. I hadn't told anyone at home how she'd humiliated me in class and forced me to use my right hand. I hated her, but I was still determined to work hard and force her to change her mind about me. In the meantime, at the laundry, I was content to imagine how wonderful life might be if I greeted the world as Lena Hern.

Sometimes I went to the back of the laundry to give Hadie shirts. What was a person's true nature? I wondered as I watched her iron in silence. Hadie's? My father's? My mother's? Max's? I thought of Simon and the relatives who congregated in the living room. And the other students in school, and even Miss Marshall. What was inside people that made them act in a certain way? And what was my true nature? Was I an artist, and if so, what was an artist like? There was no one I could ask, so I would have to draw more and find out for myself, I decided. But I couldn't wait to grow up and live a different life from my parents. Of course, I had no idea, no one did, what the world would be like then or what the next day or year would bring. Like everyone else, I would have to wait.

I told Max I was learning about the customers. We were at the Montrose Avenue Beach. The sun was shining, and a winter wind whipped off the lake. Bundled into our heavy coats and scarves, we strolled along the sand, holding hands.

"So what have you learned?" he said.

"Mr. Ernest Frieberg comes to the laundry whenever I'm there."

"He likes you," Max teased.

"No, he doesn't." I laughed. "He changes his clothes three times a day. He's having a problem with his tooth. And Mr. Abe Shusterman is rich. Like Mr. Usher Cohen. Mr. Shusterman owns a laundry, too, but he brings us his clothing."

Our footsteps crunched against the hard sand. Max and I walked easily together, as if this were the most natural way for us to be, talking, holding hands. We stopped beside a large oak tree, its wide trunk sheltering us from the wind.

"And what about the beautiful customer?" Max said. He put his arm around me. "Have you seen her again?"

I shook my head no.

"You see, Lena. Your father may have only *one* wife. But if you want an explanation, I still think you'll have to ask your father." Then Max kissed me, and we kissed for a long time.

I'd learned, too, that Mrs. Eta Glasser worried about perspiration stains that spread like puddles on her blouses. And Mr. Boris Schneider tried without success to wash the urine stains from his trousers. But I didn't stop kissing Max to tell him this.

One afternoon, when no customers were at the laundry and Hadie wasn't there, my father said, "Lena, please sit down with me."

We settled into the two chairs that faced the long counter in the front.

I wondered if he was displeased with me. But he smiled, and this put me at ease.

"I want to talk to you about Uncle William, as best I am able," he began.

"Mother said he had a nervous collapse," I replied, curious. "He stopped singing because the girl he loved left him."

My father nodded and rested his hands in his lap, large hands, dotted with freckles. The nails were thick and untrimmed, like a laborer's, but his fingers were long and slender. One day I would draw a picture of those hands, I decided. Simon's hands were a similar size and shape, and able to do the work of a man, too. Though I wasn't sure if Simon's hands contained the kindness of my father's.

"That is a simple explanation about Uncle William," my father said. "You were brave on the roof, and you deserve a complete explanation."

"I had to try to save him, Papa." When I thought of the roof now, I thought only of Max.

"Yes. Poor William. I spoke to his booking agent in California, a Mr. Brunswick. He had arranged for William to sing in nightclubs. This was just what your uncle wanted," my father said. "But he was in love, as you know, with a woman. She was not a Jew. And not a good person, but this had nothing to do with her religious beliefs."

"It was her nature," I said.

"Yes. If we begin to judge by religion or the color of a person's skin or hair, soon someone will be judging us. *Petlurias* will march down the street again." He sighed. "The woman sang with William, but they had an argument. She moved away to another city. The booking agent said that after she left, William became another person. A neighbor told me this, too. And another woman who lived in the building complained about the sobbing from his apartment." My father shook his head slowly. "Lena, I don't know what happened. While I was there I searched, but I couldn't find Maurice. Thank God, he's disappeared from our lives. William's small apartment in California had few things in it. No money. Maurice must have taken what there was. Or the woman did. William's car was gone, too. Your mother's letters were on the kitchen table. And yours. Papers were scattered on the floor. Sheets with musical notes." My father paused, then continued. "I believe

William couldn't manage on his own. He depended on this woman, on Maurice. When they left, he became full of sadness, depressed. This made him feel hopeless, I believe."

My father was quiet, as if he had given a long and complicated speech.

"It's all too difficult, Papa." Then I was quiet, too. What was there to say? We couldn't repair Uncle William, as if he were a shirt with a rip in the sleeve. My father had no answers. The rabbi had no answers.

"Even so," my father went on, "you have never seen a sky like the one in California. Everywhere, it stretches. And the color is the most blue of all. The air has the taste of purity. It's something to see." He smiled dreamily, and his red hair seemed the color of fire.

"If only the air could have helped Uncle William," I said.

"If God could breathe such air into a person, we would all have fewer troubles. We would be living in paradise then."

I nodded. I knew about paradise now. Paradise was kissing Max. *You'll have to ask your father*, he had said to me.

I sat up straighter. "What happened to the woman in the laundry? The one who called you Henry? The beautiful customer?" I asked boldly. "Maybe Uncle William's friend in California was like her."

My father blinked. "We don't know the woman who went with him to California," he said sternly. "And we have many customers, Lena. That's the end of this discussion." He rubbed the back of his neck before continuing. "However, there is a second matter."

I waited.

"I have decided to speak again with your teacher about your drawings."

"You will? That would be wonderful." I wondered for a moment if the beautiful customer had advised him to do this.

"Your teacher may not listen to me, but I can't watch her be so unfair. I would like to bring her some of your drawings."

"Oh, Papa. Would you? She's horrible to me. I don't want to show her anything. But maybe it would help. I'll give you the drawings I keep in my room."

"Good. That's what I need. I'll send a note into school and tell the teacher I want to speak with her. You and I will talk to her. Your drawings are beautiful, and she should recognize this. It's best if the three of us discuss the problem now, without your mother. I fear she may not understand."

"She doesn't understand anything," I said. "And Papa, if I work at the laundry so much, I won't be able to finish all my assignments. That won't help me with Miss Marshall either."

"Then we will have to make an adjustment." He paused and studied me. "You'll find, my Lena, that distance makes the eyes sharper. I didn't see you when I was away in California, and now it's as if you went on a journey, too, from the continent of childhood to this. I can see you aren't a child anymore. The days go slowly, but the years disappear. You're growing up, just as you should be. Thank God for that."

I smiled at him, pleased by the affection in his voice. It was because of Max, I thought, helping me on this journey, but I couldn't tell this to my father. Max was my secret.

"I *am* growing up," I said. "I wish Mother would understand."

"One day I hope she will," he said.

Still, it felt cozy and safe here, my father and I talking. I glanced at the front of the laundry and then toward the back. This would be a perfect place to bring Max. We could come here on a Sunday when the laundry was closed and no one else was here. We could be alone, not freezing on the roof or at the lake. We could kiss and do whatever we wanted here, and no one would see us. I would ask my father for the key. No. How would I explain why I wanted the key? I would find the key and borrow it.

"Lena." My father interrupted my thoughts. "The Jewish mystics say that God, in order to create the world, had to make himself smaller. To make room for the world. I'll help you with your teacher, but I want to become smaller for you, a smaller presence in your life. If only I could convince your mother to do so, too."

That afternoon when Hadie arrived, my father left the laundry to make a delivery. I lingered by the front counter. No customers appeared, so I made my way to the back. It was hot there, as it always was. Hadie was intent on ironing, and didn't seem to notice me. I wandered to the rolltop desk. Invoices were piled on top, and also pencils, buttons, thread, and needles. A copy of the *Chicago Tribune* and one of the *Sentinel*, the Jewish-English weekly, sat there. A small poster from Glickman's Palace Theater lay on the desk, too. *TEL HAYMARKET 0881 BLUE ISLAND AVE & ROOSEVELT ROAD. 1925–1926 Season. Vilna Troupe.* The rest was in Yiddish, days and times of performances. I could understand some of the titles of the plays: *Day and Night* and *The Green Fields*. I'd never seen a poster like this at home. I eyed the wooden cash box where my father kept coins and money, and I studied the compartments on the top portion of the desk, the many small slots and drawers. Then I peered at the four drawers on the lower part of the desk. Where would he keep the extra key?

"What you lookin' for there?" Hadie said suddenly.

I swung around to face her, startled. She rarely spoke to me. "Nothing," I stammered.

She stood by the ironing board, staring at me. Sweat bubbled on her forehead.

I picked up a pencil from the desk. "This. I'm looking for this. I needed a pencil to write the customers' names."

"No, you looking for something else." She nodded vigorously. "I have two good eyes. You tiptoe about this laundry like a thief."

"I was looking for a pencil, and I found it."

"What you want that for? All them pencils up front. And I seen your Daddy give you pencils to take home." She set down her steaming iron on the board and wiped her forehead with the back of her hand. "All there is here is clothes and money." Her eyes traveled to the wooden box. "You not going to steal from your daddy, are you?"

"I would never do that," I said.

"No, you looking for something specific, Miss Lena." She smiled a thin smile. "I know this place. I knows the iron and the pressing machines. I know the boredom. I could give you lessons in boredom. God makes you bored so you won't stay in one place too long." She breathed in the hot air and smoothed the collar of the shirt she was pressing. Then she walked toward me. "I know where everything is. The pencil and paper, the lists your daddy keeps. And the money. Nothing else here." She eyed the desk, quiet. Then she stared at me and raised her right eyebrow. "I know everything here."

I turned to go. "I'd better get back to the front counter."

Hadie placed a hand on my shoulder. "And I see that your daddy treats you like a little girl, but you're a woman. At least, you're moving down that road. Would be a nice place here to come with your sweetheart. Your uncle did. Before he go away."

"My uncle?" I faced her. "Which uncle are you talking about?"

"Oh, honey." She laughed and hid her face with her hands. Then she gazed at me with kindness. "The mean one. That man could not keep a secret. Not Mr. William, the man that sings. I may not talk much, but I ain't a fool. I have four children of my own. I've seen you with your sweetheart, that nice-looking boy. I seen you near the lake, walking close. You holding his hand."

I gulped, but didn't reply. When had she seen us?

"Miss Lena, you been nice to me. You're polite. You ever want something, you look here. This is where your uncle went when he want to get in this laundry, or he want to buy some special thing for a lady. I seen him go here." She pointed to the large bottom drawer on the left side of the rolltop desk. "I knows you're in a hurry, but wait." She knelt and pulled hard until the drawer slowly creaked open. Then she dug inside it, lifted out six folded white towels that lay on top of a thick wad of money and the laundry key.

One True Friend
January–February 1927

"I have the key," I said to Max.

"To your heart?" he asked.

"No," I laughed. "You already have that."

I was sitting on a green velvet sofa in the living room of Max's house while he sat at the baby grand piano. It was a large, elegant room. A shining chandelier of crystal teardrops hung from the ceiling. A blue oriental rug stretched across the floor. Winter sunlight poured in through the windows. We were the only ones at home.

"The key to the laundry," I explained. I still wondered why Hadie had shown it to me. Or was she showing me the wad of money? But she'd looked at me with kindness, so I was sure she meant to help.

"Let's see the key," Max said.

"I don't have the key with me." I felt myself blush. I'd been caught in a lie. "But I know where to find it."

"So *have* is the wrong word."

"Now you're being precise."

"You taught me to be precise," he said.

"Well, I can take the key any time I want."

"And what are you going to do with it?" Max said. "What will the key open for you?"

"Not for me, for *us*. We can go to the laundry on a Sunday." My father sometimes went to the laundry on Sundays to finish paperwork, but I decided not to tell Max this. My father didn't go every Sunday. "We can kiss at the laundry," I said, suddenly shy. "We can be completely alone there, and do whatever we want."

"We're alone now," Max said. He joined me on the sofa and pressed his lips against mine.

"Yes," I whispered.

"Sometimes we'll kiss at my house," he said. "Sometimes at the store."

We kissed for a long time. Then I eased away from him. "Will you play something on the piano for me?" I said.

"I'd rather kiss you."

"Just one song, Max. I've never heard you play piano." I laced my fingers in his. "We have all afternoon. You said everyone would be gone today."

He hesitated and then reluctantly went to the piano. I wanted to kiss Max—I longed to—but I also wanted to hear his music, to understand another part of him. When he began to play, the sounds melted into a melody so sweet it had to be meant just for me, I hoped.

"You're so good at this, Max," I said when he finished playing. "What's the name of the piece?"

"It's about indecision." He swiveled around to face me and grinned. "Where to kiss? I call it, 'A Kiss in the Laundry.'"

I laughed. "You can't put your title on someone else's music."

"This is my own composition."

"You can do everything," I said, impressed.

"No, only this. But I'd like to do something else, too, one day," he replied seriously. "Something important. I want to help people, help with life and death. I want to study to become a doctor."

"You'd be a wonderful doctor," I said. Life and death. I'd seen too much of that already. "Do you believe in God?" I asked.

He shrugged. "My parents don't go to *shul*. My father believes in free will. He says God is the opiate of the masses. Besides, I don't think a doctor has to believe in God. I don't know. Do you?"

"I'm not sure either. My parents like to give advice based on what *they* think God thinks. As if they could know."

"No one will ever know. But, if you want to hear music—this is real music. Mozart."

In the splendid light-filled room, Max played the piano again. The music began softly and then became forceful. The sounds seemed to grow, a crescendo of melody. His fingers were skipping, running, twirling across the keys. I felt guilty, suddenly, about being here. I had lied to my mother and told her I was going to the lake. I hadn't mentioned Max or his house.

The music shimmied and slowed. My heart slowed. The keys clattered. Then two high notes trilled in the room, followed by a hollow silence. He was finished, and all thoughts of my mother disappeared.

"That was beautiful," I said.

"Next time I'll play jazz for you." He sat next to me on the sofa, and we kissed again. Each time we touched, I felt as if time stood still, as though I could touch him forever. With Max, I felt safe. He was becoming the home I'd always wanted, a place I never wanted to leave.

Our mouths dipped together. We wrapped our arms around each other. After awhile, Max slid his hand to my white cotton blouse and opened one button and then another. He eased the blouse from my skirt and slipped his hand beneath my camisole. I unfastened the front of his shirt until I could slide my hand onto the smooth skin of his chest.

I couldn't bear to be silent one more second because of the pleasure of touching him and because I allowed him to touch me.

"Oh, Max," I whispered. I wanted to shout, "I love you."

Then, the front door creaked open. "Maxwell," his mother called out. "Are you home?"

Max jumped up and fastened his shirt studs. My heart hammered in my chest. I buttoned my blouse, jammed it into my skirt, and smoothed my hair away from my face.

"Maxwell?" Her footsteps grew louder.

"I'm here," he yelled, having made his way to the piano again. "I'm practicing." He began to play the Mozart piece.

"You're just starting to practice now?" Mrs. Sloan said sharply. She peeked into the room.

I took a deep breath and folded my hands on my lap.

"Oh, you have a guest." She frowned. "Max, you know you're not supposed to have guests when no one is home."

Max shrugged and continued to play the piano.

"I'm Lena Czernitski," I said awkwardly.

"Of course." She smiled. "You're Simon's sister, aren't you? We met at the school, or the Center, I think."

Max's father walked in behind her. I had seen him only once, and from a distance. He was a stocky man, with eyes like Max's. His sandy hair was speckled with gray, and he had a long nose, like Max's, too. He wore a black overcoat and nodded at us both.

"Max," he said. His face was pale; his mouth pursed in a frown. "Please play your music another time. We always welcome your friends, but I'm not feeling well. We had to come back early." He smiled quickly at me and then trudged out of the room.

"It's best if we don't have visitors now," Mrs. Sloan said anxiously. "Meyer will be home soon. He must have quiet. Your father must rest. Lena, of course I'm happy to see you. But I need Maxwell's help."

On my way home, the streetcar rumbled. I sat alone, thinking about Max. I wanted to stay at his house all afternoon. I'd been surprised to see he looked somehow younger when he faced his mother. I felt like one person when I was with my family and like a different, stronger person when I was with Max. Perhaps this was the same for everyone.

I thought of our conversation about God and my father's words at the laundry. My father wanted to make his presence small. My mother's presence wasn't small. She seemed to be everywhere in our apartment, the smells of onions while she cooked, the click-clack of her sewing machine. Her opinions. She even hovered in my mind when Max and I were together.

I could say truthfully, as I'd told Max, that I didn't know if I believed in God. Where had God been when I'd encountered Uncle Maurice? When Leah Grace died? When Uncle William jumped off the roof? And when the *Petlurias* shot my grandfather? I was confused. I didn't know what I believed. It was the kind of confusion I would have to unravel myself, I decided. If there *was* a God, perhaps this

God could breathe understanding into Miss Marshall, or gentleness into my mother.

After Leah Grace's death, my father had said that the rabbis tell us even a moment in paradise can be enough. "A moment that makes you feel grateful," my father said. I'd finally realized I was grateful for Leah Grace, but that didn't ease my sorrow, and I was so grateful for Max, but if anything happened to him, I didn't think I could bear it. Did God tell the rabbis what to say and think?

I made my way from the streetcar to Bittersweet Place, trying to untie these great knots of questions. I thought of my father again. I could see he loved people—his face glowed at the laundry. I didn't know if this was because he was away from the family then or because of his nature. Could I form friendships as he did? I could see this brought him happiness, but he and my mother were opposite in this way. She loved her sewing, while he loved conversation. She had relationships with the utensils in our kitchen, while he had relationships with the customers at the store.

At home, I sat at my desk and considered this. Was I like my father or my mother? Maybe I was like both. I had friends at school. There were the other girls from Poland and Russia who I talked with at recess, and, on occasion, I went to their apartments. Even Hadie had become a kind of friend, I supposed. But I'd become good friends with only two people, I realized: Max and Elka Amsall. They were clearly different kinds of friends. But in this way, I was like my mother, I decided, perhaps cautious about people.

Mary Hall had been a friend, but she'd laughed at me when she visited our apartment. I couldn't be friendly to her after that, even when she'd become nicer to me after Miss Healy blamed us both for teasing boys in the schoolyard. Even when she'd been kind after Miss Marshall humiliated me in class. I couldn't trust Mary Hall. What would stop her from being cruel again?

I tapped my pencil against my desk, opened my notebook, and thumbed to the page where I'd written the new list: "What I WANT by Lena Czernitski." At the end, I added: "12. Have good friends." What I yearned for were true friends, friends of the soul. Max was one of these. I was happiest when I was with him, or when I sat alone at my desk with my utensils—my pencil and notebook—or went to the lake to draw.

The week after Max played the piano for me, he and I didn't see one another. His father had developed a fever, he told me on the telephone. Max had to work at P. Sloan and Son Men's Manufacturing after school and also help out at home. Meyer was no use, Max said disdainfully—all Meyer could do was write, not talk to customers.

The next day, Max's sister gave Simon a note in a sealed envelope to pass on to me. I waited until I was alone in the living room to open it.

> Let's use the key to the laundry next week when
> I'm well. I've gotten sick. I have a fever now, too.
> Always yours, Max

I hated to think of Max ill. I read his note again, disappointed I wouldn't see him for awhile. Always yours, Lena, I daydreamed. I set his note on my desk, smoothing out the wrinkles on the paper. Then Leah Grace popped into my mind, and how ill she'd been with a fever. A foolish, stupid thought.

Two days later, Max called me on the telephone and told me he would have to stay home three more weeks.

"Three weeks?" I said. "I'm worried about you, Max." In our living room, I clutched the receiver to my ear.

"Don't be. I'm fine. We'll meet in the laundry soon." He coughed and coughed.

"You don't sound fine. Is your fever bad? Can you even eat?"

"Soup. I eat soup. My throat hurts, my head hurts—that's the worst part." His voice sounded weak. "I'll be okay. You'll see. You'll get the key, and then we'll be alone at the laundry."

"I hope so. I hope you'll feel better soon."

With Max sick, I spent more time with Elka Amsall. She joined me as I walked home each afternoon. She always wore a black wool coat with a fine fox collar and asked me questions.

Her family had come from Poland, near the German border. Amsall, she told me, meant "little black bird" in German. She was this exactly: short, with thick dark hair the same color as an ocean sky on a night without stars. She had brown eyes, round rosy cheeks, and large breasts, which she hid by wearing blouses too big for her. "I don't want people to see my shape," she confided. Her father was a furrier, her mother sickly.

Elka seemed to know everything—the details of the Boer Wars, the rules of Prohibition, the ideas espoused by a political party in Germany, the National Socialist German Workers' Party.

"What do you think of this coat?" she asked one day. "Do you like it? Will you help me with the arithmetic assignment? Lena, come for dinner at our apartment tomorrow."

I realized neither Max nor I had ever asked the other as many questions as Elka asked me. She talked without stopping, like a fluttering bird. There was something about this I liked, so I went to her apartment one afternoon to help her with arithmetic, her only weak subject.

"I know you can draw," Elka said. We stood in her long, narrow living room. "Draw a picture of me now, can you? Can you make me a little more beautiful than I really am?"

"You're already beautiful," I replied. I wondered how she knew I liked to draw. Only Miss Marshall, Max, and my father had seen my drawings, although I sometimes sketched on my papers in school.

I was about to tell Elka I couldn't draw her, but she handed me paper and pencil. "I know you can do this," she said. "I've seen you draw in class."

I was flattered that she noticed. Maybe I would need to draw for someone, I thought, for Miss Marshall. I might as well practice now. So Elka sat perfectly still in an armchair in the living room. At first, I was a little uneasy, and my lines were clumsy. But I settled into the sofa, erased and continued to draw until I made a sketch of her in her coat with the fine fox collar.

"That's great, Lena," she said, looking at the finished drawing. "You drew me just as I asked you to."

I lay awake in the drafty, wintry darkness of my bedroom. Simon was asleep in the other bed. He seemed to be able to sleep despite the whirl of his thoughts. Or maybe his thoughts didn't whirl. Maybe he was lucky. My feelings plunged as I'd never known them to. I wanted to visit Max, but he'd told me on the telephone visitors weren't allowed. He would be fine, he assured me again, though his voice sounded hoarse and tired. How did he know whether he would be fine or not? I was learning too much about illness and hospitals. I thought of Ellis Island, where I'd been sick with measles, and of my old grandmother on her hospital bed, and Uncle William who now lived in a place for people with problems of the mind, a place I'd never seen. My mother said Simon and I weren't old enough to visit there yet. And I thought of poor Leah Grace, how pale and weak she'd been before she died.

Stop thinking about this, I told myself. I wanted to be at the laundry with Max. I wanted us to walk by the lake and kiss beneath the big oak tree that grew where the grass met the sand. I could almost feel his arms around me now.

A burst of frigid air pushed into the bedroom through a crack in the window. I pulled the wool blankets up to my neck, waiting for the hiss of the radiator and its blast of heat. I waited for my thoughts to disappear.

The next day, I decided to go to the library after school to find bits of information to give to Max, to cheer him up.

I'd been to the library before to draw when the weather was bad and I couldn't sit by the lake. I'd been there, too, to read books to help me learn English. Now I didn't know what information I was looking for, so I went to the librarian. "Do you have a book on fever?" I asked. "And art," I added, an afterthought.

She was a tall, plain woman, with short red hair and a serious expression. "We have no volumes on artistic fever," she whispered. "I'll see what I can find."

I waited in the large room. Long wooden tables lined the floor and people sat reading books and newspapers. Everything about the room had a golden glow—the honey-colored tables, the paneled walls and wooden shelves. A chandelier dangled from the ceiling, casting beams of light. The room was still, except for an occasional footstep or the scraping of a chair. This seemed suddenly like a sacred place, with all this silence, and I imagined Max here or at another library, collecting information about Chicago.

The woman returned with two books and told me to use them in the library. I decided I didn't need a book on fever. What more did Max or I need to know? The only resolution was to get well. So I sat at a long table and opened one of the books: *Rembrandt's Etchings: An Essay and a Catalogue, with Some Notes on the Drawings.*

I leafed through the pages. For a moment, I forgot my worries about Max. I studied the beautiful drawings and followed the lines with my eyes, trying to understand how the shapes were made. I took paper and pencil from my book bag. I did not trace. I wanted to see if I could capture on my own some of the shapes in a portrait of a man.

My first sketch was stiff and ugly. I crumpled the paper in disgust. A man at the next table frowned and whispered, "Shhh." I nodded, and tried again and again, until some of my lines were more delicate, lovely even, I thought. Then I stopped and looked around.

A mother sat with a child, perhaps Leah Grace's age, at the table next to mine. The man who'd frowned at me sat bent over a book. I began to draw him, his shiny balding head, the way his arm pressed against the table and afternoon light settled on the folds of his jacket. I drew quickly, as if my hand had a will of its own. Then he coughed, stood up, and walked away.

My drawing was unfinished. Did real artists have problems like this? I wondered.

Even so, I'd work on these drawings, I decided, and maybe give them to Max when he was well again.

At the end of that week, Miss Marshall stood like a soldier in front of the class. I sat nervously. When she eyed us like this, we never knew what would come next. She wore bright red lipstick today, a light blue dress with a narrow skirt, and black pumps with shiny buckles. She would have been nice-looking, I thought, if she weren't so miserable.

"This morning we will present our recitations of the Gettysburg Address," she announced.

Everyone groaned. She'd given us this assignment weeks ago.

Elka's left hand shot into the air. She waved it frantically.

"Miss Amsall," Miss Marshall snapped. "You of all students know how to raise your hand properly—right hand in the air, elbow on the desk, left hand in your lap. Where is your self-control today?" Then, Miss Marshall eyed Mary Hall. "Miss Hall, put your hands behind your back for five minutes. I couldn't tell if you were raising your hand or wiggling." Mary Hall had been sitting quietly, like me. But the three of us were different from the other students—Elka was Polish, I was Russian, and Mary, Elka, and I were older than the others in the class. So Miss Marshall picked on the three of us. Every day.

A few students laughed. Mary's face paled.

"Miss Czernitski," Miss Marshall went on. "You will begin the recitation. Are you prepared?"

"Yes," I said. I stood up, squared my shoulders, and made my way to the front of the room. I had practiced the assignment over and over. Miss Marshall could do her best to humiliate me, but I was determined not to humiliate myself. I was wearing a soft brown wool dress, a new one my mother had sewn for me. It was one of my favorites, with a pale blue silk sash wrapped around the dropped waist. The dress wasn't store-bought, but I looked presentable. I stood next to Miss Marshall and faced the class, wondering, suddenly, what my family had been doing in Russia when President Lincoln had been giving this speech.

"Abraham Lincoln gave this speech on November 19, 1863," I explained, forcing myself to pay attention and not let my mind wander. My palms were sweaty. I pressed them against my dress.

"Correct," Miss Marshall said.

Some students stared at their desks, but Philip Schloss and a few other boys glared at me. Philip's blond hair was slicked back as if he'd used too much Brilliantine. His nostrils flared. He rolled his eyes at me and laughed.

Miss Marshall ignored him. I was furious, but there was nothing I could do except look away and stare at the wall.

"Four score and seven years ago," I began, "our fathers brought forth on this continent a new nation, conceived in..." My voice sounded shaky, and I suddenly couldn't remember what came next. I paused, thinking hard. Then the words rushed back to me, and I spoke in a strong voice, "...that this nation, under God," I finally concluded, "shall have a new birth of freedom—and that government of the people, by the people, for the people, shall not perish from the earth." I stopped. I'd recited without one mistake.

There was silence.

"Where did the President present this speech?" Miss Marshall asked me.

I paused, thinking, looking at her. Where? Not Boston. Someplace east. "Pennsylvania," I said quickly. "That's where Gettysburg is. On a battlefield."

"That is correct. I am surprised, but pleased," she said sharply. "You may go back to your seat."

I hurried to my desk, flushed with relief.

Mary Hall and Elka Amsall came up to me as I was leaving school. "Lena, wait," Mary called. Her silky blond hair was tucked beneath her red wool hat. She was as tall as me, but prettier with her pale blue eyes and perfectly shaped lips and upturned nose. "We're going to meet Willa Jones, Sylvia Glassman, and some other girls on Diversey Avenue. Do you want to come with us?"

"We'll look at the shops there," Elka said.

"No, I'm sorry, I can't," I said. The three of us strolled out of the schoolyard. I wanted to go directly home in case Max telephoned or Simon brought me a note from him. I was angry, too, and embarrassed about how Philip Schloss and his friends had acted in class. They'd made me feel stupid and invisible at the same time.

"Too bad. Are you sure you won't join us?" Mary Hall said. "You look upset. Are you worried about Philip Schloss and those other boys?"

"I wish they'd leave me alone."

"They won't leave anyone alone," Elka said.

Mary nodded in agreement.

Why was Mary friendly, anyway? I wondered. With girls from another country? Elka and I were so different from Mary even though Miss Marshall picked on the three of us. Mary had lots of friends. She didn't need us. I, on the other hand, was noticing how much I liked her company, despite what had happened in the past with her, and the company of the other girls. I was lonely without Max. I smiled, thinking I was like my father, who enjoyed having friends. "Another time, I'll come with you," I said. "It's nice of you to ask."

"Sure. Don't let Philip Schloss bother you. You could join us more, if you wanted," Mary Hall said. "I always see you with that older boy."

"Sometimes I'm with him," I said, surprised she'd noticed.

It was chilly as we walked. Even though the sun shone and the sky had a bright blue tint, it seemed like winter would never end. We were bundled in coats and gloves, Elka wearing her black coat with the fox collar, Mary in a fine red wool coat that matched her hat. We trudged ahead. When we reached the turn that led toward Diversey Avenue, I waited for them to go their own way, but instead Elka stopped.

"I'm so unhappy," she stammered. "I don't know how to tell you both."

"What's wrong?" I asked. I remembered how she had waved her hand in class, so unlike her. "Are you ill?"

"Did someone die?" Mary Hall said.

"No, no," Elka said. "It's…we're moving away, in three weeks." There were tears in her eyes. "Just three weeks."

"Oh, Elka, I'm sorry," I said.

"To where?" asked Mary.

"Wisconsin…Milwaukee." Elka's voice was a little stronger. "My father told me last night. My uncle lives there. He and my father will open a fur business. But I don't want to go. What should I do?"

Wind pushed against our faces. Mary pressed her arms across her chest. "I think you have to go, Elka," she said.

"There's no other way," I said. I knew I had to encourage Elka, but I didn't want her to leave. "You can't live without your family. At least Wisconsin isn't far, not like Poland."

"Winter lasts ten months a year there." Elka scowled. "It snows every day. It's worse than Chicago. It's a living hell, my mother says. The business will do well, my father says. He'll become rich."

"Then your life will be easier," I said.

"There will be nothing wonderful for me," she said. "My father will still drink whiskey."

I didn't know what to say. Mary Hall was silent, too.

"You'll have to see what happens," I finally said. "At least you'll be free of Miss Marshall. And when you're older, you can live where you want."

This seemed to cheer up Elka some, and her face relaxed. "I hope so." She sighed. "Are you coming with me to Diversey now?" she said to Mary.

"I'll meet you," Mary replied. "I'll walk a little further with Lena."

"All right. I'll see you both later." Elka sprinted away from us, her black hair spreading behind her like an opened fan.

I was ready to hurry home, but Mary Hall trailed beside me. I was like my mother and father both, I thought. I enjoyed the company, but only for so long.

When we reached my street, I stopped. "I've got to get home now," I said.

"Too bad about Elka," Mary said softly. "Maybe we'll never see her again. That would be sad."

"I hope she'll like it there," I said, a little sad myself and surprised by Mary's wistful tone.

"She might." Mary dug her hands into her coat pockets. "I want to tell you something, Lena." Her pale blue eyes met mine. "I saw how Philip Schloss looked at you in class today, how he laughed. You think I'm like him and the other kids at school who hate Jewish people. But I'm not."

"He's awful," I said, startled that she mentioned this. "And you're his friend."

"Well, I'm not like him. If people are friendly to me, that's fine. If not, that's swell, too."

"So you want to avoid problems in school?"

"Of course. Miss Marshall doesn't like you. She barely likes any of us. She's the most hateful to you. You did a great job with the speech today, and she wasn't even nice about it. But you should know, she's not fair to anyone."

I shrugged as we rounded the corner onto Bittersweet Place.

"Remember when we studied about our forefathers?" Mary said. "They aren't my forefathers either. My grandmother came from Ireland."

"Really? I thought your family had been here since the Pilgrims."

"No. My grandmother came here to escape from a famine. She was poor and very religious. Catholic. My other grandparents are from Sweden. We have relatives in both places still. Really, I'm not so different from you."

I hadn't known about that. I stopped again, in the middle of the block.

"My grandparents even talk with an accent," Mary said.

"Like my grandmother does."

"Maybe like everyone's grandmothers."

We both laughed.

I didn't tell her that my old grandmother barely knew English, or that she barely spoke at all now. Or that my parents spoke with accents, and my mother could hardly read or write English. "I have to go," I said again. "But thanks for the company. And for telling me about your family."

"I want to tell you one more thing," said Mary. "I hate when kids call you an ugly Jew. I'm sorry they do." She paused. "I'm sorry if I've ever done anything like that. Your brother…" She looked suddenly stricken.

"You know Simon?" I asked.

"I've met him," she said. "I've heard kids calling him names. But I want you to know that I'm sorry for anything I've done and for what those other kids say to you."

Hearing Mary's apology made me queasy. "They're stupid, prejudiced morons," I sputtered.

"They're cruel," she said, "and they're wrong."

"Why are you in Miss Marshall's class anyway?" I said. "You're almost as old as I am."

"I hate it. Does it bother you to be older?"

"Sure," I said, thinking about how hard I'd worked to get promoted an extra grade every year. "When we came here, they put me in the youngest grade because my English wasn't good. I felt terrible about that. Ashamed. What happened to you?"

Mary was quiet. Her pretty face crinkled into a frown. She tucked a few stray wisps of blond hair beneath her hat. "I was sick when I was younger," she finally said. "I had scarlet fever. They thought I might die. They thought other kids would get sick, too. They put me in the hospital. I had to stay there a long time. I couldn't go to school or anywhere."

"Oh, no." I scanned her face, her blue eyes, her body clothed in the fine red wool coat. "Are you all right now?"

"Mostly. Please don't say anything about this. Some kids, if you tell them…"

"Will be cruel," I said, finishing her sentence.

"Yes. Well, I just wanted to tell you." She turned away and retraced her steps, disappearing onto Clarendon Avenue.

I continued home slowly. I'd never imagined this about Mary—her family, her illness, her apology—and couldn't understand why she'd told me. I didn't know what to believe about her now. I thought of my mother's words. She'd once said: You can't know about people from the outside. She was right. Then I thought about Elka. She was moving. I would miss her. What if Max had scarlet fever, too?

But how did you understand what was inside a person? My mind leapt to Max again. I wanted to know him inside and out, but I wasn't sure how to do this. Mary Hall had once seen her parents kissing and having sex. She'd told a group of us last year that she'd opened the bedroom door to ask them a question and there they were, heaped on top of each other, naked, like grunting lumps of clay. *Shtupping*, I thought. Was that how you understood another person?

How I wished I could talk to my mother about this, just as I'd wanted to talk to her about Uncle Maurice. Tell me a story about it, she would say. But what good were stories when something was real? *Shtupping*—sex—what I feared my father had done with the beautiful customer, what Uncle Maurice might have wanted of me, what had led to the ruin of Uncle William, I was sure. And even so, I knew in my heart I wanted to do this with Max.

I didn't care what anyone said, I couldn't wait.

I walked past a tree now that stretched toward the sunlight and air, the very things that would nourish it and cause it to grow. Then I hurried into our building and climbed the stairs in the musty hallway. Someday I would be alone with Max in the laundry. I would proclaim my love for him. When he was well. And he would be well again, soon. He had to be.

A Visit to the Rooming House
February 1927

"Decency" was a word my mother rarely used. I didn't know the exact Yiddish equivalent. It wasn't really *sechel,* sense about the world. Or *balebatish,* to be modest. "Decency" meant proper behavior, all those things required to live an acceptable life. I had looked up the word in the dictionary. I knew decency formed the basis of my mother's beliefs. It permeated all she did, from her glances of disapproval to her demands we be polite. "You sit with your pencil and books too much, Lena. You will turn into a person who does not know how to talk to other human beings," she'd told me, as if even failing to participate in conversation was an indecent act. She held a long list in her head, I was sure, about what constituted proper behavior and what did not.

She would have considered my visit to Max's house and his fingers on my breast indecent. If she had known, she would have punished me. And because I had encouraged him, her censure would have been severe. I didn't care. I only cared that Max and I would be at the laundry alone, and soon. He was finally feeling better, his fever and cough gone, and we had made a plan to meet.

At school and at home now, I felt as if I were a horse locked in a corral, longing to run free. I had read about places like this. They existed in the west, in wide stretches of open land. Montana. Nevada. Colorado. California. Like those pent-up animals, I was wild inside.

It had been almost two weeks since Elka had told us she was moving, and I was working at the laundry today. I felt sad she would go away. Each day, she sat stone-faced next to me in class.

My father wasn't at the laundry, nor was Hadie. While Aunt Razel spoke to a customer at the front counter, I wandered to the back, carrying a few shirts I'd folded and my coat draped over my arm. I set the shirts on the ironing board and went to the rolltop desk. I knelt and pulled open the bottom drawer slowly, trying to avoid making a sound. I was lucky. The washing machines vibrated loudly. I felt certain my aunt couldn't hear me.

I dug my hand beneath the folded white towels as Hadie had shown me, rooting around. Finally, I felt the cold metal of the key. I lifted it out and eased the drawer shut. I jammed the key into the pocket of my coat. Max and I would meet at the laundry on Sunday. In three days. I wasn't sure how I would bear the wait.

I took a circuitous route home. I wanted to be alone with my thoughts, and at the apartment I was always ambushed by interruptions—by my mother, my father, even Simon. And since the family club had resumed meeting in our living room, the relatives and the *landsleit* interrupted me, too.

The wind whipped against my face. The streets and sidewalks were dry and gray, like the sky. I wore a long black cardigan sweater over my brown dress, my heavy coat, and thick rayon stockings for warmth.

I swung onto Cornelia Street. Cornelia was a grand street, with two- and three-story brick houses, and some larger apartment buildings, too. Many of them had carvings above the windows and large, gracious courtyards in front.

Whenever I walked up this street, I pretended I lived in one of these houses. I imagined my room, the big windows and bright light, a crystal chandelier in the living room. A closet filled with new clothing. I imagined the quiet in such a house.

I noticed a man a few yards ahead, walking in the same direction as me. I glanced quickly at his back. I knew that coat, I realized, the blue tweed pattern. I knew the sway of the man's arms.

"Papa," I called out in surprise.

"Lena," he said, turning around. "I thought you were at the laundry. That's where you should be."

I fingered the key in my pocket. Did he know? Had he found out about Max and me? "I *was* at the laundry," I said carefully. I would talk to my father as though he knew nothing. I wouldn't let my nervousness show. "I have too much schoolwork today, so I couldn't stay."

We stood facing each other.

"I was walking down this street because," he began, as if he needed to explain, "I have many memories here." His voice was quiet and wistful. "When I first arrived in America, I sold grain like I did in Russia. And I had a route here, delivering milk. I lived in a rooming house then, on this very street."

"The rooming house where you learned English," I said, relieved. He didn't know about Max and me, I was sure. He was only out walking and thinking, like I was. "Which house was it?" I asked.

"You, your mother, and Simon were in Russia. I drove a wagon with a horse. A fine one. It could have been a race horse if I'd had the money." He gazed up the street, but he didn't answer my question. "On a street full of memories, one can feel young again," he said. "Almost as young as you are. This you will understand when you are older. But this is not the fastest way home. We should choose another route."

We'd walked a few paces when my father suddenly turned and pointed back in the direction from where I'd come. "We will go this way," he said.

A door opened a few yards from us. A woman walked out of the building. My father stopped, swung around again, and glanced at the woman. I followed his gaze.

The woman wasn't wearing a coat. She wore a slim black dress and a long strand of pearls. She was tall and slender. She wrapped her arms around her chest, as if for warmth. Then she waved at us. "Would you like to come in?" she called out.

Her blond hair was swept back from her face. Her blue eyes regarded us kindly. I knew that face. Those eyes. It was the beautiful customer.

My father hesitated, as if to protest, but then started up the sidewalk toward her. "Come, Lena," he said.

I followed, astonished.

As we approached her, he said, "This, Lena, is the rooming house where I was a boarder. Now a family lives here. There are no boarders anymore."

The woman watched us. "I'm pleased to see you, Henry," she said, shivering in the chilly air. "Come in, please. It's freezing outside today." She spoke without an accent. Her eyes were the color of the ocean. I could tell by the way she looked at my father and smiled that she liked him. I could tell that he liked her. My eyes flitted from her to him and back. She was the woman my mother had screamed about, and I hated the woman because of this.

In the hallway, the beautiful customer reached to shake my hand. I stepped back. How could I touch her when she had hurt my mother, when she could hurt our family? Yet, I was drawn to her sweet perfume, her kind voice.

"Don't be shy," she said to me. She opened the door to her apartment. "I won't hurt you. Your father has told me about you. Lena? Is that right?"

"Yes," I said.

"I'm Millie Farber. And your father was correct. You're lovely. Beautiful."

I felt color rise to my face. "Thank you," I said. I wanted to tell her I wasn't beautiful at all. I was often clumsy and ill at ease, except when I was with Max. I wanted to tell her I longed to be as she was: blond and pretty and without any cares. She didn't wear an apron. Her hands weren't chapped. Her nails were polished a sparkling bright red.

My father remained silent as she ushered us into a parlor. The beautiful customer—Millie—was more slender and graceful than I'd imagined she would be. When I had seen her at the laundry, she'd been wrapped in a brown overcoat. I could smell her perfume now, like lilacs, stronger and sweeter than the scent of my mother or my aunts.

"I'm glad I saw you both," she said.

"We haven't much time," my father said quickly. "We're expected home. And Lena has school assignments to complete."

"But this is a welcome coincidence. I was going to stop by the business to tell you. It may be quite some time before I see you again." She looked at me. "And I may not have had the chance to meet Lena."

"Another laundry, you are switching to?" my father said, his voice tinged with regret. He sat stiffly in a blue velvet armchair.

"No. In a moment I will explain." She left the room.

My father and I sat in silence. He took off his coat and set it on his lap. I took off my coat and sweater and laid them next to me on the sofa with my school bag. I peered at the books lined neatly on the wooden shelves in the room. There were leather- and cloth-bound volumes in English and even Yiddish. I spotted the book Max had mentioned, *Illinois Poets*. On the same shelf was the book my father and I had once read about in the newspaper, *An American Tragedy*. And I saw a gray book with words I couldn't understand, French words, I was sure: Balzac *Contes Drolatiques* Paris. I noticed a small poster on another shelf, for Glickman's Palace Theater, *1925–1926 Season*. It looked like the poster I had seen in the laundry. I wanted to look at it closely and check, but the beautiful customer came back into the room.

She carried a white china teapot, a crystal pitcher filled with orange juice, a plate of poppy seed cookies, and three china teacups and saucers, all balanced neatly on a silver tray. These were finer than anything I had ever seen, and I knew I had to be careful with them. She set them all on a low table. The poppy seed cookies were perfectly round. The napkin she gave me was made of thick cloth with pink embroidery on the edge.

"I want you to tell me about yourself," she said kindly. She sat across from me, in another blue velvet armchair. "But first I will answer your father's question." She looked at him. "Henry, I wouldn't willingly give our business to another laundry. We are moving away. To Colorado. My husband has relatives there. It's a new frontier, he tells me, with many opportunities for people like us." Her voice seemed to shake. She stared at her wrists, as thin and graceful as the necks of swans.

"Ah," my father said. "Opportunity." He looked pale.

I glanced from one to the other uneasily.

"If I had a reason to stay in Chicago," she said finally, "I would stay here. Whether my husband decided to go to Colorado or not. I would prefer to be *here*."

A stillness settled in the room, so profound I felt as if Millie Farber had fashioned a cushion of silence and pinned my father and me to it. My father seemed oddly rooted to his chair, his red hair curling and dull, his eyes glowing, his fingertips tapping against his lap.

I held my breath. What could he say? *He* was the reason she wanted to stay here, I was sure of it. I saw the way Millie Farber looked at him, the affection in her eyes. I saw the way she pursed her lips and waited for his words. And I hated her for it, hated the long strand of shiny pearls that hung from her neck. Hated her silky blond hair, her blue eyes and her smile. I hated that we had stopped here.

"One can always find a reason to stay in one's home," my father said. "In some instances, this is simpler to do than in others."

"Oh, yes." Millie stood up to fill a glass with orange juice. "What are they anyway—arguments and reasons?" she demanded. "They're just a collection of words. Words you tell other people. Words you tell to the heart. Words you use to lie to yourself."

I thought I saw tears in her eyes.

But she blinked and smiled. "Tell me, Lena. Your father has said how beautifully you draw. Is this something you would like to do when you grow up?"

I was surprised she knew about my drawing. And though I wanted to be a great artist someday, I hadn't really thought of drawing as a grown-up activity, not like working in a laundry or being a teacher. It was something I did to escape—from home, my thoughts, the misery of school. From losing people I loved.

They stared at me, as if waiting for me to carry the conversation away from the difficult subject Millie Farber had introduced. I decided I would do this for them. For my father.

"The drawing. I don't know." I shrugged. "Maybe I'll continue to do it when I'm grown up," I said, as if no passion or anger had flared in this room. "I mostly draw by the lake. Once I drew a picture of a friend. But my teacher doesn't believe I created the pictures myself. Really, it's a great problem. A terrible one." I felt suddenly bold, as I often did with Max. "I don't know how to solve the problem," I said. "Maybe you can help me."

"You might try to draw at places other than the lake. So you're comfortable with your skill everywhere. I hope one day you'll find someone who can teach you more about drawing. As for the teacher you have now, I wish I could be of help. Some people are stubborn. Cruel. Evil even."

"Evil," said my father. "No. This teacher is stupid and full of prejudice."

"Perhaps," said Millie. "You won't know until you talk to her, will you? And you must. Henry, you must defend your daughter."

"Of course, I am planning to do this," he said. "I will talk to her again."

"You can't let this woman ruin Lena's future. Lena is almost an adult, but she's still a child. If the parent doesn't help the child, who will? God, who you love to talk about?" She shook her head. "I don't think so."

"I am not so superstitious to believe God would intervene." He lifted a hand in the air, as if daring God to contradict him. "Even when I first came to this country, I had no superstitions like that."

"I don't know what to think about you anymore." She sighed and sat next to me on the sofa. "Lena, would you like more juice? A fruit perhaps?"

I shook my head no and thanked her. The two of them were having a private conversation, I realized, a private argument about something they had discussed before. No. They were discussing Millie's moving away. It didn't matter what words they used. There was an intimacy in the way they spoke, the way they looked at each other, a familiarity that made me uncomfortable. It was as real and solid as any object in the room.

I thought to mention the schoolwork that I needed to get started on, but instead, without even meaning to, I slipped a pencil and a few sheets of paper from my book bag. "I think I'll start to draw here," I said. "I will try your suggestion, Mrs. Farber."

"Good," she said.

My father seemed content to sit. Millie Farber seemed content to sit as well. So I studied the pitcher of juice and the diamond pattern of the crystal, how it glittered in the light of the room. Then, I began to sketch.

An Important Announcement
February 1927, later that afternoon

On our way home from Cornelia Street I clutched my drawings beneath my arm. I had given Millie Farber a drawing of my father's hands. He'd sat motionless in her parlor. As the sky had dimmed, I tried to reproduce his fingers on paper, the graceful arch of them, the rough texture of his nails, the patterned folds and shadows on his skin. I tried to capture the way his thumbs touched each other. I spent the most time on this drawing. Millie Farber had especially liked it, so I had left the drawing with her.

A deep silence had settled into her apartment while I drew, interrupted only by the scratching strokes of my pencil. My father and I continued this silence as we made our way home.

Finally, I said, "She's a kind woman, Papa."

"It was at her rooming house where I lived when I first came here," he said. "Of course, the reason I was able to come to this country was because of your grandfather, may he rest in peace."

"Oh," I replied. I wanted to discuss Millie Farber. The way they had looked at one another...they had once lived under the same roof! I knew what I knew, and I could imagine the rest, though I couldn't bear to. Maybe it was better not to talk about this. "I know that story," I said impatiently. "You were commissioned into the army. You bribed a soldier with *Zaide's* money. Then you ran home, said goodbye to everyone, and left for America."

"If only it were that simple." My father's arms swung restlessly at his sides as we walked. "I was conscripted, not commissioned. Forced to go into the army," he said. "You know what happened there. Men were swallowed in the Russian army. Never heard from again."

"So you ran to the forest and hid, then used the money Grandfather gave you, so you could leave for America," I said, finishing his thought.

"No," he replied, shaking his head. "Your grandfather had bought a ticket, passage for one person on a ship to come to America. He planned to bring all of us here one day. But he wanted first to see for himself if we could live here, if it was a good place for us. He gave *me* his ticket. Your mother will not talk about it, to this day. In one flash of a second, I escaped the army and was on my way."

I stared at him.

"Yes. Then the war came. It was impossible for anyone to leave Russia, to join me. And your grandfather wasn't…he wasn't blessed with luck when the *Petlurias* came to Belilovka."

"He gave you his ticket for the ship?" I repeated, amazed.

"Yes. The ship was called the SS *Chemnitz*. I will never forget the name. It brought us to the port at Baltimore." My father nodded, as if reliving this voyage. "In Russia, when Uncle William took me to the ship and left me, I was all alone, and I cried. Then, when I came to Chicago, I worked and saved. Every month I sent money to your mother so she could come here when the war ended, when it was safe to bring you, Simon, and the others. But I learned much later that the banker, the man I trusted, ran away with this money to Mexico. It never reached her. If only I'd known." My father sighed deeply. "But she was smart; she'd hidden jewelry and money in a pillow. Enough to get all of you to Poland, and you know the rest…" He eyed the drawings in my hand. "Enough of these stories. We will bring these drawings to your teacher."

Darkness spread across the sky like a black curtain. I pushed away the memory of my grandfather slumped and dead in the white wooden house in Belilovka. I didn't know what to say to my father. He'd been safe on Cornelia Street with Millie Farber. My mother had stood face to face with the *Petlurias* then, waiting for money that never came. I thought of my mother's beautiful black Persian lamb coat. She'd worn it on our journey through the forest and into Poland. But she'd traded it on the ship for money. All this information made me feel weak.

I yanked open the door to our building, pulled off my gloves, and jammed my hand into my coat pocket. The laundry key was still there. I didn't want to think about the past or my grandfather's ticket, about my father or mother or Millie Farber. Except to tell Max.

In my pocket, the sharp edge of a piece of paper scratched against my fingers. I had forgotten about the note from Miss Marshall. With all that had happened today, I'd neglected to give the note to my father. I dug it out as we climbed the stairs and handed it to him as we reached our apartment door.

He unfolded the piece of paper. "Ah, your teacher," he said. "She is finally responding to the note I sent, when I told her I wanted to talk with her again. She asks that I meet with her tomorrow. That's when we will bring her the drawings, Lena. We'll bring some others, too, that you keep in your room."

I nodded. I didn't think anything good would come from a meeting with Miss Marshall, but maybe I was wrong. Maybe my father could defend me. After such a difficult afternoon, it made me happy that he wanted to try.

Voices chattered in the kitchen. I retreated to my desk, placing my drawings face-down on top of it.

"Chaim, Lena...is that you?" my mother called.

"We have been waiting." Uncle Abie's voice boomed. "I have come to make an announcement."

Uncle Abie, Aunt Ida, and my mother were sitting at the kitchen table. Simon stood near the stove. He had been working more and more for Mr. Usher Cohen, so it was strange that he would be home. It was strange that so much family gathered in our kitchen today. I looked at Simon, grateful he was there. Next to him stood Uncle William.

"Uncle William," I said, astounded to see him here.

His arms hung limply at his sides. His eyes looked painted on his skin, glazed and vacant, and were the shape of two flat black almonds. He didn't speak. His crumpled white shirt and gray wool trousers were too large. He was so terribly thin.

I glanced at Simon again. He shook his head and shrugged.

My father walked in. "William, you are here?" he said with

astonishment. "Reesa, what is this? What's happened?"

"They allowed William to come home for one night," my mother began. It was clear Uncle William couldn't explain this. "The other relatives will be here soon to see him. Go walk with your uncle, Simon." She gestured toward the hall. "Please. We must discuss important matters."

Simon frowned, but he linked his arm in Uncle William's, knowing better than to argue with my mother's request.

"We will bring him back to life," she said to my father.

"Hello, William," my father said, stepping closer to my uncle.

Uncle William didn't reply. It seemed to me he would not be brought back to life. He stumbled toward the hall with Simon, and I sat down next to Aunt Ida.

"He'll stay in the apartment tonight?" my father asked. "This is your intention?"

"Yes," my mother replied. "If the doctors cannot help him, we must help him. I cannot bear for him to be in that place day and night."

"We will have whatever discussion you wish." My father sat next to me. "Then I'll bring William back to the Dunning Hospital. Even if I have to carry him on my back. He can't stay here all night."

"William needs to hear Abie's announcement," my mother said.

Uncle William began humming in the hallway, loud enough for us to hear. Then he sang a tuneless melody: "She loves me. She does not. I have a voice. I do not. One day in the future, I will sing again…" His voice trailed into a whisper.

"He won't understand what we talk about," Uncle Abie said. "My poor brother. It's a pity what happened to him, to his mind." Abie patted his wide belly and ran his hand through the thin wisps of his gray hair. He smelled of sweat and tobacco. He reached for one of the glass bottles on the kitchen counter and sighed. "*Schnapps.* I love it. Or vodka. It makes me happy. It helps me forget." He unscrewed the lid of a bottle of *schnapps*, poured some into a glass for my father and into one for himself.

"Tell us your news already, Abie," my father said, pushing

away his glass. "You'd live better—all of you—if you made your announcements without speeches."

Like Millie Farber had done, I thought.

"Chaim, where is your patience?" my mother said.

Aunt Ida sat quietly. A book lay on her lap, *So Big* by Edna Ferber. She fingered it nervously.

"Since you are in such a hurry," Abie said, "I will begin. When the others arrive, I will tell them, too. There are two items. Which is most important? I can't say." He eyed my mother. She handed my father a sheet of paper that had been resting on her lap.

He set it on the table and read it aloud. I pulled my chair closer to him and read along.

> My dear family,
>
> I have been away from California for many months. I had a business opportunity in Louisiana, but this was a wild land. It did not work out. When I returned to California, ready to move in again with William, he was gone. Mr. Stanley Brunswick, his booking agent, told me William had fallen into madness. I must know where William is! He owes me money. If I cannot settle my affairs here satisfactorily, I will need to come home. I also have matters to settle with Mr. Usher Cohen.
>
> Of course, I have missed everyone, Mother, Reesa, Abie, the rest. There is no time to write a long list of those who are always in my heart.
>
> Yours,
> Maurice

My heart stopped.

"I hope to God he stays away," my father muttered.

"Let me speak with honesty." Abie took a long breath. "Maurice is a man who takes advantage of people. All of us, we know this. And Mother, if she were not at death's door, would agree."

If Uncle Maurice came home, what would I do? I looked to my father, but he stared at his lap, lost in thought about Millie Farber, I supposed, and the feeling of being young, which he could recapture on Cornelia Street. He wouldn't help me, I thought, not with Uncle Maurice or with Miss Marshall. I would have to be the needle that mended my own life. I would have to make my own plan. I could depend on no one, except myself and maybe Max.

"Abie," my mother admonished. "Maurice is your blood."

"You always see the darkness, Abie." My father drummed his fingers on the table. "Everyone in this family does. If Maurice comes home, we'll put him to work in the laundry. He owns part of the building, after all. And I have a personal matter to discuss with him. If he never returns, even better. And Abie and Ida, why work like slaves at that piano store instead of helping at the laundry? Why is this family always filled with arguments and reasons?"

My head was spinning. Maybe I was my father's personal matter. Maybe he would protect me. So Uncle Maurice owned part of the laundry building. Some day he would come back. I willed myself to be calm.

"We won't solve the problem of Maurice until he is standing right here." Uncle Abie broke the silence. "So I will go to the second piece of news. Ida and I have decided to move away."

"Abie." My mother clutched her heart.

My aunt watched her husband with a tender expression. Move away, I thought. Like Elka Amsall and Millie Farber. Was there no certainty, even here in the *Goldene Medina*?

"And where are you going?" my father asked.

"Yes, where will you go, Uncle Abie?" I said. Colorado? I thought. Wisconsin? California?

"You cannot be a Jew in America," he replied, gulping his *schnapps*. "You may be free, but this is the land of heathens. Not just on Independence Boulevard. A man can't be observant. Can't pray. You can't hear God in this country. The whole place stinks of Christ. No, the truth is, you can't even be a good Christian. Money is the God here."

"Go back to your village then," my father said. "Shut out the world. What train will you take to this paradise?"

"No trains." Abie slipped a folded paper from his pocket and smoothed it open on the kitchen table, on top of Uncle Maurice's letter. It was a map. "And the Rabbi Hirschfeld," he scowled. "The man is a living Golden Calf."

"Stop this talk, Abie," my mother ordered.

"Our father, Reesa, may he rest in peace, wouldn't carry even a handkerchief on *Shabbos*," Abie replied. "Look at how we live, working on Saturdays. He would never have been happy here." He eyed the map. "Mielitz," he said proudly. "Ida and I are moving to Poland."

My mother gasped.

He slid his wide fingers over the map. "Here." He slipped a pencil from his shirt pocket and marked a large "X" on the map.

"Abie, you are jumping off the roof, too," my mother cried.

"Poland," my father spit. "It's no better than Russia."

Uncle Abie gazed at my father with pity. "Ida and I have made the decision. Her family lives in the village of Mielitz. We will, too. I won't work seven days a week sweating in that laundry or at the piano store so I can buy a loaf of bread. I'll work in a mill and fish. We'll live in the country again."

Aunt Ida smiled. "Where the air is pure."

There were so many places to visit, I thought. Colorado, Wisconsin, Poland.

"You'll see what happens there," my father warned. "The same things that happened to us in Russia. You're diving into Hell. Better to go to Palestine. But do as you choose. You always have, Abie."

"Don't go." My mother's voice trembled. "It's true, you and Ida came to Chicago with Razel and Charlie a full year before we did. But we are here now, all of us, together. The way we should be. You won't be happy, Abie. Ida, tell him, please."

"I will make a home wherever we go," Ida said. She pressed her thin lips together. "Once you move from your country, Reesa, you can do it again and again. Places mean nothing."

"Let us go where we want," Abie said. "In life, you have to know when to stay in your home, and when to leave it."

I pulled the map toward me and studied it. There were rivers, roads, and villages, the names in Polish. Places that seemed dark and small, like Belilovka. Would Mielitz be different? I imagined sailing on a boat to visit Uncle Abie and Aunt Ida. She would stand on the shore waiting, a book of poetry in her hand, children at her side. Abie would run to greet me, clutching pink roses. Trees and flowers would grow everywhere. We would be far from Uncle Maurice, Miss Marshall, and every other trouble. Max would be there, too. The streets and synagogue would glow with light.

I remembered how I had stood on the deck of the ship that brought us to New York, and watched Poland disappear. We glided away on the green-gray sea. Gulls flew. The sun set. The boat bounced on the waves. We slept below. Too many people were crammed together and hungry, and terrible odors rose. But the air on the deck near the ocean had been fresh and sweet and hopeful.

I knew this about Russia and Poland: They were far away, across an ocean, places I never wanted to see again. I knew them only in memory. That was enough. Then I remembered the synagogue in Russia. There was no synagogue in Belilovka. We traveled to the town of Ruzhin and sat in the small wooden synagogue there. The rabbi and cantor never smiled. My mother prepared lunches for us, weeping on Yom Kippur because only through tears could she convince God to forgive her, forgive us. Gizzard and liver for the children. Bitter foods, bitter lives.

"William had his nervous collapse because people have no respect for religion here," Uncle Abie was saying.

"I don't think that's the reason a person has a nervous collapse," I said, looking up from the map.

"I'll take all of you with me," Uncle Abie replied, ignoring my comment. He draped an arm around my father, one around my mother and drew them into his big body as if they were children. "We'll go to the synagogue, walk on *Shabbos*," he said, his voice dreamy. "Maybe it will help Ida. We have always wanted a child. Why not there?"

"I believe in facts," my father said. He pulled away from my uncle. "Do you think life is better in Poland? Do you *know*? No.

Do you read, Abie? Newspapers and books? Do you listen to the radio? Vladimir Jabotinsky and other intellectuals travel through Russia and Poland. They say nothing is getting better for Jews there. They understand the world. And you? You'll blunder through life deciding this or that based on sentiment. I've read that a book has been published in Germany. They call it *Mein Kampf*, and it's filled with venom against Jews. That such a book is published tells you what people are thinking. Poland is right next door. One day, we'll rescue *you* from Poland. I'll be sending you money there."

"Really?" shot back Abie. "Two years ago the Ku Klux Klan marched right here, in Washington D.C. The very capital of this country. Do they like Jews? I don't think so, Chaim. They hate us. They hate the Negros. They hate anyone who isn't a Christian, who doesn't have white skin."

"Abie, I'm surprised," my father said, smiling wryly. "You do know a little about the world. You must read the newspaper after all."

"For God's sake, Chaim," my mother bristled. "What are these ideas? You aren't the man we knew in Russia. Don't speak to my brother that way."

"He has his ideas," Abie said. "I have mine. The days are brothers, but no two are alike. What's the harm?" He chuckled. "We're having a little debate."

"Where is the help we give each other?" she lamented. "This is not a family anymore. This is a gathering of people who care only about themselves. That is why William jumped off the roof." She pulled herself up from her seat and turned her back to us.

"The future is better in Poland," Abie insisted. "You will see this. I promise. You'll come to visit, Reesa, with Lena and Simon. We will treat you as if you are the czarina, better than the president."

"Where is the *shalom bayit*?" My mother swung around to look at us.

"There is no peace in this home," my father shouted back.

"There is no family anymore," she yelled. "What's happened to this lovely family?"

Everyone began speaking in heated voices, one over the other, in fiery layers. Simon walked into the kitchen with Uncle William. William was still humming. My mother grasped his hand, and Simon, suddenly free, ran from the room.

Soon the front door opened and closed, and more voices poured into the apartment.

"We are here," called out Uncle Charlie from the entryway.

No one answered him. Everyone in the kitchen was arguing.

It seemed to me that when people in our family argued, their words talked of one subject when they were really speaking about another. I was sure this was true of my mother and father. Of my father and Millie Farber. True for everyone in the kitchen now, everyone in the family club. Perhaps even true of Max and me.

Uncle William stopped humming. He stood next to my mother, his arms dangling helplessly at his sides.

I couldn't bear to look at him and so returned to staring at the map. There was no place for my father in this apartment, I realized, no place of comfort. And there was no place for me either. I was a stranger. I had no home.

I shut my eyes and imagined the future. Max and I kissing in the laundry. Aunt Ida and Uncle Abie living happily in Poland. Uncle Maurice leaping off the roof instead of Uncle William. Our apartment quiet and peaceful. My father and Millie Farber sitting close in her parlor. My mother at the sewing machine, clutching Uncle William's hand—forever trying to stitch our family together, still waiting for money from my father that would never come. Simon off working with Mr. Usher Cohen.

"What will the key open for you?" Max had asked me at his house before he got sick. I didn't need to explain to him. The door would take me far from here, from Bittersweet Place. Max and I would walk through that door together.

Miss Marshall's Edict
February 1927, the next day

I had learned the word "retrospect" in school. It was a ten-dollar word, Miss Marshall told us. The sounds of it fell from my tongue like a poem, but also like a warning: By looking backward, you could see the bleaker, truer meaning of a day. Now I understood this.

My father and I were on our way to see Miss Marshall, and I was nervous. I reviewed the events of yesterday in my mind. In retrospect, they seemed enormous—talking with Millie Farber, learning about Uncle Abie's leaving, about Uncle Maurice's possible return. I felt a great foreboding about the future. Would my father run off with the beautiful customer? And if he did, what would become of my mother and Simon and me? Would I be trapped alone in the apartment with Uncle Maurice?

Last night, I'd had trouble sleeping, and so I went to the kitchen for a glass of milk. Next time, perhaps I would have a glass of *schnapps* or vodka instead of milk. Simon drank it; why shouldn't I? Poor Uncle William hadn't stayed in the apartment. My father had taken him back to Dunning Hospital. "Don't ever bring him home again," my father had warned my mother. "He's not well, and we cannot be responsible. Do you not remember what happened the last time?"

"If we do not help him, who will?" she had said. "I will not let him rot there."

"You heard me, Reesa. That is the end of it."

As I'd made my way back from the kitchen, the light in my parents' bedroom shone beneath their door. I tiptoed past their room and heard the clatter of the sewing machine, so slow, as if it were dying. I heard voices. Don't listen, I told myself. Just go to your room. Then I heard my name.

"Lena's teacher," my father said. "Tomorrow I will meet with Lena's teacher again. She sent me a note to arrange the time. I want to talk with her alone."

"Alone?" my mother replied.

"Lena and I," my father said. "We will go to the school, with her drawings."

The sewing machine stopped. "What drawings? The drawings the teacher told us about?"

"These." Papers rattled.

I stood motionless in the hall.

"These are hers? Lena's?" my mother said.

"Yes."

I squeezed my eyes shut and sucked in a breath.

"She has never given me them or told me." My mother sighed, her voice like the purr of a wounded kitten.

"She considers it private." My father's voice was matter-of-fact. "Everything is private at her age. That's how children are."

There was a long silence.

"When I was that age, there was no 'private'," my mother finally said. "These are beautiful." Papers rattled again. "She is my daughter. Why did she not tell me? What have I done to cause such secrets? Haven't I loved her enough?" She started to cry. Long, low sobs that began in the heart.

"Reesa, please," my father said.

"And the glass cup, the ballerina made of porcelain, what I brought from Russia—they are gone, Chaim. I have not had a moment of quiet to say this to you."

"Gone?"

"Lena broke them by mistake, an accident, she said. At least she told me." My mother had sobbed again. "What is there left anymore of our old life?"

Walking with my father to see Miss Marshall, I shivered to think of my mother's sobs. I kicked a piece of ice from our path. It was snowing, and the wind blew stray flakes in our faces. My skin burned from the cold. I would reconsider my behavior, I decided, my silence with my mother. I hated to remember the broken cup and ballerina. I couldn't remake her past or give her all she'd left in Russia, but one day I would draw a picture of the broken objects for her, I resolved. In that way, I could almost give them back to her. I had given a drawing to Millie Farber and not to my own mother. I would draw many pictures for my mother. That's how I would try to make this up to her.

My father stared ahead into the whiteness, and we plodded toward the school. Class had ended for the day, and I'd gone to meet him as he walked here. We were going to talk with Miss Marshall together. He pulled open the door to the building. We entered the dim warmth of the hallway and cleaned the snow from our coats. I remembered my mother's tears again, and Millie Farber's radiant smile. My father's face had glowed in Millie Farber's parlor. But at home, with my mother, he coiled any tenderness into himself as if he were a snail. My mother was living with absence, I thought. I was sure this must be true, and I suddenly wondered: Was absence worse than loss? I didn't know. Silence and secrets were everywhere in our family.

"Which is the way?" he asked. He carried my drawings. He had wrapped them between two pieces of board and tied them with rope. He was dressed in his heavy gray overcoat. He had combed the wavy curls out of his red hair, but they'd sprung back in the dampness.

"This way," I said.

We turned the corner and I led him through another hallway. I unbuttoned my coat and smoothed my blue wool dress, the one my mother and I had bought at the department store, a flapper-style dress. It was knee-length and had a long, low waist. I wore my rayon stockings and boots for the snow. I would wear this dress when I met Max at the laundry on Sunday. Philip Schloss once told me the dress looked just like the one the school janitor's daughter wore. I didn't care what he said. The dress made me feel beautiful.

"Well, it is a pleasure, I'm sure, Mr. Czernitski," said Miss Marshall. Lipstick coated her wide red lips, and she wore a pale yellow dress with a lace collar. She sat at her desk, smiling with her lips clamped shut, so she showed no teeth. "Please sit down."

"I wish my reason for being here was a pleasant one," he replied.

My father and I each settled into a desk. He placed the package of drawings on his desktop and slid into his seat, thrusting out his long legs from the side. He looked odd and uncomfortable in the small wooden desk, but this didn't seem to concern Miss Marshall.

"You wanted to speak to me." She folded her hands on her lap.

"I wish to talk to you about a misunderstanding. Lena's assignment to draw a picture of a landscape and a portrait."

She nodded.

"I brought to you," he said, "other examples of her work." He placed his coat on the desk next to him. Then he untied the rope from the package, peeled the board from the papers, and handed her four sketches of the lake and a sketch of the crystal pitcher from Millie Farber's apartment. "Lena drew these," he said. "She drew the ones she gave you for her assignment, too."

Miss Marshall eyed the drawings and dropped them one by one onto her desk. "Very nice," she said. "However, I don't believe these are yours." She addressed these remarks to me, then smiled flirtatiously at my father. "I have taught many children and seen many drawings. Lena may be older than the other students in class, but still it's impossible for someone her age to draw this. I know what a child her age can do. I am not implying you are a liar, Mr. Czernitski. Surely, a parent wants to believe the best of a child. However misguided this may be. All of these pictures were traced. Again."

My father's jaw tightened. Anger flashed in his eyes, but he answered with an even tone. "Believe what you want, Miss Marshall. I saw Lena draw the crystal pitcher. I was there every second while she drew it. I must defend my daughter." He turned to me. "Lena, show her how you can draw."

I had been afraid it would come to this.

Miss Marshall frowned. The skin on her forehead pinched into itself. She rapped her fingers on the top of her desk. "Of course, I would like to help you. However, I don't have time today for this, Mr. Czernitski. I'm sorry." She stood up.

"I don't think you are one bit sorry," he said. "I won't allow you to deny me a chance to defend my child." He rose and faced her.

I looked from one to the other. I thought he might slap her.

Miss Marshall stared impatiently at my father, then at me. Finally, she sat at her desk, pulled two pieces of paper and a pencil from the drawer and handed them to him. "I won't deny you then. She has five minutes to draw." She crossed her thin legs and eyed the clock that hung on the wall. "I don't have endless time or patience. Five minutes, Lena."

I reached for the paper and pencil. I felt sure my face was bright red. Just draw, I ordered myself. You are Lena Czernitski, who can draw almost anything. Max has seen you do this. Leah Grace. Elka. Millie Farber. Pretend you are at Lake Michigan. I took a deep breath and began to study my father's hands in the dreary light of the classroom, so different from the light by the lake or the graceful light in Millie Farber's parlor or even the soft light in our apartment on Bittersweet Place.

"No, Lena. I would like you to draw a picture of *me*," Miss Marshall said.

I grasped the pencil tightly. I wanted to sketch my father's hands again. I was certain I could improve on what I'd done at Millie Farber's apartment. But I wouldn't have that choice. So I stared at Miss Marshall. I would have to draw her as if she were an object, as if she were a table or chair or someone I did not know—someone I did not hate. I would try to capture whatever soul of hers—if she had one—lived inside her.

This was a hard task, almost impossible to draw in so little time. I could hear Max advising me: *Be strong.* I told myself I was made of iron. I quickly sketched the shape of her head, the narrow slope of her nose, omitting the tiny hairs that flared from her nostrils. I drew her wide cold eyes, her squat ugly neck. Her shoulders were square, as if made by rulers. I sketched her arms, then her mouth, like the wrinkled petals of a flower. I returned to the outline of her face and added her brown hair, not in a bun today, but styled in a long flapper's bob, and then went back to her arms, elongating them, until I reached her hands. Hands were still a mystery to me. The only ones I had been able to draw were my father's.

I slowed down, puzzled. I glanced at my father again, and left Miss Marshall without hands. On the second sheet of paper I began to draw my father. The wavy red hair that sprang on his head. The large ears and span of his nose. The arch of his shoulder, the lean line of his arm. Head, chest, arms. I stopped and inserted the back of the chair. I knew I should return to the picture of Miss Marshall; I could sense her watching me.

"That's enough." She yanked both sheets of paper from me and squinted at the drawing of her. "Is this how I look? Peaceful? This woman has a peaceful expression." She paused before finishing her thought. "It is a person, Lena. It seems you can do this, as you said."

I had been holding my breath, and let out a long sigh. "I think you would really like to be more peaceful," I said. The words burst out by themselves.

"She didn't intend to be disrespectful," my father said. "She meant that…"

"Well," said Miss Marshall, placing the drawing on top of the others. "What matters is what you think, Lena Czernitski, I suppose. That you see me like this…I am surprised and pleased to learn I was mistaken."

"Thank you," said my father. "I was certain you would understand."

"I will reconsider," she said, fingering the collar of her dress. "I'll think more about the problem with the assignment."

"Think more," he said. "What is there to think about?"

"So Lena can draw a person, but a landscape? A lake?" she snapped. "I'm sorry to say, this is a different skill entirely. Look at the great painters." She waved as if these painters stood behind her, waiting to be introduced. "Some painted portraits, others the outdoors. The picture of the lake, was it traced? It was too perfect, the shading, the shapes. The detail and perspective. The grass, the shadows. I told you, it's impossible for someone her age to draw that. Did she use another picture and copy it? I say she did. You people are always trying to get away with something."

Fury flickered in my father's eyes. He closed a hand into a fist. "That's not true."

"You may have done a reasonable job reciting the Gettysburg Address, but I am waiting for your apology about the drawings," she hissed at me. "And why do you tease Philip Schloss and the other boys? I see how you look at them in class, trying to make them laugh. You and Elka Amsall. You only create trouble."

"I've never done anything to him or any of the boys," I said with anger. "I didn't trace the picture. Why can't you believe me?"

"Lena," my father said, grasping my arm. "Stop this. She is your teacher."

"Why can't you say the picture is good and beautiful?" I shouted at her. "I'm a prisoner in your stupid classroom." I pulled myself from my father's grasp. "We have rights in America. You're not the final judge of anything. You don't treat me like a human being."

Miss Marshall pressed her lips together, her face white. "If you acted like a person, you would be treated as one."

"Miss Marshall, she's a child," my father said.

"You may look peaceful in my drawing," I pushed on, screaming at her, "but I have come to hate you. Hate, hate you. Fail me. Every day of my life, fail me. I don't care. I don't need your stupid edicts." I stormed out of the room.

The snow slowed me down, but I ran, charging to the streetcar, which I rode, gulping back anger. I jumped off at the stop near Independence Boulevard, near Max's house. If Miss Marshall hadn't planned to fail me before, now she certainly would. I felt badly that I'd left my father with her. Still, I held onto the hope that my father might somehow help me. I had no faith in Miss Marshall's nature. But I believed in his charm.

The lights in Max's house glowed. It was almost Friday night, *Shabbos*. I should be home with my own family, not on the sidewalk in someone else's neighborhood.

I stared at the graceful white fence surrounding Max's yard, at the lights in his windows shining like stars. The brightness in Meyer's room flickered and then darkened. I imagined him making his way downstairs, Max close behind him. Benny and Sophe would be trailing close behind, too. The family would sit in the beautiful dining room. Fine china plates filled with meats, sweet cakes, and hot *kugel* would cover the table. Over dinner there would be laughter and quiet conversation. Meyer might even recite his poems. And afterward Max would play the piano. Why couldn't I live here? Live such a happy life?

The wind hummed, and a chill raced through me. I climbed the stairs that led to Max's porch, but then stopped. I didn't belong. I was a stranger here.

I took one last look at his house, then swung around and began my journey home.

A Kiss in the Laundry
February 26–27, 1927

Snow fell all day Saturday, until the city was drowning in white. The wind howled. I watched from my desk in the living room. Frigid air pushed its way through the cracks around the window. Young children played on the empty street, tossing snowballs, laughing and shouting. Suddenly I missed Leah Grace.

After awhile, I began to appreciate the storm's silence. No cars or people hurried about; the world seemed at rest. It was at just this moment, when calm settled in me, that I realized the storm might prevent me from meeting Max tomorrow. The streetcar might not run in these high drifts, and I *had* to meet Max.

My mother joined me in the living room.

"You cannot ignore what happened with the teacher yesterday," she said, standing next to me. "You may have ruined your future, Lena."

I nodded. I didn't want to talk about it with her.

"I can't speak to you standing on one foot." She frowned. "How can I talk to you if you will not talk to me?"

My father came into the room then and said, "Lena's words to Miss Marshall were not ideal, but Reesa, you know as well as I do, futures can change in a minute."

My mother turned to face him. "Who will wait for such a future? Tell me, Chaim, who?"

They regarded each other cautiously, towering over me as I sat at my desk.

"The future is an unopened book," my father said. "I've told you many times."

"But you are ripping out the pages. Always, you want to rip out the pages." She placed a hand on my shoulder. "If you do not wish to apologize to the teacher, Lena, I advise you not to," she said to me quietly. "I have given this thought. The worst are the secrets. Next time, don't talk with such bitter words. Hate creates hate. You will have other teachers, and a long life, may the Almighty will it, to undo what happens now."

I stared out the window. "I don't think I'll apologize," I said. I knew I wouldn't. "No, I won't apologize. She's the one who's wrong."

"You must," my father insisted. "Go to school Monday. Be polite. Tell her you didn't mean what you said. I've told her already."

"You will make up your own mind, Lena," my mother said. She sighed, then went on with force. "You will see: Necessity will teach you what is trivial in life, to sew or cook or clean. But only education teaches what is important. Do what you want about the teacher, but think carefully. Do not throw away your education."

I didn't reply. My mother wore the green housedress with the frayed collar; stains smeared the bodice. She looked worn, not smiling and pretty as she'd been a few months ago, on the day Rabbi Hirschfeld had visited us.

I eyed the window again. Snow swirled to the ground. What was trivial? Sewing. Cooking. Cleaning. My mother's life. I felt a terrible sadness for her. She didn't have time for tenderness. And when she spoke of education, her voice vibrated with longing, as if she wished it for herself, as if she wished she were me. I would never live such a life.

"You will make your own life," she went on, her words aimed at the back of my head. "I will have to step away so you can do this." Then she muttered, "In this world, this is what parents do, and so will I." Her hand disappeared from my shoulder. Her footsteps thudded across the floor. Soon the sounds of her chopping echoed from the kitchen.

I heard my father sink into the sofa, the cushions contracting with sighs. Perhaps he had advised my mother to make her presence small.

But somehow, in the light of the storm, nothing she did seemed trivial. I imagined her in Russia, the wagon ride. My own fears about Millie Farber—were these my mother's fears, too? I suddenly felt disgusted by my father and the beautiful customer.

My father left the room in silence. I would draw a picture of my mother someday, I decided. I would try to see her in that way I could only see a person or a thing when I tried to draw it.

"And we still have not heard from Maurice again." Her voice burst from the kitchen. "I feel in my heart, he will come home soon."

"I won't allow him in these rooms," my father declared.

Whispers erupted from the kitchen, an angry jumble of English and Yiddish. For the rest of the day I sat drawing in my notebook meant for words. I drew the knobby blue fabric of the sofa, the smooth arch of the doorway, the oval slant of lamplight spilling onto the floor. I couldn't bear to think about Uncle Maurice. I couldn't bear to think about Miss Marshall. Why did Miss Marshall hate me? I supposed I'd never know her reasons.

I slammed my notebook shut.

On Sunday it was hardly snowing at all. I was determined to see Max, and informed my mother I was going to the lake.

"In this storm?" she said.

"The storm is over. I want to think about what to do on Monday when I see my teacher. I need to breathe fresh air."

"There is plenty of air in this apartment. We are going to visit your grandmother today. She will not live long, Lena, you will see. You should be there with us. Simon will come after his work with Mr. Usher Cohen. But do as you must," she said with resignation. Then she whispered, as if talking to herself, "No matter what age they are, your parents, you always want them here."

I left home anyway, eager to go to the laundry. I would visit my grandmother another time. The worst are the secrets, my mother had said. But sometimes secrets are essential, I thought, and can't be helped.

Instead of hurrying to the laundry, as I imagined I would, I took my time, kicking loose snow, peeling spirals of ice from trees. I stopped to finger the key in my pocket. I felt guilty and nervous.

This guilt wasn't because I had stolen the key or lied, but because my grandmother was sick and I'd left the family to go off with Max. What difference would one more person make in that room with her? I thought. Oh, I could do what I wanted, I told myself. I was no longer a child. I had kissed Max many times. I was grown up, with a woman's shape, breasts and hips.

But where was my decency, my loyalty?—I could hear my mother demanding to know. I loved Max too much to answer her, even in my mind. I loved the absolute comfort I felt when I was with him. And I loved the pleasure of kissing him. If a kiss felt like this, and being close to Max did too, wouldn't the rest feel wonderful?

Maybe Millie Farber and my father met somewhere, I thought as I climbed onto the streetcar. Maybe they met at her apartment that had once been a rooming house. I sighed, a whistle of sadness. Why didn't my father love my mother? I loved my father in spite of his actions, and in spite of myself, I liked Millie Farber.

Max was waiting in front of the laundry. The other stores on the street were closed. "Oh, Max," I said, thrilled to see him. I took the key from my pocket, but it wouldn't turn in the lock.

"The lock is frozen," I said.

"Let me try." He jiggled the key from side to side.

I tried again. Then he did. Back and forth we went, until finally, I was able to move the key in the lock. Something caught and clicked, and I pushed the door open.

The laundry was dark, but warm. An odd, sharp smell floated in the space, a smell I didn't recognize. I would have opened a window or switched on the lights, but our visit was a secret. We locked the door behind us and made sure the shades were pulled down. The "Closed" sign hung in the window. In the faint afternoon light, I felt terribly shy. We hadn't seen each other for weeks, since Max had gotten sick. Now we were finally, safely alone. We threw our arms around each other.

"Max, I've missed you," I said.

"I missed you," he said.

We kissed, and after awhile, I stepped back, shed my coat and said formally, "I've decided to become an artist." Then, I told him about my screaming at Miss Marshall.

"She deserves it," he said, laying his coat on the front counter.

"I wish my parents could help me."

We sat next to each other in the chairs at the front. We held hands and whispered, as if even the laundry walls knew we shouldn't be here.

"If your parents were artists, it could be harder to be one," Max said. "What if you wanted to sew? Your mother is such a good seamstress, how could you sew like that? Maybe you're lucky your parents know nothing about art."

"I would never sew." I studied Max's eyes. They were brighter today, as if washed with sunlight. "It's useless work." I paused. "Not useless. But it hasn't made her happy."

"Everyone is unhappy. Sometimes I'm unhappy. Other days not. This is an unhappy time for your mother."

"She's always been this way."

"You don't know that. What about when you were a child?"

I shrugged. We were both solemn and awkward today, I thought.

"My mother is unhappy, too," he said. "My father whistles, and she screams and worries."

"Maybe one day they'll switch. She'll whistle."

We laughed.

"I don't think so," he said more seriously.

"What does she worry about?"

"She was worried when my father and I were sick. She worries about Meyer. And she's upset about the store, P. Sloan and Son Men's Manufacturing Company. Business is bad. My father and his brother aren't speaking to each other. They're dividing up the store now. My uncle is starting his own business. She worries about that. My father worries about nothing. He says, 'The business will turn out swell.'"

"Do you think it will?"

"I don't know. My mother could be right."

"I hope not. You have to believe your father." I thought I heard a noise, like a faint footstep or scratching from the back of the laundry. I told myself it was the wind rushing through the windows.

"Did you hear that?" I whispered uneasily. "That sound? Do you think anyone is here?"

"No. No one is here, just us."

"Listen," I said.

He squinted and turned his head. "Rats," he whispered. "Mice."

"Max, that's awful," I said. The laundry seemed wild now, unpredictable. Not safe. "Maybe it was a bad idea to come here."

"They won't hurt." He leaned close to me and sang in a whisper:

The worms crawl in
The worms crawl out
The worms play pinochle on your snout
The mice crawl in
The mice crawl out
The mice play pinochle on your snout...

Max brushed his hand up my arm, his fingers like mice scampering. I laughed.

One long leg of his was crossed over the other. He braided his fingers with mine. I knew Max was waiting. We would lay towels on the floor in the laundry, I had told him weeks ago, so we could lie down together. I wanted to kiss him again. I loved Max. I had already given him my soul, but what would he do with it? What if I gave him the rest of me and he never wanted to see me again?

"You look like you're thinking about something important," he said. "The solutions occur in the silence. That's what my father says."

"It's never been silent for me."

"No?"

"The noise in our apartment. All the relatives. The roar of the city."

"A city doesn't roar," he said.

"Not one place." Then I reconsidered. "A library is silent. A hospital is silent, and a *shiva*, but that's an unhappy silence."

"Then some day we'll go to where it's silent and safe and beautiful."

"Where?"

"California. By the ocean. It has the kind of silence you've never heard."

"You've been there?"

"My parents have. I've read books, seen photographs."

"I couldn't go," I said grumpily. "You can't hear silence anyway."

"Why can't you go there? After school is finished, I'll study at the university and then go to California. Illinois became a state in 1818, but California didn't until 1850, so it's younger, somehow, a more hopeful place. It was the thirty-first state, and used to be part of Mexico. It's beautiful, I think. You'll come with me."

"Oh, Max. I'd love to. But…there's an uncle of mine who lives in California," I said quickly. "He might still be living there. I can't see him again."

"Why not?"

I tried to repair my words. "He wouldn't want to see me." That was the only way I could explain Uncle Maurice to Max. I felt I could tell Max almost anything, but I couldn't bear to tell him this. "He doesn't talk to the family," I said. "But this has nothing to do with us."

"California is a big state, Lena. He won't even know you're there. But like you said, he has nothing to do with us." His voice was soft. "Let's just be us."

I gazed at Max. Something rose in me, fell, rose. I struggled to push away the feeling, but it raced through me. "Yes, let's be us," I whispered.

My heart almost burst as he kissed me. I would go anywhere with him. To his house. California. The moon.

We fell into each other's arms. He was unfastening my blue dress and finding my camisole. My fingers rushed over his arms, down his legs. This was more brazen than I'd ever been. I was ashamed and giddy and delighted.

A door creaked, the wind blew. Time stopped. My breath was

wild. I shut my eyes. In the darkness I saw ruin in my future. I heard my mother's words echoing through my mind—decency. "No," I finally whispered. "Let's wait."

"Wait?"

"Someone is here. Listen." I heard the noise again, like scratching, something more than wind. I was sure of it. My father must have come to work on receipts instead of going with the others to visit my grandmother. He often entered the laundry through the back and worked there. Or was it Hadie who had come to do some ironing? Had the family come looking for me? "They'll find us, Max."

"They will not." He kissed me again.

A person makes a decision, I thought. My father had said this about the beautiful customer. I didn't know if I trusted his words, or if I trusted Max. But at that moment, I couldn't trust the future or the safety of the laundry.

"Next Sunday," I murmured. "We'll come back here, when we're sure."

Max's face was flushed. "Sure of what? I'm not a toy, Lena. If you want to do this, fine. If not, that's how it will be. Make up your mind. I've made up mine."

I gulped. If I could have, I would have run to Millie Farber and asked: Was I going to ruin my life? Was I wild and indecent? Cheap? I was a little afraid of Max, of what we would do together, of what I *wanted* to do with him. "We need to be sure we're really alone here," I said, and more quietly, "and to be sure how we feel about each other."

"We? I'm sure we're alone, and I know how I feel about you."

Max didn't wait for my answer. He snaked his hands along my waist.

Pregnant, I could become pregnant, I thought.

I heard a sound again, a creaking, like footsteps. "What's that noise?" I said. Almost a scuffling. And voices. A door slammed.

"It's nothing," Max whispered with impatience.

"No. Someone is here." A new smell crept into the room. At first it was faint. A putrid, sharp scent. It grew stronger and thicker, and we breathed in the heavy air.

Max sat up straight.

"It's smoke," I said. "Something is burning."

"From next door, I think."

"No, it's here," I said. Max was wrong. "Somewhere here." I didn't bother to button my dress, but bolted from the chair and started toward the back of the laundry, running. I pushed past the rows of clothing crammed together and hanging, bar after bar, past the stacks of boxes and supplies. The dark shadows of the machines stood like monsters. And beyond those I saw it, a dancing pile of flames, spreading even as I watched. "Max!" I cried. "There's a fire!"

"Come on," he called to me from the front. "Let's get out of here."

The odd, sharp odor I had noticed when we came in—I recognized it now. Kerosene. The floor in the back was wet with it. Before I could do anything, flames shot up by the back door. The room filled with smoke. Fire leapt, skipping, growing larger before my eyes. Then I saw a figure, like a phantom, a man standing beside the rolltop desk in the corner, fumbling madly with papers, coughing. My father.

"Papa," I called frantically. "Is that you?"

"No one's there," yelled Max, pushing his way through the smoke and heat to get me. "Let's get out."

"He's here." I ran from Max, toward the rolltop desk where I saw my father rummaging through piles of papers. I grabbed his hand. Smoke stung my eyes and throat. "Papa, what are you doing?" I shouted. "You could kill yourself. All of us."

He looked at me as if shaken, as if he had aged years since this morning.

"Lena? Why are you here?" he whispered hoarsely. "It was Maurice. He did this. I tried to stop him. I must get the money I left here and the important papers or we will have nothing and be ruined."

"We've got to get out of here!" Max shouted. He pulled my hand, and I pulled my father.

The flames were rising almost everywhere, so we crouched low to the floor as we wound our way in panic to the front. The heat pursued us. Max grabbed our coats from the counter by the door.

I saw the floor behind the counter was moist along the edges, too. Max pushed us until we were standing beneath the pale light of a streetlamp outside. The snow glistened. Even in the crisp air, the grim smell of smoke hung in my hair, on my clothes.

My father broke away from us, running on the snowy sidewalk to the grocery next door. He pounded on its door, trying to rouse the owners who lived upstairs.

Max wrapped my coat around me as if it were a shawl. I stood mesmerized. The foul smell of smoke grew stronger. Then, we heard a terrible sound, like the roar of a train, and seconds later, the laundry burst into flames.

Circles of bright orange flame leapt along the doors, the windows, everywhere on the building, suddenly glowing like thousands of burning Sabbath candles.

An Offer
February–March 1927

On Monday, I didn't apologize to Miss Marshall, and she didn't mention my yelling at her or the meeting with my father. The fire made my problems at school seem unimportant. As soon as she saw me, Mary Hall ran up to me in the classroom and said, "I heard about what happened at your family's store. You saved your father."

"Max Sloan saved us," I corrected her softly.

"No. You were there, too. I couldn't have done what you did." She smiled without mocking me.

Miss Marshall stood nearby and told us to be quiet. She looked right through me. She didn't say a word about the fire.

Elka came up to me, too. Her move had been postponed; we were all grateful for that. She flung her arms around me. "Oh, Lena. I am so sorry about the fire. I wish I could be here to help. I hate to move, but you can always come to Milwaukee. Maybe you can live in Wisconsin, too."

"Thanks." I knew she meant to be kind, but I was tired of talking about the laundry fire and thinking about what it meant.

In the afternoon, Miss Marshall told me to go to the principal's office. She had no sympathy for anyone, I thought.

"Come in, come in," Mr. Bender called out when I knocked on his door.

He was a tall, stooped, gray-haired man, and he sat hunched at his desk in the drafty room. His desktop was covered with piles of papers and folders. "Sit down, sit down," he said. "Lena, correct?"

"Yes." I sat in a chair opposite from him.

"We've all heard about this fire. I'm sorry. I truly am." He frowned. "But everyone has problems, young lady. You might as well get used to it. This doesn't excuse your behavior with Miss Marshall. I want to talk to your parents, but I'm not going to bother them now. They need time to resolve what's happened, I'm sure."

"They do," I said uneasily. I didn't think either of them could come to school for a long while.

"In the meantime, I expect you to attend class and exercise self-control. Demonstrate respect. A student can't yell at a teacher. I don't allow deceit." He opened a folder that sat on his desk. "Last year, you received the highest possible grades in Deportment, Character, and Citizenship." He eyed me. "I don't know what's happened to you. I've told Miss Marshall to keep careful notes on students, especially you."

"I know what's happened," I said, determined to explain. "She's not fair, she—"

"A teacher is in charge of her classroom," he interrupted sternly. "But I also expect teachers to be fair. We have bigger problems here. Negroes who can't read. A boy brought a knife to class. Diphtheria in Chicago. What if the disease spreads to schools? Don't add to the problems. I'll investigate what's fair or not." He pointed to the door. "You can go back to class."

I left, and a wave of relief rushed through me. Mr. Bender hadn't issued a punishment or failed me, yet. But even this meeting seemed less important than what was happening at home.

I didn't see Max all week. My mother had instructed Simon and me to come directly home after school. "If your father needs you, you must be here," she said. This time, Simon and I didn't argue with her.

I didn't tell my parents about Mr. Bender either. I didn't want to add to their worries.

My father had been resting in bed since Sunday, unable to walk without wheezing. My mother made him a batch of guggle muggle, but even that didn't help. On Tuesday, a doctor came to our apartment, the first time a doctor had visited here. Smoke had collected in my father's lungs, the doctor said. He needed to drink hot liquids and rest. I knew something else was bothering my father, though. He was brooding. It was as if he had seen a madman in the laundry that Sunday, and this had shaken him. Perhaps my father had seen something terrible, had really seen Uncle Maurice there, and luckily, in the confusion of the fire, my father hadn't asked why Max and I were at the laundry. My mother, however, had been curious.

"How did you get into the building?" she had demanded when we came home that Sunday, dazed and smelling of smoke. "Why were you at the laundry, Lena? You said you were going to the lake. And you came home with the buttons of your dress unfastened. Even in a fire there must be decency."

"I changed my plans," I'd said quickly. "I remembered I'd left papers for a school assignment at the laundry. Max Sloan was supposed to help me with the assignment, so he went to the laundry with me. I took a chance," I said, pleased with my lie, "that the front door would be unlocked." I shrugged, trying to think of what else to say. "It was lucky, I guess. And my dress…I don't know what happened to it. Everything was so confused with the fire."

She seemed to consider the explanation. "Well, I still don't think I understand why you were at the laundry, but perhaps God placed you there to save your father."

I had turned away, thinking about Max. I didn't want her to see the blush spreading across my face.

The knocking at the door to our apartment didn't stop all week: policemen, neighbors, relatives, friends, the doctor again—as if we were hosting a *shiva* for the laundry. The policemen arrived for the second time on Thursday afternoon, eyeing my father suspiciously. They questioned him again, demanding to know why he had been at the laundry when the fire broke out. I didn't know if he'd told them about Uncle Maurice. I could see they thought my father might have been involved with the fire. I didn't know what to think about their suspicions, and pushed their prying questions out of my mind.

Sunday night, a week after the fire, I sat at my desk in the living room, trying to concentrate on an assignment for school. Yet another knock interrupted me. I hurried to the door, my mother's footsteps trailing behind me. My father was still resting in his room. Simon was in our bedroom. He'd told me he didn't want anyone to bother him. "I can't think about that stupid fire anymore," Simon had said. "I've got to finish this assignment."

I knew none of us could bear to see one more sad-faced guest offering words of sympathy. But I swung open the door anyway.

Rabbi Hirschfeld tipped his head. "Good evening," he said.

"Oh, it's you," I said, thinking about the afflicted and wondering what he would tell us now. "Hello."

"Please, come in," said my mother from behind me.

The rabbi reached past me and clasped her hand. "I heard about the unfortunate event at your business," he said as he walked in.

"Yes," she replied. His expression was grave, but my mother seemed composed, as she had since the fire. The misfortune seemed to have given her strength.

"Things happen in this world for a reason," she told the rabbi. "No one is dead, thank God. Our world is still here, our family. Of course, the livelihood…" Here she paused. "But a person can begin again. When you have had to once, you can begin over and over, even if you prefer not to."

He nodded in surprise. "I wanted to see how everyone was managing and how I could help."

"That is very kind. Lena, can you please bring the rabbi tea?"

I trudged to the kitchen, amazed at the injustice of this. Why should I bring the man tea? After all, I had been the one in the laundry, the one to see the fire and feel the terrible heat of it. My mother hadn't been there. Yet, the rabbi seemed uninterested in comforting me.

But I did as my mother asked and brought two cups of tea to the living room, one for her and one for the rabbi. She and the rabbi were engaged in a philosophical conversation when I returned. He sat on the sofa; my mother sat across from him, leaning forward to listen. His gold ring sparkled.

"What can one say? The fire was a horrible event," the rabbi said. "Even a learned man, a rabbi such as myself, has no answers. My personal view of life is: *Altsding lozt zich ois mit a gevain.* Everything ends in weeping." He sighed extravagantly and sipped his tea. "I have seen that in my own life."

"Your ideas are so wise, Rabbi," my mother replied.

He smiled. "Then, as you have told me eloquently, you begin again."

I sat on the other side of the sofa. Let the rabbi and my mother have a romance with words, I thought. I knew the loss of the laundry would have a terrible effect on us. I wasn't really sorry about it, though. Oh, I regretted the destruction. Regretted that Max and I had been interrupted, that the fire placed a new burden on my father—because of this I knew he couldn't possibly have started the fire himself. And Hadie. I felt badly for her. She would need to find new work. The relatives and my father would need to find work, too. But my father would somehow earn money, I was sure. For now I was tired of thinking gloomy thoughts. Besides, a new happiness whirled inside me. I longed for the world to disappear. I longed to be alone with Max. To make time stop again.

I returned to the kitchen to prepare more tea for my mother and the rabbi. I couldn't bear to listen to them talk about the fire. I felt certain Uncle Maurice was responsible for it, like my father had said. Even though there had been no sign of my uncle, even though no one knew where he was, I was sure he'd destroyed the laundry.

I'd heard my parents talking last night. The insurance company would pay the owners of the laundry for all they had lost. When the money appeared, that's when Uncle Maurice would appear, I was sure. He and Mr. Usher Cohen owned the building. They would be the ones to receive any money, my mother had said.

"Your father's name is not on the papers for the laundry," she had said again this morning. "I begged him to change this. But your father is a stubborn man."

It was then I had remembered that Simon worked for Mr. Usher

Cohen. Was it possible Mr. Usher Cohen had something to do with the fire? And what about Simon? The more I thought about this, the more uneasy and upset I became.

I returned to the living room carrying the two cups of tea rattling in my hands.

"I will ask Chaim to speak with you now," my mother was saying to Rabbi Hirschfeld. "I know you can be a help to him." She stood up and turned to me. "Thank you for this, Lena. Be careful with those cups or they will spill. Can you please bring something sweet for the rabbi, too?"

As I carried a plate of round butter cookies from the kitchen, I overheard my parents talking in their bedroom.

"The rabbi would like to speak to you," my mother whispered.

"Tell him I am ill," my father replied hoarsely.

"He is here."

"And what will he do? Does the man have a contract with God? Will he bless the charred remains of our store and make everything right? Is he going to find me a job? Will he pay our rent? We'll lose the apartment if I don't find work."

Lose the apartment? I gripped the plate of cookies.

"The rabbi knows Mr. Usher Cohen," my mother said. "Maybe Rabbi Hirschfeld can help learn the truth of what happened. Mr. Cohen may have learned something about the fire. He owns part of the laundry, after all. The rabbi could talk to him."

"I told you, Maurice started the fire," my father snapped.

"And I told you, he is in California."

"I saw him, Maurice," my father insisted, coughing. "I've told you already: I went to the laundry to finish work with receipts. There was a smell, an unusual smell. I went to the desk, but the floor was damp. I couldn't work. Something wasn't right. At first, I didn't see him there. He was hiding. It wasn't until Maurice tried to sneak out that I got a good look at him. I wanted to stop him, but he had already done the damage, Reesa." My father paused to cough again. "And there was no time. I had to try to save the money and papers we'd left there. So I let him get away."

"Chaim, hush," she whispered sharply. "You must have seen a ghost. And I have told you, I have taken in more sewing work. I am doing everything I can to help. For God's sake, be polite now and talk to the rabbi."

"I'm well past that. Please bid the rabbi goodnight and send him on his way."

I hurried back to the living room.

I handed the plate of cookies to the rabbi and sat at my desk. My father had just said we could lose the apartment. I felt weak. My notebook lay on my desk. I opened it to my list of fears. What would we do if he couldn't pay the rent? Where would we go?

Just then, someone knocked on the front door. I raced down the hallway, relieved to escape from the tension that had collected in the apartment like rainwater after a storm. I was hoping someone would appear and bring good news.

In the dreary outer hallway stood Max's father.

"Mr. Sloan," I said, surprised.

"Good evening, Lena." He wore a black overcoat and a gray felt hat. "I hope to talk with your father, if I may. Of course, I don't wish to intrude, but Maxwell assured me I wouldn't be bothering anyone."

"Is he with you? Max?"

"No, he's not."

I regarded Mr. Sloan cautiously. Did he want to talk to my father about why Max and I had been at the laundry? Before I could get a sense of this, my mother and the rabbi joined us at the door.

"I see you have company. Good evening to all," the rabbi said. "I hope to see you in synagogue. You, Lena, especially," he finished, and walked out.

My mother eyed Mr. Sloan with suspicion.

"Mrs. Czernitski," he said. "I am Maxwell's father. He's a friend of your son and daughter. I own a clothing business on Roosevelt Road. Perhaps you know it? P. Sloan and Son Men's Manufacturing Company. It used to be called P. Slovansky and Son. I may need help at the store. I, too, have experienced unexpected changes." He spoke with slow precision. "I hoped to discuss this with your husband."

"We appreciate that," my mother replied. "This is very kind." She nodded. "But my husband is not able to talk to anyone, not tonight. He is not feeling—"

"Reesa," called my father from the bedroom. "Send the man in, please."

My mother escorted Mr. Sloan through the hall into the bedroom. She left the two of them alone.

I helped her bring the cups and plate of cookies from the living room to the kitchen. She whispered to me there, "The man, that Mr. Sloan, is an intellectual. You can see this right away, Lena. German Jews. That is their *yichus*. They are not really *unsere leite*. One of us. We do not belong with them."

"Intellectual?" I set the cups in the sink. "That doesn't matter. He's my friend's father. Max was here the day the rabbi came to talk to you about Uncle William."

"That polite young man?" She wiped her hands on her dress. "Even so, I can see the father is full of ideas. No matter what store he owns. People like him eat ideas instead of bread. What could be the future of such a store?" She sank into a chair at the table. "There is a place for all people. But ideas are not a way to change the world. I have heard the rabbi speak of repairing the world. *Tikkun Olam*. He is absolutely correct. You do one good deed at a time. You go to *shul*, and listen to Rabbi Hirschfeld's words. Collect charity, like Aunt Feyga. You have children. That is how to change the world. Ideas will not help a burnt laundry." She nodded with conviction. "Listen to what I say. You must learn to dance at home, Lena, so you know how to dance in the world. *Nadan kenen elteren geben, ober nit kain mazel.* A parent can give a dowry, but not luck. "

"Luck has nothing to do with this. Mr. Sloan is here to offer Papa something. Something important." I stretched my arm toward her as if I held his offer in my hand. "He might need help in his store. He's being kind. Why can't you be grateful for that?"

"You will see, Lena. Everyone in their life is searching for luck. Who feeds you? Gives their lives for you? Your father and I. I do not care what the man offers. We do not want charity. An offer is merely an invitation. Thank God, Ida and Abie are leaving for Poland. Maybe it is better that they do what they wish. The piano store is closing. They have no work here. And the rest of us? We will see if your father can find a job that has a future."

"I happen to like ideas," I pushed on. "To think. To look at the world. Even the fire. In a way, it was beautiful. The fire was like a picture. The colors, the flames."

"Pictures." She rose and rinsed the rabbi's cup in the sink. "They have only gotten you into trouble. I have yet for you to show me one picture of yours," she said bitterly.

We were interrupted by a soft thump on the front door.

"I will hang a sign to warn people to go away. But for now go, Lena. Please tell this person politely to come back tomorrow."

When I swung open the front door, Millie Farber stood in a dark green overcoat, facing me.

I didn't know what to say and stared at her.

Millie Farber's short blond hair was pulled back behind her ears. Her coat was unbuttoned. Her long strand of pearls glittered against a soft blue dress. Everything about her was color and light. She clasped a black pocketbook at her side.

"Don't be afraid, Lena," she reassured me. "I've not come to interfere with your father. I may be able to help your family."

"I don't think you ought to come in," I whispered with regret. I stepped into the hall. "I don't think my mother will talk to you, and my father isn't well."

"He's not well? I didn't know." She scrunched her lips together. Her eyes filled with tears. "I can come back when he's feeling better. He will feel better, won't he? It's not life-threatening?"

"The doctor said he needs to rest. The smoke and…he should be fine."

"That's something to be thankful for."

"I don't think my mother will ever talk to you."

"Of course." She nodded. "It was foolish for me to think she would. Presumptuous. It's only that I wanted to see your father again. I wanted to help all of you. He loves you, his family, so much.

But I was wrong. I shouldn't have come here."

My mother approached the door as we spoke. Her breath heaved, as if she were tired.

"What is happening here, Lena? Come inside," she said. Then she noticed the beautiful customer. She grasped my arm. "Please come inside right now, Lena."

I stepped in. The two women faced each other.

"You *choleria,*" my mother snapped at her.

"I don't know what that means, Mrs. Czernitski. I can imagine. But you should know I have no other motivation than to help." Millie Farber paused and whispered, as if talking to herself. "I gave up on the other a long time ago."

"How dare you," my mother said. "You are not wanted here, ever."

"Things happen that perhaps should not," Millie Farber said.

I could see my mother debating with herself. She pressed her hands on her hips, tightened her jaw, and glared at Millie Farber. My mother's need to be polite, her pride, battled with her desire to scream at the woman and slam the door. The two were so different— the rawness of my mother and the gracefulness of Millie Farber.

Mr. Sloan and my father emerged from the bedroom and walked toward us.

"Very kind," my father was saying. "I will consider it and am sorry we've had to meet under such circumstances. I have yet to learn why Max and Lena were at the laundry." When he and Mr. Sloan walked into the entryway, my father's face paled.

"Henry," Millie said with that tenderness. She took a step forward, then stopped. "I've come here," she said formally, "because my husband's grocery needs a manager. We are moving away, and he has decided not to sell the business yet. Would you consider," she said, her voice rising with excitement, "taking that on? And Mr. Sloan." She seemed to know him. "There could be a place for you as well if this was ever needed." She spoke with dignity and charm.

I could see that she loved my father, and because we were his family, perhaps she loved us, too. I could see the bittersweet way they regarded each other. They were both happy and sad in the same moment, I thought. Looking at the two of them, I no longer felt angry or ashamed.

"That's a generous offer," replied my father quietly.

My mother folded her arms against her chest.

My father brushed a hand through his hair, trying to pat it flat. He wore rumpled black pants. His old white shirt was torn at the elbow. Seven days' growth of beard shaded his face, and a dazed expression rose in his eyes, the expression I had seen during the fire. "It is something to consider," he went on, his voice unnaturally hoarse.

"Please send my wishes to your husband, Mrs. Farber," said Mr. Sloan. "I hope to remain in the clothing business and to see him in our store again."

"Of course," Millie Farber said. "Perhaps he will stop there once more before we move away."

The hallway light flickered, then dimmed. A winter draft pushed into the small entry of the apartment where the rest of us crowded together.

There were no outbursts now, no little volcanoes or big ones. No more words. Millie was not invited in, and she made no move to enter. My father and Mr. Sloan stood motionless.

My mother wrung her hands together and pursed her lips, but said nothing. There had been a change between my parents, as though the fire had tempered my mother's anger and my father's betrayal. Suddenly, I wanted to protect her, but I said nothing either.

Standing in the uneasy silence, I felt a wave of terrible sorrow for the laundry, for all of my family's hard work ruined.

Millie Farber backed away. "Well then, good night."

"Please thank your husband," my father said. "I will give this thought."

"Good," she said. "We will wait to hear from you."

The beautiful customer swept toward the stairwell and perhaps out of our lives. What would happen to us? The world is a narrow bridge, I told myself. The most important thing is not to be afraid.

A Misunderstanding
Mid-March, 1927

The day after Millie Farber's visit, we returned to the laundry. The building was a charred, foul-smelling skeleton. My father searched frantically for the wooden cash box in the debris. He tore his pants and became black with ash. But the box was gone. Piles of burnt wood and twisted metal lay on the floor of what had once been the family business. Only the large pressing machines had survived the flames. The scorched, awful smell of ruin and ashes stuck to my clothing and hair.

That week, the family club disbanded. There was no money for pinochle or even a bottle of *schnapps*. My mother, thinking it best for the family it seemed, forbid any frivolity. And by the end of the week, my *bubbe's* condition became worse.

My father had told me once that life never stops. "It pushes forward," he'd said. "You have no choice but to go on. If it's not one trouble, it's another. There are always troubles in life." I had thought him overly pessimistic; his view of the world was as dark as Uncle Abie's, but now I considered my father's words carefully. "My Lena, you'll live through many things," he had said, "and survive them with courage. This is your legacy."

Two weeks after the fire, my old grandmother was near death, my father still hadn't decided about a job, Miss Marshall continued to be miserable to me, and Elka Amsall had finally moved away.

"This is the end of the discussion about work," my father said harshly to my mother. The three of us were in our coats, leaving the apartment to visit my grandmother. "We all know we'll lose the apartment if I don't work," he said. "We won't be able to pay the rent. There's nothing more to discuss."

He had been talking more and more about losing the apartment.

"Mr. Seligman himself works at the Rogers Park Hotel," my

mother said quickly. "Do not forget, he is a member of the family club, Chaim. There may be a job with him. And Charlie and Razel want to use their money and start a new laundry. Feyga and Myron have a little money to add, too. Why won't you think about that?"

"I'm aware of the problems in each," my father replied. "Where will we get the money to contribute to a new laundry, Reesa? We don't even have money to continue the family club. We're not charity. I will not become a peddler or a knife sharpener or milkman. I'm well past that. I will seize the best opportunity. The best for the family and myself."

"How many opportunities do you think exist in the world for you?" she said.

"It's enough, Reesa. *Oif morgen zol Got zorgen.* Let God worry about tomorrow."

I wished they would both stop talking about this. For days after Millie Farber had appeared at our door, my parents hadn't said a word to one another. Now, they bickered and argued as though hurling their worries back and forth would make these worries less. Part of me missed Millie Farber and her offer of another life.

In Aunt Feyga's living room, my old grandmother lay asleep on the edge of the bed. Her coarse hair curled in peaks like beaten egg whites. Her mouth hung open. A few long white hairs, thin as thread, sprouted from her wrinkled chin. Her breath was so labored; it seemed at any moment her heart would stop. And her body was so thin.

A sharp scent soiled the air, not kerosene this time, but urine. The room was uncomfortably hot. I stared at her. One of her arms lay beneath her head, as if her own skin could bring comfort. Even with her eyes shut, she coughed, a sound like choking.

My mother and father, Aunt Feyga, Uncle Myron, and I huddled around the bed in gloomy silence. My father looked tired, but he had finally shaved and was dressed in clean clothing. Aunt Feyga seemed heavier than usual; one giant breast hung lower than the other. I felt embarrassed for her. Her red lipstick smeared off her lips and onto her skin. She gazed forlornly at her mother.

Simon hadn't come with us. He was working for Mr. Usher Cohen, even though it was Sunday, and because this brought money into our apartment, he was allowed to stay away. Still, I worried about Simon. What did he do for Mr. Usher Cohen, anyway? And who would the police blame for the fire?

We watched my old *bubbe* breathe, just as my mother and I had done in the hospital room. Now it didn't matter whether we spoke or were silent. There was nothing we could do to help her.

I stayed for a while, then whispered I was going to see friends. My mother didn't ask where I would be or with whom. And I didn't tell her. I took one last look at my grandmother and then tiptoed out.

My parents planned to return to the laundry after leaving here. They were going to speak to the police again, but I wanted to see Max.

An hour later, Max swung open the front door to his house. Just as he had told me it would be, the great red-brick house was empty. His family had gone out for the afternoon.

"Do you want to come to my room?" he asked. "Or listen to the piano?"

I knew he was asking whether I wanted to continue what we had begun in the laundry. Of course I did, but I replied, shy again, "I'd like to see your room, I think."

"Good." He smiled and held my hand.

Max led me to the wide staircase and up to the second floor. I thought of my *bubbe*, my family surrounding her, while the chair where I had perched sat empty. I told myself there was nothing I could do to help her. Why shouldn't I be with Max?

His bedroom, which he shared with Meyer, stood at the end of the hallway, across from Meyer's study. The study door was open. Ten pencils with points as sharp as blades rested in a row on the desk, waiting for Meyer's return.

"That was awful, the fire," Max said.

"You saved us." We stopped at the door to his room, still holding hands.

"No, I told you, you did. I would have ignored the smoke."

"You wouldn't have," I said. "You pulled us outside just in time. You did, Max. That's the truth of what happened."

As the days had passed, the fire seemed worse and worse to me. I didn't want Max to know how difficult things were for my family now, but I was so upset by all that had happened that I shed my pride. "Max, the cash box is gone," I said. "Everything is gone. Nothing is left of the laundry. My father still hasn't decided what to do about work, and if he doesn't get a job, we'll lose our apartment. We won't be able to pay the rent. I don't know where we'll go."

"He'll find work. He could help at my father's store a few days a week. My father liked him."

"Why did your father come to see us?" I asked. "Did you ask him to?"

"It was his idea. You know, something happens, and everyone hears about it. Lawndale, Maxwell Street, the world. My uncle left the clothing store to open his own business on Roosevelt Road. My mother thinks my uncle is a thief. My father says it's a misunderstanding between them. He wants Meyer to help in the store. Meyer hasn't yet, and my father can't work at his store alone."

"I'm sorry," I said. Would Max's family have to leave this beautiful house if something happened to Mr. Sloan's store? "Will Meyer really be able to help? What does a poet know about clothing?"

"That's what my mother says," Max replied, leading me into his bedroom. "What does Meyer know about inventory and damaged goods? Delivering packages? Accounts receivable? Credit? She recites a list."

"He'll have to learn."

"We'll see. He doesn't want to learn. He's worthless. My father is having problems, and Meyer is writing poems. My mother says Meyer was born to write, not to be in business. All I know is there's too much yelling in the house."

"I'm sorry," I said again. It was hard to imagine disagreement in this grand house. "Maybe things will change."

"I don't know. I'm going to help at the store, too."

"Do you want to work there?"

"No, but I have to. Some days, after school. Besides, it's the right thing to do."

"It is," I said, impressed, and I held Max's hand tightly. There was so much I wanted to tell him. That my father's two wives had met. I didn't really know if they were both his wives, but they had stood face to face. I wanted to tell Max that my father said Uncle Maurice had started the fire. I wanted to explain that Mary Hall had spoken kindly again to me. And that my grandmother hovered near death. But I had talked enough about my family already, too much. So I said, "Are you sure no one will come home this afternoon?"

"They went to play Hearts at their friends' apartment and to have dinner there."

"Sophe and Benny? Meyer, too?"

"Not Meyer. He has a girlfriend now, and he's at her apartment, reading poetry to her. He stays there all day. Shall I read poetry to you?"

"Silly," I said. "Do you even write poems?"

"Only songs."

"That's better than poetry."

"Maybe."

I glanced from Max to his room. Two beds stood side by side, covered by soft brown blankets. A wooden board hung on one wall with articles from newspapers tacked to it. Max must have saved the articles, about Louis Armstrong and Al Jolson and jazz. Three typewritten poems hung there also. Against one wall sat a wooden dresser. Books were piled on the night table along with a copy of *Freiheit*, a Yiddish communist newspaper. I recognized it because of Uncle Abie. He had said only the most godless, radical thinkers read it.

"That's Meyer's," Max said, pointing to the newspaper. "He's a socialist." Then Max pulled back the blanket from one of the beds.

We sat down, side by side. He kissed me quickly. We were formal
and awkward, as we'd been in the laundry at first. I supposed we
were both shy.

But I whispered boldly, "I don't want to become pregnant. I don't
want it to hurt. That's what I was trying to tell you in the laundry."
I immediately regretted my words. I sounded like a child. "We have
to be careful."

Max scooted next to me, until our thighs were touching. He
wrapped his arm around my back. "I know what to do."

"Max, have you done this before?"

"It's instinct, Lena. How did you know the way to kiss me? Did
you read books? Practice? And if you practiced, then you should tell
me with whom!"

I laughed. I wasn't growing up in private anymore, I thought. I
was growing up with Max.

We sat as close as we could while we talked. "When will your
family come home?" I asked.

"I told you. They won't be home until tonight." He paused. "If
you don't want to do this, tell me now."

"No fires here?" I took a breath.

"Let's not talk," he whispered.

I gave him an uncertain kiss, then a confident one. Max reached
for the buttons on my white blouse, popping open one after the
other. I slid my hands over his arms, his back, kissing him. Then I
remembered something I'd read. Or had I heard it? I wanted to ask
if Max had told me this: The Greeks say that friends have one soul
that lives in two bodies. But instead I murmured, "I want to know
you always, Max."

He ended our kiss and sat up. "There is no always," he said.
"Nothing is forever."

"I didn't really mean forever." I corrected myself. "I meant that I
like you."

His face became serious, his eyes darkened. "If we do this, we're
very good friends. But I'm not really promising you anything."

I dropped my hands in my lap. I said, "I didn't ask for a promise."

"I didn't know what you were thinking, and I don't know what you expect."

"What about California? You said you wanted me to come with you."

"I do. But that's a long time from now."

I thought about California. Had Max changed his mind? What was he telling me? That this was the last time we would see each other? That I would give myself to him, give everything, and then he would leave me? Emotion rose in me like a storm. I frantically fastened a button on my blouse. "Are you saying this is the last time we'll be together?" I bit my lip. I felt like screaming at him, but I knew this wouldn't solve anything.

"No. I just meant we're young. We're not getting engaged. I'm trying to be practical and honest."

"Maybe I wouldn't get engaged to you," I said angrily, though I knew nothing would please me more. I tried to calm myself, but I blurted out, "How do I know you won't have two wives?"

"I would never. But no one knows the future." He softened his voice. "We're still young, Lena. That's all I meant."

"Yes, we're young," I said more calmly, "but in ways we're grown up."

"Let's not argue." He linked his fingers in mine. "We're wasting time."

"This isn't an argument. It's a debate. A discussion."

"Let's not talk about this anymore." He leaned against the pillow. "If I started this debate, I'm sorry." He put his arm around me. "Let's just be us again."

Max leaned to kiss me, but after a minute I pulled away. I hadn't known I was capable of stopping the pleasure of our kisses. Always was a long time, and who knew about anything in this world? Love made people do unpredictable things, terrible things, I was sure. I thought of Uncle William, of the girlfriend who'd left him.

I was about to explain this to Max, but he stood up, marched to the other bed, and sprawled onto the mattress. He picked up a book from the night table, *The Three Musketeers*.

"Are you going to read *now*?" I said.

"Yeah, for a few minutes. So you can decide if you want to do this," he replied matter-of-factly. "I happen to like you very, very much and I want to do this, but maybe you don't. Practically speaking, we don't have endless time. My family will come home. Either yes or no, Lena. Whichever way…" he sighed with impatience, "is fine. I don't want to be a beggar."

"Oh," I said, surprised.

He began to read.

"It's rude to read now," I said.

"You wanted time to think. So think." He didn't look up from his book.

We lay on our separate beds. Max was being difficult on purpose, I thought. Still, we'd never had a misunderstanding before, and this one seemed to be my fault. A million thoughts burst into my mind—about broken hearts, Uncle William and his girlfriend; about Uncle Maurice's big-breasted, ruined women. I thought about my mother's modesty, and Millie Farber. Were there proper ways to live? How did you reconcile—a ten-dollar word—what you *wanted* with what was decent? What you absolutely *wanted* with what you knew your family, your mother, thought was best. This seemed an unsolvable problem.

I shut my eyes and imagined a large brown woven basket, one I could throw worries into, big enough to hold every thought of mine. I tossed in my doubt and hesitation, my shame and anger, my fear and guilt. Then I flung the basket to the ceiling, into the sky, until it disappeared. I let the flames in the laundry burn up my shame.

"Well, maybe I am being a little rude," Max said. He shut his book and stood up. "You're right, and I'm sorry."

"Come here, Max," I said, satisfied with his words. I loved him, I knew. And I wanted him to love me, body and soul.

He sat next to me and then we lay in each other's arms.

After awhile, we shed our clothing. He'd never seen me naked, and at first, I was embarrassed. I had never seen him. His bare skin, the fine, golden hairs, every part of him.

"I hope we'll be safe," I murmured.

He didn't answer. I knew I didn't want words. I wanted him so close to me that it felt as if we were the same person. When he fumbled, trying to ease himself into me, I helped him find the right spot. Then I felt it, a pull, something broken inside me. I gulped a breath so I wouldn't cry. Then all thought fell away. The weight of Max's body pressed against me. I wrapped my arms around him.

"Oh, Lena. I love you," he said.

I rocked my body with his and rested my head against his shoulder, against his soft, wonderful skin. Oh my God, oh my God. Time was a whisper, I thought dreamily. You listened, and it was gone.

Three Secrets
April 1927

My mother was wearing her good turquoise dress. She had been about to go to synagogue when the officer knocked on our door. My father was dressed in his overcoat. The policeman slouched in the doorway of our apartment and faced my parents. I stood between the two of them, waiting to hear what the man would say. It was Saturday morning, almost three weeks since my visit with Max at his house. Officer McGuire wore a dark-blue uniform with shiny brass buttons. He was heavy, with thin white hair and tiny slits for eyes.

"I'm glad I found you home," the officer said heartily. "I have good news for you. We have arrested Mr. Usher Cohen." His large belly heaved as he spoke. "Mr. Cohen was on the lam, but we found him. Even his wife didn't know where he was. We have determined he was responsible for the fire at your business."

"Oh, no," gasped my mother. Her body sagged.

My father stared at Officer McGuire and nodded slowly.

"There's nothing to worry about," the officer went on. "The man is in jail."

I wasn't surprised by the policeman's words. Mr. Usher Cohen's name had been in the papers as part owner of the laundry, after all. If the insurance company paid for the damage caused by the fire, he would receive money. It wasn't clear to me, though, if he'd be entitled to insurance money now because he'd been arrested for causing the fire. Still, he had been our friend, sat in our living room, drunk our vodka and *schnapps*. I thought uneasily about Simon again.

"Well. We have many questions about this," my father said.

"Would you like to come in?" my mother offered weakly. "Please do."

"No, ma'am. I'm only here to report our progress." The officer took a step back, so he stood firmly in the outer hallway. "We discovered

Mr. Cohen has been selling liquor, too, not Noxzema creams. All those Noxzema boxes he was transporting were jammed with bottles of whiskey. He was the one who bought the kerosene used in the fire at your business, but we believe someone else is responsible for the fire. Someone helped him."

"Have you found that someone else?" asked my father. "I told you who helped him."

"I can't tell you anything more, but we'll investigate and find the person or *persons* and keep you informed." The officer smiled confidently. He stood up straighter. His silver star gleamed against the blue uniform. "If you have more information, you need to let us know immediately. Do you understand?" He waited, as if to see whether my parents would add anything. "You, too," he said to me. "If you have information, call us right away." Finally he shook their hands and left.

"So Mr. Usher Cohen has been selling whiskey," my father said bitterly. He slammed the door. "I had to scramble to get liquor for the family, and Mr. Usher Cohen never said a word. He knew how hard it was to get and how expensive it was. It's one thing to buy whiskey, but to sell it is another matter entirely. This is a lesson, Lena. You think you know someone, but you don't. And he bought the kerosene. That bastard. *Gonif.* I could kill him."

"He always seemed honest," my mother lamented. "We treated him like family. He is even a member of the family club, Chaim. That he would do this to us, it's a sin. More than a sin."

"What about Simon?" I asked.

"What question is that?" she replied frowning.

"Maybe he knew what Mr. Usher Cohen was doing." I felt in a panic saying this. "Maybe Simon will be arrested." My words tumbled out. "What exactly does he do for Mr. Usher Cohen? Maybe Mr. Cohen tricked Simon into helping with the fire." I knew I shouldn't say this to my parents, but I couldn't contain my fear.

"Simon carries boxes to a car," my mother said gruffly. "He would never look inside them. And the fire? Where you get your ideas, Lena, I do not know."

My father shrugged with what seemed like bewilderment, but he said nothing more.

I felt suddenly frantic about Simon. He'd left early this morning. Had he heard about Mr. Usher Cohen's arrest and run away? What if we never saw him again? No. Simon was probably at the Jewish Center, playing basketball, where he always went. But still, after my parents left the apartment, I hurried out to find him.

Outside, a warm April wind shimmied around me. The sun was bright and lit up the sky. Birds chirped. Small blades of grass grew, and a few tiny buds, like peas, dangled from trees. Shadows from the branches stretched across the sidewalk.

I loved this mild weather, although I knew the weather could change at any time, become cold again, even snow. Spring was fickle but full of hope. In a way, this was like my family. I was worried about Simon, but I felt happy and hopeful about my father. He was finally working—at Millie Farber's grocery and on Saturdays at Mr. Sloan's store. My mother made no secret of her wish for my father to quit the grocery. But with these jobs we wouldn't lose the apartment. And my grandmother hadn't died, although she barely held onto life.

Rushing to the Center, I thought of my list of fears. New fears, like my worries about failing in school and losing our apartment, had replaced old ones. But I'd finally mastered one fear for good; I *had* known happiness, that day with Max in his room. Nothing bad had come of it yet. I'd learned something new about life, something wondrous. I loved Max. But did he love me? Oh, I hoped so. He had said so. But he had also said he wasn't promising anything. I wanted a promise, of love everlasting.

Groups of boys were playing basketball in the auditorium. Most were lightweights, almost the same size and build as my brother. They dashed across the floor, fiercely pursuing the ball, yelling to each other. The room smelled sour; footsteps thudded and echoed. I expected to see Simon running in the auditorium, too, but he wasn't there. I recognized short Nookie Michaelson and broad Izzie Berger.

"Has anyone seen Simon here today? Izzie," I screamed. I ran onto the edge of the gym floor. "Have you seen him?"

Izzie was out of breath and running. He looked my way, but didn't answer. Nookie Michaelson bounced the ball and raced across the floor. He yelled back to me. "Nah. Hasn't been here today. Sorry."

"Sorry," echoed Izzie hoarsely.

"Are you sure?" I yelled out.

"We got eyes," Nookie shouted, dashing toward the basket. "He hasn't been here all day."

I hurried from the Center, hopped onto a streetcar, then got off at the stop near the Montrose Avenue Beach, my favorite spot and Simon's, too. Families strolled there. Gulls swooped low to the water, their wings like white sails. Foamy waves splattered against the sand. But I didn't see Simon anywhere.

Now I began to feel a terrible panic. Had Simon been arrested and locked up in jail? Or beaten and hurt? Why didn't my parents *do* something? I didn't know where else to look, so I charged home, desperate to find him. I would decide on a plan there.

In the apartment, I found Simon sitting at the kitchen table, eating.

"Where were you?" I said breathlessly.

"Out," he replied calmly.

"They've arrested Mr. Usher Cohen." My voice was a screech.

"I heard. You don't have to be dramatic. I know who he is, Lena."

"Oh, Simon, maybe they'll arrest you, too."

He didn't reply. He bit into a *corshecloff* cookie and chewed loudly. Then he took a gulp from a glass of milk, indifferent to the news.

"You work for Mr. Usher Cohen," I blurted out. "Maybe they'll arrest everyone who works for him."

"I don't work for him. I quit months ago."

"You did?" I sat in the chair next to Simon. "Do Mama and Papa know that?"

"Well, not exactly," he said. "I told them Mr. Cohen owed me money, and that I hadn't gotten paid for awhile."

"Then where do you go after school?"

"Library."

I picked up a cookie and set it back on the plate. "Do you really go there? To the library?" I inched my face close to his and squinted at him. "I don't believe you, Simon."

He shrugged and looked at the table.

"You probably go to play cards or basketball or drink whiskey," I said. "I'll bet you drink all the time and smoke cigarettes."

He shrugged again. "Prohibition."

"You're lying, Simon."

He gulped more milk.

"I know you're lying."

He was quiet and then turned to me. "Between you and me, Lena. I've met a girl."

"Really?" I smiled, pleased with this news. "Who?"

"Can't tell."

"You won't tell me?" I said, disappointed. "I won't say anything. I absolutely promise."

"No."

"I can keep a secret. You know I can."

He stood up, raised his arms, and stretched. "I can't talk here."

"No one is home. The walls don't have ears. Where are you going?"

"Out. Come with me. Maybe I'll tell you."

We walked out of the apartment, down the stairs, outside, to the next block.

"Are you telling me or not?" I said, stopping.

"I haven't decided." He continued to walk, and I followed. Finally, he said, "There's a problem."

There didn't seem to be much of a problem now that Simon wouldn't be arrested. "What's the matter?" I asked.

He didn't answer.

A cloud passed over the sun. I felt chilled. I'd been so eager to talk with him that I'd left the apartment without a jacket. "I'm going home, Simon. I'm not following you around the city. You'll have to fix your own problem." I swung around.

"Come back, Lena. We're only a block from home."

I stopped.

He walked up to me. "She's not Jewish," he whispered.

"Oh, Simon, no." I didn't know what to say. This wasn't just a problem, it was unsolvable. I imagined my mother's furious censure, my father's angry disapproval. Yet I liked this girl because Simon liked her, and besides, I was curious.

Simon's red hair blew in the breeze. He looked not so much troubled as resigned. "You can't tell them or anyone," he said. "Promise me with your life."

"I won't say anything. Who is it?"

"I can't tell you."

"Someday I'll find out. I don't even want to know anymore." I wrapped my arms around myself for warmth. "Have I met her?"

A man walked past us. We were quiet until he turned the corner.

"You're not going to California with her, like Uncle William, are you?" I asked. "His girlfriend was…"

"For God's sake, Lena. Don't be so glum."

This was the longest conversation Simon and I had had in years. He had drifted so far from us he was hardly a presence in the apartment, or my life.

"We never talk to each other anymore," I said to him. "Sometimes I feel like I don't have a brother."

"Don't be stupid. You have a brother, and I have a sister." He slid off his blue wool jacket and draped it around my shoulders. "Here, it's getting cold outside," he said. "We don't have to cling to each other, Lena. We don't have to be like Ma with her family."

I nodded. I'd missed him. I had a brother, and I needed him.

He whispered, "It's Mary Hall."

"Her?" I stared at him in disbelief. "Simon, how could you?"

"She's not who you think. She's so much nicer than you know; she's really swell. I can talk to her, Lena. We really talk, and she's smart, kind, she's…don't tell her I told you."

"How long has she been your girlfriend?"

"That's it. I can't say another thing about this."

We walked to Bittersweet Place in silence. I thought of how Mary Hall had told me about her illness and family, how she'd been kind to me. But she wasn't *unsere leite;* she wasn't one of us.

It was clear to me Simon was done talking about this, so I asked him, "Do you ever think about what happened? To us? I mean, our grandfather. The Cossacks? That awful night?" This may have seemed disconnected from our conversation to Simon, but it wasn't. I was still thinking of Mary Hall, how her life had been so different from ours, no matter where her grandparents were born.

"Nah," he said. "I want to live, not regret. What can we do about it anyway?"

"The way Mother talks—you'd think it happened yesterday."

"She lives in two worlds. Just forget all of it, Lena. You have to live *as if...*"

"What do you mean?"

"As if people didn't hate each other, as if the world were absolutely safe."

"Oh, as if Uncle William were healthy, as if the fire never happened..."

"Yeah, that kind of thing, that's right," he said. "Don't think about any of it. Besides, maybe something good will come from the fire."

"I don't think so. The way they argue about it, it's awful."

"Our parents have created their own hell," Simon said. "Haven't you noticed?"

I shuddered. I had never thought of them in this way.

"But they love us. They work hard for us—so we can have a better life," Simon said.

"I know." This made me feel guilty. "But what good could there be from the fire?"

"We won't have to go to the laundry. That's good." He grinned and swung his arms carelessly. He seemed like a man to me. Tall, thin, with an air of confidence.

"Something is different about you," I said. It must be because of Mary Hall, I decided.

He laughed softly. "Don't know. But there's something different about you, too."

"I have my own secret." I felt a flush, an excitement that Simon and I could talk about our lives.

"So?" He stopped and eyed me.

"Max Sloan is my boyfriend," I said.

He raised his eyebrows. "I thought that might be."

"You did?"

"Now that you tell me, it makes sense. I brought you those notes from him when he was sick. And he's always busy with something. You."

I blushed. "Promise with your life not to tell anyone."

"Two secrets then." He laughed. "Lucky you, lucky me."

Instead of going home, we wound our way to the lake. The sky stretched across the water, like a painting that radiated with shades of blue light. The space Simon had once occupied in the family had been empty for so long, but I realized now I'd been waiting for him to fill it up again.

"You seem happy," he said as we strolled on the sand.

"I am, except for our family—the troubles. It's nice to have a secret, this kind of secret." I sighed.

"A boyfriend. A girlfriend."

"Yes." I nodded and took a breath. I thought about what else was hidden. My real, ugly secret. What would it mean to anyone who didn't know Uncle Maurice? I couldn't decide if I had the courage to tell Simon. I was so ashamed, but I resolved to try. After all, what if my uncle came home? Who would protect me? My mother was often gone, delivering her sewing repairs. My father worked at two jobs and was hardly home anymore. "I used to *not* be happy," I went on, carefully choosing my words. "There were things in our family…"

"Millions of reasons to be miserable there," Simon said.

"This was different." I stopped, debating. "Uncle Maurice…" I paused again.

"That *shmuck*. He thinks he's so American. I know he's our family, but he's no good."

How could I explain? Maybe Simon would blame me for what had happened. My mother would, I was sure. I still felt it was my fault. If I hadn't been bathing. If I hadn't been in the hallway. I should have known better. All these thoughts thundered in my head, but I forced myself to go on. "He touched me, Simon," I burst out. "He kissed me." The words exploded. "He yanked away my towel. I'd been in the bath. I didn't have clothes on and he…" Tears gushed in my eyes. "He made me…" I gagged.

"Damn, Lena." Simon clasped his arm around me. "Did he hurt you, I mean did he…?"

"No." I shook my head.

"That bastard. He's worse than a criminal. Did you tell them? Mother and Father? What did they do?"

"I told Papa a long time afterward. Uncle Maurice had already moved to California." My throat was dry, my voice raspy. I tried to sound strong. "Papa said he would kill him. Maybe he has."

"I don't think so. But I would."

"Don't tell anyone. Please."

"No." He dropped his arm away. "Listen to me." His voice was firm. "What happened—that's one of the things you don't think about. And whether you'd been wrapped in a towel or not, he would have done the same. That's the kind of person he is."

"Maybe yes. Maybe no." I could hear the roar of the elevated train, feel my uncle's cold fingers. Hear his awful laugh. "I hate him," I said. "I wish he were dead."

"Who knows? Maybe he is."

"Simon, what if he comes back? If he can't settle things in California, he wrote in his letter that he'd come home."

"You don't have to worry," he said. "I'm here. You're not alone. That's a promise."

I nodded, grateful.

We meandered in silence, as I often did with Max and had done with Leah Grace. Our bodies cast rubbery shadows across the sand. Waves rose lazily in a soft whooshing rhythm like instruments playing a lullaby.

"Why was his name on the laundry papers with Mr. Usher Cohen?" I asked, changing the subject.

"I don't know." Simon shrugged. "I guess they were friends."

Finally, we circled home.

I plopped onto the bottom step of our building by the entrance. "I need to think," I said. "Before I go in."

Simon eyed me. "Are you all right?"

"Fine." I glanced up at him.

He knelt and brushed his hand so gently against my head, smiling in such an unexpectedly tender way that I smiled back. Then he bounded through the door, slamming it behind him.

I closed my eyes. Telling him had been a great relief, I realized, but I wasn't ready to go to our apartment yet. I sat for a while and then I walked to the end of Bittersweet Place, rounded the corner, and wandered from block to block until I reached Cornelia Street, as if I would find an explanation for Uncle Maurice there. I peered at the buildings. What had become of Millie Farber? I wasn't brave enough to find out. And what would become of Simon and Mary Hall?

The sun was sinking and the breeze had picked up. I pulled Simon's jacket tightly around me and started for home. Talking was a slow unburdening, I thought. You needed courage and someone you loved to listen, someone who would understand. You needed to use as few words as possible. At least, I did. I hadn't imagined I would tell anyone about Uncle Maurice, especially Simon. But things always happened that I didn't expect. I had told my father, but I had spoken to him out of anger. What would my mother say if I told her? Or if I explained to Millie Farber? What would they say about what I'd done with Max?

I could imagine my mother's anger and bitter disappointment. What would she say about the kind of person I was? If only I could please her.

Millie Farber's soft smile opened in my mind. I liked her and I hated her. "Thank you for telling me, Lena," she might say. Perhaps she would sigh, and talk to me as if I were grown up, capable of understanding the world. And I was. She would be sympathetic, but she would have no answers about Uncle Maurice or about my behavior with Max. "That's how life is," she might say. "Sometimes cruel, sometimes happy. We're afraid, but we love anyway."

Unexpected News
April–May 1927

We had expected my grandmother to die, but when she did, I was unprepared. Not for the fact of her death, but for my mother's tears, and for my own. My grandmother had been disappearing for years, only now she had truly vanished. I didn't know if I believed anymore in billions of souls scattered in the sky. My old grandmother was air, she was water, she was dust, like Leah Grace, like my grandfather in Belilovka.

When I told Max about her death, he draped his arm around me. We were walking on the grassy area that bordered the sand by the lake. "I'm really sorry," he said. He seemed a little sad, a little shaken. He hadn't faced much death in his family. "She was old. She lived long," he went on gently. "There is no 'always,' is there?"

"No," I said.

"Yeah. Well, maybe I was wrong. Maybe I do want to be with you, however long 'always' is."

"Oh, Max." I stepped closer to him. "I'd like to know *you* always. You know that."

My mother insisted Simon and I go to the cemetery. "You are both old enough to be at a burial," she said. My father agreed.

At the funeral, we were a small group. The cemetery was a flat expanse of land, with just a few trees, and absolutely quiet. Beneath a blue April sky, we crowded around my grandmother's grave—the aunts, uncles, and the four of us. The coffin sat in a hole in the ground so deep it seemed like a wound in the earth. Rabbi Hirschfeld led us in prayers, and this time, he didn't try to teach us any lessons.

The very next day, the family shrank again. Uncle Abie and Aunt Ida prepared to board their train for New York City. They would sail to Poland from there.

In the late afternoon, after school, my parents, Simon, and I went with Abie and Ida to Union Station. The other aunts and uncles couldn't join us, a reminder of another sadness. They were preparing to sit *shiva* for my grandmother.

My mother and I had accompanied my father to Union Station when he left for California, but I had been too upset then to notice the world around me. Now we walked into the main hall of the gigantic station, and I stared up, up at the huge ceiling where windows let in a rush of sunlight. The ceiling was so tall it seemed to graze the heavens. We were dwarfed by the height of it, by the crowds that hurried past on the pink marble floor, people racing to find trains or buy tickets, running up and down the long staircase. Some travelers called out for redcaps to help with luggage. Others huddled on the wooden benches waiting for their trains to appear.

We stood next to a row of tall white columns to say our goodbyes.

"So," said Uncle Abie. He wore a navy suit and a black wool overcoat. Aunt Ida stood next to him in a gray dress, a gray wool coat, and white gloves, their three suitcases on the floor beside them. "The time has arrived," he went on. "Ida and I are going to the land where God is still respected." Tears gathered in the corners of his eyes. "Even so, my soul will ache for each of you."

My father clasped Abie with emotion. "We often disagree," my father murmured, "but that doesn't take away the love."

"No." Abie hugged my father tightly, and I marveled to myself that two people who argued so much could still feel such affection for each other.

Then my aunt and uncle hugged each of us. The longest embrace was reserved for my mother.

"You will visit us," Abie beamed, stepping back from her. "Simon and Lena will bring their own children to us someday. Can you imagine? Life is sweet. No matter where we live, we will remember the joy of each of you."

"Go in health," my mother said quietly, as if she were speaking for all of us, for my old grandmother. "And live in health, too."

My grandmother's *shiva* was held at Aunt Feyga's apartment. I was allowed to stay home because of schoolwork. Nights, I sat at my desk completing assignments. Sometimes Simon joined me in the living room. He and I hadn't talked more about Max or Mary Hall or Uncle Maurice, but a silent understanding arched between us. His presence was a comfort.

I worked hard. Two months of school were left, and I was determined to do all I could to change Miss Marshall's mind about failing me. She still had no sympathy for me, despite the fire. Mr. Bender hadn't contacted my parents yet, and I was glad for this temporary reprieve. It was hard for me to concentrate, though, with so much happening—my aunt and uncle gone, Simon returned to me, the new *shiva*. Sometimes I opened my notebook and drew instead of doing my assignments. I wasn't a seamstress who wanted to sew the world shut, like my mother. I wanted to rip open the world, to draw what I needed to remember and what I wanted to forget.

I sketched my grandmother, pale and curled into herself like a baby, and Uncle William, thin and broken, although I couldn't create a good likeness of his face. Then I drew the fire. Page after page. I had no colors to use, so I shaded the shapes, and drew thin curving lines and wide angular ones. Tall rippling flames, the thick, suffocating smoke, my father huddled at the rolltop desk in the back, and the huge, scowling pressing machines.

As I sketched, I wondered: How much could one person bear in life? Would my life be burdened with one misfortune after another? I thought of Rabbi Hirschfeld. We were all afflicted, I decided.

Nadan kenen elteren geben, ober nit kain mazel, my mother had once said. Parents can give a dowry, but not luck. Luck was a stupid superstition, like chewing on thread so your brains wouldn't be sewn away. But what if I was wrong? Could you change your luck? I remembered my father's words. *Oif morgen zol Got zorgen.* If there was one—let God worry about tomorrow.

Despite the difficulties created by the fire, the days began to fall into one another with an odd calm. My grandmother's *shiva* ended. Max and I met after school. We often walked along the lake in the milder weather, kissing, holding hands. We had gone to his room on another Sunday when his family was out. I still worried that my behavior with him wasn't decent, but even so, I wanted to stay in his arms, close to him, forever.

Sometimes my mother, Simon, and I visited ABC Grocers on Broadway, where my father worked. I went to help him in the grocery on Saturdays, too. My mother said I didn't need to do this. "But I want to help the family," I told her. "I have to. Too many difficult things have happened to us."

Max told me that Broadway seemed to be the only street in Chicago without a suffix. It wasn't a place or an avenue or boulevard or street, he said. It was just Broadway, named after a famous street in New York.

The grocery was wedged between a laundry and a clothing store. Foods sat on floor-to-ceiling wooden shelves. The space was warm and cozy and dim, with narrow aisles. Piles of garlic, apples, and onions were heaped high. Butter, cheeses, milk, flour, and sugar were organized like *landsleit* on shelves. Sweet smells of spices and sharp scents of cheeses drifted in the air. My father helped customers, gathering items they wanted into brown paper bags, placing money into a shiny cash register.

Millie Farber and her husband were never at the grocery. She and my father seemed to have nothing to do with one another now, though I didn't know for sure. Perhaps she had moved away after all. If so, that was just as well.

When customers trickled in, my father's face glowed with happiness like it had at the Granville Laundry. But still, I sensed something was missing. He wasn't at ease as he used to be; there was no laughter or talk about guggle muggle here. At the grocery, no one shared the details of their lives.

From the day he started to work there, my mother went, like a detective, to check on him. She brought him an apple, a sandwich, her *corshecloff* cookies, but really she was spying, I was sure.

"He works in a grocery," I said. "He doesn't need your food."

"He enjoys it," she replied. "I bring what he likes." She pressed her offerings into his hands and sometimes kissed his cheek, as if making amends for something I didn't understand.

My parents had created a jumble of hurt and confused feelings. Simon had called it "their own hell." Miss Marshall would say his assessment was a cliché, but Simon was right. There seemed to be more affection between my parents now, and I longed for this to last.

The family club still didn't meet. The gatherings had stopped after the fire. There was no money yet for *schnapps* or sweets, and no one seemed to have the spirit for laughter or pinochle. The aunts and uncles were still scrambling to find work, and of course Aunt Ida and Uncle Abie had gone to Poland. Only Uncle Myron had started a new job, at an apron factory. The few times the relatives stopped by the apartment, they talked in low, anxious whispers about Mr. Usher Cohen.

We hadn't heard more from the police about who helped Mr. Usher Cohen with the laundry fire. He was still in jail. Some nights, in bed, in the darkness, I wondered if my father could have been involved. This didn't seem possible, but he had been in the laundry on the day of the fire. He continued to tell us that he had seen Uncle Maurice there, but we hadn't heard a word from my uncle. My father was so grieved by the loss of the laundry, though; his tall frame bent when he spoke of the horrible event, his voice quivering.

In my mind, I kept weighing what evidence I had.

One afternoon someone knocked on our apartment door. I swung the door open. A policeman in a blue uniform stood facing me—a tall young man with blond bushy eyebrows and short blond hair. His narrow green eyes stared at me. He removed his hat and pressed it against his chest.

"Are you Mrs. Reesa Czernitski?" he asked.

"Not at all." How could he think I was my mother? I stopped myself from smiling at his mistake.

"Who is there, Lena?" my mother called out from her bedroom.

"Can you please wait a moment?" I said to the man. "I'll get my mother."

I found her at the sewing machine and told her, "A policeman is here." I was sure his presence marked the end of our calm.

My mother lifted her foot from the treadle. "So perhaps now we will learn more about the fire," she said.

"I'm Officer Peterson," said the man when we returned to the door. He hesitated, as if he didn't know what to say next. It seemed to me he was new at this, young, without the confidence of the other policemen, of Officer McGuire.

"You have a relative, a brother, Mr. Moshe or Morris Rubolsky?" he finally asked.

"Yes." Her eyes flickered with anticipation.

My heart did, too.

My mother wiped her hand impatiently on the side of her green housedress. "Maurice," she said. "His name is Maurice Roberts here, in America. He likes this name better."

The policeman nodded.

"Do you know where he is?" she said. "We have not been able to find him."

"I have unfortunate news," he said.

"What has happened?" She blinked, her face impassive. "But please come in. Lena, show the man in. The neighbors do not need to hear all about our lives." She lumbered down the apartment hallway.

I followed her. The policeman shut the door and walked behind me.

"I was afraid of this," she said to the man as we entered the living room. Although he was taller than my mother, he looked like a boy next to her, perhaps just a few years older than I was. "Is this about the fire?" she asked.

"Fire?" Officer Peterson rubbed a hand against his cheek and raised his bushy blond eyebrows. "What fire?"

"The laundry fire. Our business burnt to the ground," she explained. "Nothing left of it. The Granville Laundry."

"I don't know about a fire." He pulled a small pad of paper from his uniform pocket and flipped through the pages, reading them. "Nothing about a fire here."

"But what is your news then?" she said. "Where is my brother? He is in trouble, isn't he? I could feel this all these months."

I glanced from my mother to the policeman.

"I am sorry to tell you." He looked as if he would rather not continue. He frowned and cleared his throat. "Your brother is dead."

"No." My mother squeezed her eyes shut; her face curdled into grief. She leaned against the wall. Her body wobbled. I worried she might faint. Out of duty and concern I reached for her hand. But a trill of delight, surprising and delicious, shot through me. My uncle was dead.

She slid her hand from mine and breathed deeply. "Excuse me," she said to the policeman. She gripped an arm of the sofa and sat down. "So many things unexpected."

"A shock, I suppose," he said sympathetically.

"Yes. How could he be dead? Tell me what happened," she said. "But please sit down. There is no need to stand."

He joined her on the sofa. I sat in a chair opposite them.

"I know only a few facts," the officer began apologetically. "Your brother was found in his apartment on Diversey Avenue three days ago, no longer alive."

"Diversey Avenue?" my mother repeated.

"In Chicago?" I said.

"Yes, in Chicago," he replied.

"Are you certain this man was my brother?" she said.

"Yes." He nodded vigorously. "His apartment was on the second floor, above a tailor shop. The landlord needs to talk to you about the junk—excuse me…" He stopped, his face rosy with embarrassment. "I mean the possessions your brother left behind."

"Possessions? I do not understand." My mother opened her hands as if her palms held the answers to these mysteries. "My brother lived in California."

"He wrote us letters from there," I explained.

"I don't know about California, ma'am," the officer said, looking from my mother to me. "And I don't know anything about any letters. I do know he rented an apartment here on Diversey Avenue for two months."

There was silence. My mother was struggling to absorb this information, I could see. Two months. Uncle Maurice had been here all that time, but I hadn't seen him, and now I would never see him again. I felt giddy with relief.

"He never told us he was living in Chicago again," she said. "And now he's dead. How could that be? He had an illness?"

"Mr. Rubolsky died of a coronary. The landlord found him on the floor. The rent was late."

"The heart, the heart," she murmured. "My poor brother." She sat straighter and snapped out of her melancholy. "His heart was weak since he was a boy. I suppose it was a miracle he lived as long as he did. Not such a good life."

"I don't know what kind of life he had." The officer shrugged, weary and out of patience. "You'll need to decide on the funeral arrangements, and you'll have to collect his possessions." He handed her a piece of paper. "Here's the person to contact at the police station, and the landlord's information." He stood up. "I'm sorry," he said awkwardly.

Uncle Maurice dead. I felt relief in every part of my body. I wanted to shout with joy. Maybe my secret could die now, too. That's what I wanted.

My mother escorted the officer out.

When he was gone, she turned to me, determination glowing in her eyes. "Lena," she said, "I will talk to the person at the police station. I will tell the others in the family." Her voice was strong. "Then after I speak to the landlord, you and I will go to Uncle Maurice's apartment."

"I can't," I said. "I won't go to that apartment. I don't want anything to do with him." How could I go there, and see and touch the things that belonged to him?

"You heard the policeman. Your uncle is not alive. I need you to help me."

"Papa will go. Or Simon," I said.

"If they can, they will come, too. But I do not know if they will be able to help when the landlord says we must go to the apartment. I need to have your help, Lena. It is a *mitzvah* to help in this way."

"I won't go there. Maybe I won't be able to go there when the landlord says. I don't want to pack up Uncle Maurice's life. If he had secrets, I don't want to know them."

"I am sure Maurice, of all people, had secrets. Secrets are tucked in everyone's heart. But secrets or not, I need you to go with me to the apartment, Lena." She studied me carefully. "I do not understand the problem with this. Can you tell me? I want to understand you."

"There is no problem," I muttered.

"Many times I step aside for you, against my good judgment," she said, as if the matter was settled. "But this, a visit to your uncle's apartment, I cannot do myself."

The Decision
May 1927

"Maurice was no good," my father pronounced, cutting the fried liver on his plate at the dinner table. "People create their own misery. His heart gave out because of the terrible things he's done."

Simon shot me a look.

"Whoever Maurice was," my mother replied, "he is first our blood, our family."

I was sitting next to Simon at the table. I grasped my fork, pushing my rice and meat to the center of my plate.

"He started the fire, no matter what the police say about it," my father said. "I saw him. And he's been here all this time in Chicago. God and Maurice are playing tricks on us."

I mashed my rice, flattening it, as my parents continued to talk. The visit to Uncle Maurice's apartment loomed like a curse. My mother hadn't made arrangements to go to the apartment yet. The landlord had become ill and would telephone us when he was well. I didn't know what we would find there or exactly what I was afraid of, but I wanted nothing to do with my uncle's memory or his possessions.

After dinner, as my mother washed the dishes and my father drank tea in the kitchen, I whispered to Simon, "Come with us to that awful apartment. Please. Will you, Simon?"

He gave me an understanding look. "Sure. Of course, I'll go with you. I won't leave you alone there."

I went to my desk, and Simon sat on the sofa. My mother walked into the living room then and said to us, "The two of you will come to Maurice's funeral."

My father followed behind her. "Let them be, Reesa. There's no need for them to show respect for Maurice. He doesn't deserve any. They have memories, good and bad. That's enough."

She said nothing more about it.

The afternoon of the funeral, I came home from school and the apartment was empty. Simon was off with Mary Hall. My parents were at the cemetery. Max had to help at his father's store. I had told Max about my uncle's death while we strolled along the lake. And then I had kissed Max—because I wanted to, but also because I wanted to end the conversation about Uncle Maurice.

The apartment seemed dreary. Outside, a light rain fell. I didn't feel like tackling schoolwork, so I decided to look through the mail. Among the envelopes, I was surprised to find two addressed to me. I carried them to my desk. The first was addressed to "Lena C." I knew right away it was from Elka Amsall. I recognized her handwriting, the smooth loops and lines. I pulled the letter from the envelope. She had written on heavy lined paper, the kind we used in school.

Dear Lena,

> Milwaukee isn't as bad as I thought. I will write more soon. I hope you are happy. I am almost happy! Say hello to Mary Hall and the rest. You and I are friends forever!

Elka

The letter was disappointingly short. Elka didn't seem as miserable as she'd expected. I was glad about that. I flipped the paper over to see if there were more details about her life. The back of the paper was empty.

The second envelope was addressed to "Miss Lena Czernitski." This sounded official and important. I didn't recognize the handwriting. Inside was a sheet of thin blue paper, carefully folded into thirds. I slid the paper out. It was so delicate, I was afraid I might tear it if I wasn't careful. The letter was written in a neat, round script.

My dear Lena,

I hope I am not intruding. It was so good to meet you. In other circumstances, I would have enjoyed talking with you more. We are living in Colorado now. I am writing to thank you for being kind when I visited your apartment. And to tell you: You have so much talent. Don't forget that. I have the drawing you made at my house here with me, and I admire it every day. Remember: If you find the pearls, the necklace will follow. I hope we will meet again. Please be good to your father.

All my regards,
Millie F.

I smoothed the paper, trying to press out its wrinkles. I was surprised Millie Farber would write to me. I felt an intimacy with her, one I couldn't understand. That tenderness Millie felt for my father spilled into this letter, but I also remembered my mother's fury when the woman had stood at our door. I both liked and hated Millie Farber. Either way, she had solved a mystery for me. She lived in Colorado now.

I decided not to tell my father, or even Max, about the letter. I read it three times, then gently folded it and laid it at the bottom of the wooden box beneath my drawings. *If you find the pearls, the necklace will follow,* she had written. What did she mean? I had no jewelry; my family owned so little of anything. I shut the lid of the wooden box. Millie had brought my drawing with her to Colorado. Maybe my drawings were my pearls, I realized. Maybe that's what she was saying. I was sure of it now. Perhaps a necklace would follow then. But how? And when?

I carried Millie Farber's words in my mind when I went to school the next morning. I decided to think about her letter whenever Miss Marshall spoke to me.

But Miss Marshall wasn't in the classroom. Instead, the principal, Mr. Bender, stood stooped at her desk. "I am here to tell you," he announced, "that Miss Marshall has become ill. She will not return to school. A new teacher will be here tomorrow."

I could hardly believe this news. Students began to whisper with surprise and relief.

"That's enough," he snapped. "Do not gloat in other people's misfortune." He shot a glance at me.

Mary Hall sat next to me now that Elka had moved. We hadn't spoken about Simon, or much at all the last few weeks, but she turned to me and said, "Miss Marshall has a nervous disorder. The school is trying to hide it."

"I didn't know that," I said.

Another student called out that Miss Marshall had been struck ill in the heart. Still another claimed the woman had broken her arms and legs.

The old witch was gone. Whatever had happened, I was thrilled. But who would take her place?

"I want no more speculation about Miss Marshall," Mr. Bender ordered. "I can't discuss the nature of her problem. It is a private matter and will remain that way." He informed us that he needed to go to his office. "I'll return in a few minutes. I want all of you quiet until I come back."

As soon as he left, students started whispering again. The voices grew louder.

Suddenly, Philip Schloss charged to the front of the room. He grabbed a piece of chalk and wrote on the blackboard in big bold letters:

MISS MARSHALL IS SICK AND A PRICK
BECAUSE SHE IS AN EVEL JEW!!!

He stared at the class, snickering, and then strutted back to his seat.

An odd hush settled in the room. Even his friends were quiet. My eyes filled with tears, but not of sadness. Of anger. I struggled to blink them away. Would the world never be free of this? Maybe my mother was right to hold onto our family so tightly. Even so, I'd had enough of Philip Schloss and his cruelty. I knew I might jeopardize myself in school, but I had to tell him what I believed. I stood up. "How dare you write that," I said. "You're cruel and prejudiced and wrong."

He laughed again.

I opened my mouth to tell him more.

But Mary Hall jumped up, marched to the board, and erased the words. She faced us. Her expression was hard and uncompromising. She seemed to dare him to write the words again.

The other students looked from Philip Schloss to Mary Hall to me.

"Young ladies," boomed Mr. Bender, walking in. "One more transgression and you'll be in my office for the week. Get back to your desks. What were you doing?"

I sat down quickly.

Mary's face reddened, but she proceeded calmly to her desk, without an explanation.

I looked at her with admiration and affection even. Her actions were because of Simon's influence, I was sure.

Mrs. Paulina, our new teacher, appeared the next day. She was young and beautiful, with thin lips, shining white teeth, and hazel-green eyes. Her wavy brown hair was wound into a neat knot at the back of her neck. Her smile looked bright with happiness. She wore a soft pink dress with a white sash wrapped around the dropped waist. "I've just gotten married," she told the class. "This is my first teaching position."

She had a private conversation with each student at her desk where she murmured and smiled at everyone, except me. She told me to stay after class.

Later, I stood nervously next to her desk in the empty room, the other students all gone home for the day.

"Miss Marshall left reports about everyone," she began. The wide wooden desk had always made Miss Marshall seem invincible, but the large surface swallowed Mrs. Paulina. She seemed small and fragile.

I felt small and fragile myself.

"She wrote pages about you, Lena. There was a problem with drawings for an assignment. A landscape. A portrait. Telling lies. The drawings weren't yours, she wrote here. You traced them. The lines were too perfect for a girl your age, it says." Mrs. Paulina glanced at a notebook that lay open on the desk, then leaned toward me, looking at me intently. "She was considering failing you. She wrote that you lied to her. Are you aware of this?"

Millie Farber's words echoed in my mind: *If you find the pearls, the necklace will follow.*

"Yes, she told me. But I didn't lie to her. Miss Marshall was wrong." I struggled to control my voice. I didn't want to scream as I had done with Miss Marshall. "The drawings I gave her for the assignment are my own. I did them myself. I didn't trace anything. I told her that. My father talked to her about this, too."

Mrs. Paulina frowned and folded her hands on top of the desk. "She wrote that when she spoke to you about this, you became upset and cursed, used terrible language." She read aloud from the notebook, "'I am afraid of this girl.'"

"Afraid of me?" That was the lie, I wanted to tell Mrs. Paulina, but I forced myself to speak in a measured, strong tone. "That's not true. What Miss Marshall wrote about me isn't true. I explained to her that I did my own drawings. I even showed her. I got upset because she wouldn't believe me, even when I drew a picture while she watched me. But I never used terrible language. I never did anything to make her feel afraid of me."

"And the principal spoke to you about the drawings as well."

"Yes," I said.

"I don't know what to tell you." Mrs. Paulina pointed to the notebook in exasperation. "Miss Marshall writes one thing. You tell me another. In fact, she stopped this report in the middle." She showed me the page with the last entry unfinished. "I'll have to decide for myself," Mrs. Paulina said.

"I see," I said cautiously.

"I won't tolerate dishonesty," she said, her voice rising, as if this offended her deepest instinct. She no longer looked fragile. She rapped her pale pink nails against the desk just like Miss Marshall used to do. "I'd like you to write a report about the problem. And to bring in more of your drawings. Tomorrow, I would like to see both. And I want to speak to your parents in two weeks."

That night while my parents went to Uncle Maurice's *shiva*, I labored over my report. I didn't tell them what Mrs. Paulina had said, just as I never told them how Miss Marshall punished me because I wrote with my left hand or that Mr. Bender had spoken to me in his office. My parents couldn't help me then, and I was sure they couldn't help now. I didn't tell Max, or Simon, or Mary Hall. This was my problem, and I wanted to solve it myself.

At my desk, I added and erased until I was satisfied with my words.

Report for Mrs. Paulina

I began to draw before Miss Marshall even gave us the assignment. I drew with my cousin, Leah Grace. One of the drawings for the assignment is of Lake Michigan. I sketched this at the Montrose Avenue Beach. The other is a portrait of my cousin.

The drawings are my own work. I didn't trace them. I am an honest person. I don't understand why Miss Marshall hated me. Perhaps this is the wrong thing to write. I don't think she hated only me. She didn't like immigrants or Jews. That's what I believe.

Here are some of my private fears that I've listed in my notebook:

I will never speak good English
I will never grow up

I will never ever know happiness again
I WILL FAIL IN SCHOOL—and no one will
   help me

I've resolved most of these fears, but not the
one about failing in school. I work hard in school,
and I would never lie to you or Miss Marshall. The
drawings are my own. I hope you will believe me.
   Sincerely,
   Lena Czernitski

I set down my pencil, thinking of the lies I constructed in order
to be alone with Max. I wasn't so honest after all. But how else could
I experience life?

The next day, I gave Mrs. Paulina the report. I gave her three
drawings, too, one of the fire, a sketch of my grandmother, and
another of the lake. She told me again that she wanted to talk to my
parents.

That night, I spoke to my father after the *shiva*.

"The new teacher wants to talk to you about Miss Marshall
and my assignment," I said to him. "Please don't tell Mama." He
and I were sitting in the living room. My mother was finishing her
mending in the bedroom. "She doesn't need to know. You can meet
with the teacher yourself."

"I'm not happy to keep this from your mother." He laid the
Chicago Tribune on his lap. "But it's true, she's busy with your uncle's
death and the landlord. I'll consider what you ask, Lena. Your mother
may not have patience for this now."

My father came to school two weeks later. I knew he hadn't spoken
with my mother because she hadn't mentioned anything to me, and
she was still preoccupied with Uncle Maurice's death.

When the other students left the classroom, my father and I met
with Mrs. Paulina. He gave her more of my drawings, pictures of the
fire, the lake, and the one of Miss Marshall.

"Please sit down," Mrs. Paulina said as she took the drawings.

"And you, too, Lena. I hope you'll be comfortable, Mr. Czernitski, in one of these student desks."

"Yes, thank you," he said.

She placed the drawings next to each other on top of her desk, as if they were pieces of a puzzle.

"Lena can draw a picture for you right now," my father said.

"That's not necessary." Mrs. Paulina looked at me. "Your mother wasn't available?"

"No," I replied, feeling a sudden stab of guilt for having kept her away from this meeting.

"I prefer to speak with both parents," Mrs. Paulina said. "However, you're here now, so I'll study these. In fact, there's plenty of time to..." She didn't finish her sentence, but returned her attention to the drawings. "There's time to decide on a grade for this assignment," she finally said. She lifted one of the drawings and looked at it.

"A grade?" my father repeated.

"Then you're not going to fail me?" I said hopefully.

"Decisions are difficult," she replied, as if discussing the problem with herself. "I don't want to encourage dishonesty, but I don't want to penalize you unfairly either." She set down the drawing and brushed her hand against the pale skin of her forehead. "I've observed Lena in class," she went on. "She's polite and studious. I haven't been at this school long, but I can see that you're thoughtful," she said to me. "Intelligent. Although you often draw in class instead of listen."

"I didn't mean to be rude."

"But I'm impressed by you, by the discussions we've had, and by these drawings," she said. "I've decided not to fail you, Lena."

"Thank you." I wanted to throw my arms around her.

"We're grateful," said my father.

"I'll give Lena an 80 for this assignment," she said to him. "That's an approximate average of what Miss Marshall was considering, and what I would do."

"That's fair," my father replied, clearly pleased.

"Yes," I agreed, amazed. If Mrs. Paulina was giving me an 80, it meant she really wanted to give me an even higher grade for the assignment.

"However," she warned me, "if I see any evidence of tracing, I may change my decision."

I nodded.

"If you lied to Miss Marshall about these drawings," she said, her face puckering in disapproval, "someone will find out. But if you didn't, which I hope, then after today you can go forward with a lighter heart."

"I'd like to have such a heart."

"Wouldn't we all," she said.

"You won't have to change your decision," I said. "I never lied to Miss Marshall. I even tried to explain to her why I drew the lake and the people in the way I did, so she would understand. But she didn't."

"You can't force someone to understand," Mrs. Paulina replied kindly. "Art is a creation for the eyes. It can't always be explained with words."

"Oh," I said. I'd never thought about my drawing in this way. I wanted to discuss this with Max. Did he think music a creation just for the ears?

"Since these are your drawings," Mrs. Paulina said, "you should sign them. Write your name and the date you did them on the bottom of the paper. Or at least the year. Miss Marshall gave the assignment last fall, so you should write 'Lena Czernitski, 1926' here." She pointed to the lower right corner and handed me one of her black fountain pens with a shiny gold nib.

I did as she instructed, writing my name and the year in narrow, neat letters on the bottom of each drawing with the smooth black ink. And for a moment, I felt like a real artist.

Mrs. Paulina was an artist herself, I discovered the next week. She painted with watercolors, which I learned about when she gave the class a demonstration, painting lilies and roses, so lifelike and delicate. She told us about the new great painters in Paris and Europe, who wanted to capture the world in light. And about an American woman, Mary Cassatt, who created images of children and mothers. "A painting of hers is in an exhibit in a museum right here in Chicago. The Art Institute," Mrs. Paulina told us with excitement. "Some of you may have been to the museum. Artists study at the Institute. Paintings and drawings are displayed there. Perhaps I can arrange for the class to visit someday."

She passed around a pamphlet about Mary Cassatt's painting and others.

"Girl Arranging Her Hair," and "Little Girl in a Blue Armchair," I read when it was my turn. The colors were beautiful. In one, scribbles of orange, red, and green were woven into turquoise chairs. In another, a girl arranged her long red braid. The folds in her white blouse draped against her like layers of satin. Her arms reached upward, graceful as swans. She looked so alive, but when I studied the picture closely, holding it up to my face, I realized she was only a collection of colors and shapes.

"It's important to find an interest in life bigger than yourself," Mrs. Paulina said to the class. "To help people, or create something that is all your own, either with your hands or your mind. That," she glanced at me, "will bring you happiness."

After school, she stopped me in the classroom as I was leaving. When the other students were gone, she shut the door.

"I read your report again, Lena," she said. "And I want to say something about it. I believe Miss Marshall is an unhappy woman. You weren't the only student she treated poorly, but she was the most unfair to you. I feel I owe it to you to explain. Maybe I shouldn't tell you…but I want you to keep what I say between you and me. Please don't discuss this with the other students."

"I won't," I said, curious.

"Events in life can make people who they are. You need to understand this. Miss Marshall is a bitter person. I know her from… it doesn't matter where. When she was young, her family was forced to move. They were evicted from the apartment where they lived. The landlord was an immigrant. Jewish. Her father became ill but the landlord forced them to leave. The father died a few months later. She had loved him very much."

"That's terrible," I said, trying to take this all in. I thought of my mother's distrust of the police and government, as if they were *Petlurias*, too. "Miss Marshall didn't like anyone from another country. Who's Jewish."

"Unhappy people often take out their unhappiness on the world," Mrs. Paulina said. "She had other disappointments, too. She wanted to be an artist, but circumstances didn't allow it. People aren't always who they seem to be."

"People's natures," I said, surprised about Miss Marshall.

"That's right. We don't always understand a person's nature or how the world affects it. We all have to figure out who we are and guard this against what happens in life. Difficult circumstances aren't an excuse, but they're an explanation. Sometimes there isn't an explanation for why people act as they do, but in this case, I believe there is. Miss Marshall carried that bitterness about the landlord inside her. Unfortunately, she learned to be unkind, to hate, to make people into scapegoats, just as you said."

"Scapegoats?"

"To blame people who remind her of the landlord. She's gone through life blaming others."

"There's a word for it," I said.

"Yes. That's the beauty of language. English or Russian or whatever language you speak. You can take an emotion—a hurt, a joy—and find a word for it. This cushions a feeling, I think, if you can name it." Mrs. Paulina paused, and then leaned closer to me. "I also want to talk to you about art. You know, you may be a real artist. In fact, I think you are. You mustn't believe what Miss Marshall wrote about you." She smiled and leaned back.

"I won't," I said. "At least, I'll try not to."

"Good. She was wrong."

I arrived home that afternoon thinking about Miss Marshall and how events can twist a person's nature. I thought about the colors and shapes in Mary Cassatt's paintings, too, and about what Mrs. Paulina had said in class, thinking about happiness. How could you find your own happiness? I wondered. And did life always give you that chance?

My mother was sitting in the kitchen, drinking a cup of tea. I was going to ask her about all of this, about happiness and life and blaming others, but before I could open my mouth she looked up at me and said, "We will be going to Uncle Maurice's apartment on Sunday."

All my thoughts and questions disappeared.

Diversey Avenue
June 1927

"Damn this door," barked Mr. Prime. He jiggled the key in the lock. "I'd just as soon you haul everything out today."

Mr. Prime, the landlord, was a tall, fat, ugly man with gray hair like a wild mane. Although Diversey Avenue sparkled with people and life in the afternoon sunshine, the hallway outside of Uncle Maurice's apartment was hot and dim and empty. The air smelled of sardines and mold, an oppressive odor of decay.

"We will do our best," my mother said.

Simon, my mother, and I watched as the man continued to struggle with the key and curse. Finally, something clicked. He shoved the door open and pushed into the apartment.

My mother and Simon followed, but I stopped with dread in the doorway. It was only when Simon came back and took my hand that I could bring myself to venture inside.

The apartment was dark and smelled awful, like the hall. Mr. Prime switched on a lamp. We wandered from room to room—the living room, bedroom, and kitchen—in the gloomy light. They were small spaces, each a perfect, dreary square. Patches of gray paint had peeled off the walls and ceiling. Dust gathered in clumps on the floor like dirty, discarded clouds, and clung to the bottom of the kitchen chair and sofa legs. No curtains hung around the windows; each one faced a brick building so tall it blocked all of the daylight.

A half-full glass of water and a folded white napkin sat on the kitchen table. A fork and a stale, hardened crust of bread rested on a plate, as if Uncle Maurice had planned to return to this meal. I shuddered and looked away.

"The carpet, that lamp, they belong to me. Table and chairs. It's just the personal items," Mr. Prime informed us gruffly. "I'll give you privacy, but don't try to take advantage of my generosity." He thrust a piece of paper and pencil into my mother's hand. "I hate greedy people," he ranted. "I want to see a list of what you plan to take away."

"Certainly," she said.

"Thirty minutes or so, I'll be back. And the last month's rent is due. You'll have to pay that." He marched out and slammed the door.

"My God," she murmured, pressing a hand to her lips. She gazed at the grimy kitchen. "The rent. This apartment. That Maurice's life came to this." She paused and took a deep breath that filled her chest and pushed her shoulders higher. "We will begin," she said, her voice booming and strong now. "You go to the bedroom, Simon. Lena, you to the sitting area. I will be in the kitchen." She handed me the paper and pencil. "Write a list, please, so Mr. Prime does not think we are thieves."

It didn't seem there would be anything of value here. Why couldn't we throw it all in the garbage and be done? I knew my mother wouldn't do this, though. I went to the sitting area and stared numbly at two armchairs and their torn coarse green fabric. Time stood still. I was in Uncle Maurice's apartment, as close to him as I'd ever be again. I smelled the stale odors he had smelled. I touched what he had touched.

This made me queasy, made me long for Max and his sure sense of the world. My memory whirled to that horrible day in the hallway of our apartment. I could still hear the roar of the elevated train, see the hair on the back of Uncle Maurice's large, creeping hands. I felt such revulsion, such sorrow, feelings I longed to forget. My body slumped, as if a great weight pressed against my back. I was small, a child again. Helpless with no one to protect me. I backed away from the armchairs and tried to swallow my tears.

"Are you all right? Being here?" Simon asked, walking in. He put a hand on my shoulder.

"Not really," I whispered.

"I'll stay here with you."

"Thanks." I nodded gratefully and told myself: Uncle Maurice is dead. What happened is dead. Lena, erase the past from your mind.

On the floor, old, yellowed copies of the *Chicago Tribune* stood in high, uneven piles. Loose sheets of paper with what looked like musical notations lay scattered there, too. To distract myself and pull myself back to the present, away from my memories, I bent to pick up the sheets of paper. The words "By William Rubolsky" were written neatly at the top of some.

"These were William's," Simon said, looking over my shoulder.

"Like the ones Papa said he found in California," I replied. Simon's presence made me feel steady, more like myself. "Look at this," I continued, "it's—"

"Children, come here quickly," my mother interrupted. Her voice, warm and urgent, quieted all of my memories.

In the kitchen, Simon and I found my mother waving a piece of paper with writing on it. "See what was here on the counter," she said to us. "Simon, read it to us, please."

He read aloud:

> My dearest Reesa,
>
> Please forgive my long absence. I know about all that has happened to William. It is a great pain in my heart. I cannot help but feel responsible. I struggled in California so, and had to come back. But I have had a piece of luck. I am sure this will bring money I can use to repay you, to repair my past sins.
>
> Whatever I have, I will leave to you. Do what you wish with it. The gambling debts and Usher Cohen may ruin me. In a moment of weakness, I became involved with him and his business. I should never have done what he asked me to do. Still, there will be money left.
>
> I know you must have waited for letters from William and me. We were such hotshots then. But I have been thinking about the family. I miss them and you very much. When I see you again, you will

understand my silence.

Sometimes, Reesa, I fall into such deep melancholy. I can't explain why. I hope to live a long life, but tomorrow is promised to no one. You see, I have given great thought to

Simon stopped and turned the paper over.

"Continue," my mother said.

"There's nothing more."

She opened one kitchen drawer and then the next, fishing through them furiously. "Simon, Lena, help me find the rest of it."

He and I searched first the drawers, then the cupboards and counters. Past sins, I thought. Did that include me? Perhaps Uncle Maurice had given great thought to what he'd done to me.

"He didn't finish the letter, Ma." Simon flipped the paper from front to back. "He stopped in the middle. There's nothing else here."

"No ending to it," she said. "No date. What debts? What did he do for Usher Cohen? Maurice was the smartest of us all, but a fool. He didn't use his luck, and Mr. Cohen is… Past sins…well. We must collect your uncle's possessions, no matter what. Lena, please help me in here now."

I felt happier knowing my uncle had fallen into melancholy. I yanked open drawers and began to list the contents: five spoons, four knives, two forks, three dinner plates, pots, pans, and so on. My mother bustled about, sometimes stopping to touch an object, brushing her hand gently across an empty pickle jar or around a white saucer, instructing me to add this or that item to the list. Then she eyed the small wooden icebox. She pulled on the icebox door, trying to open it. Like the front door, it was stuck. She pulled again and again until finally, it popped open. A sharp, rancid odor of rotten food seeped into the room.

"I will begin with what is least pleasant," she said. She frowned at the foul smell, fanning the air with her hand. "This is a lesson no one wants to learn. Begin with what is least pleasant and look forward to what comes next."

She removed food from the icebox, one item at a time: the withered skeleton of an apple, three cheese rinds crippled with blue mold, two putrid chunks of raw chicken. She placed these on the table. I stood a distance back at the doorway to the kitchen, overwhelmed by the odor. Suddenly, my mother's back stiffened, and she stepped away from the icebox.

"Children!" she shouted, although I was just behind her. "Come here right now. Hurry. Please." Her voice trilled with emotion, as it had the day Uncle William jumped from the roof on Bittersweet Place. Simon came running into the kitchen. When my mother swung around I half-expected to see Uncle Maurice leaping out from the icebox.

But my mother just looked at us. Her face was flushed, her forehead shiny with sweat. She clutched a brown paper bag to her chest, the top of a large milk bottle peeking out of it. "Here," she said breathlessly, and shoved the bag toward us. "Look. Oh, my God." She reached in and pulled out a fistful of paper money. She slid the milk bottle out of the paper bag. Ten- and hundred-dollar bills were jammed and crumpled inside it, shoved against the glass.

I stared, amazed. I had never seen so much money.

"This was some luck," Simon said.

"Do not tell the landlord." She turned the bag and milk bottle upside down, shaking them. Bills fell to the floor, and my mother grasped them and hid them in her pockets, beneath her housedress, in her underclothes. She told Simon and me to do the same.

How could we take this? This was evil, stolen money, I was sure. But my mother continued to press bills into my hands, and in my shock, I said nothing.

When Mr. Prime appeared, she handed him the list I had written for her, and said we would return in an hour with boxes in which we'd put the items we wanted to keep.

"You'd better hurry," he warned. "Otherwise, I'll throw it all out. And you'd better bring the rent, too."

"We will," she replied. Then the three of us slouched past him, our pockets and clothing stuffed with money.

The Prize
April 1928

Ten months had passed since our visit to the Diversey Avenue apartment. I was learning that sorrow could pull time apart and make the minutes creep along, and then the days could speed by like galloping horses, leaving the dust of happiness behind. I longed to hold on to time as it was now—to always be sixteen, arching toward the future.

Uncle Maurice had hidden money not only in the milk bottle, but also in books we found on a table in his bedroom. My family never learned where the money came from. My father insisted Maurice had gotten the money illegally, from his disgraceful dealings with Mr. Usher Cohen.

"They sold liquor," my father told us. "Whiskey, beer. And gambled on horses. They even gambled at the laundry, the policeman told me. Maurice didn't believe in banks." My father shook his head in wonder at the irony; the insurance company hadn't paid anyone for the loss of the laundry since the fire was caused by a crime.

My mother had divided up Uncle Maurice's money. I didn't know how she'd decided on the amounts. She gave money to Aunt Razel and Uncle Charlie and their sweet baby, Leonard George, and to Aunt Feyga and Uncle Myron. She even sent some to Ida and Abie in Poland.

She bought clothing for us and herself, and used forty dollars to enroll in a class to improve her English, to buy books, and also to donate books to the synagogue. The class was held at the synagogue two evenings a week. Rabbi Hirschfeld personally taught the students. He also agreed to give my mother special tutoring in both English grammar and Hebrew prayer. Nights now, she studied at the kitchen table. Her chopping board lay bare. She talked gaily of the rabbi and the others in her class. "Rabbi Hirschfeld is a wise and kind man. Even a lawyer and banker study in the class," she told me.

"Why are they studying there?" I asked.

"Everyone wants to improve themselves." She frowned. "No, everyone wants to improve *herself* and *hisself.* No, no. *Himself,*" she corrected, and laughed. "Someday, I will know everything, Lena. Just as you do. That is my wish."

"I wish I did know everything," I said, and smiled at her.

She began to cook for the synagogue. She prepared large trays of steaming roast chickens and pans of sweet noodle *kugel.* "I want to help the true poor," she told me. "We have been blessed in an odd way, Lena. Sadness and happiness are brothers. Remember this. They walk hand in hand. After I finish my studies, I will join the *chevra kadisha,* the society to dress the dead. At the synagogue I will help people who will not even know I am helping them."

"That sounds awful," I said.

"No. You will see. The more you give to people, the more you repair the world and yourself. And I want to do a kind of penance for Maurice's poor judgment, his wasted life."

I thought about Uncle Maurice then. He had done so much evil, yet in spite of this, he'd helped us.

Everyone had found their own piece of happiness, even my father. He had used his share of the money to rent a large space and new washing and pressing machines, and had opened another laundry on Granville Avenue. Old customers returned and new ones flocked in. He stopped working at the ABC Grocery and Mr. Sloan's store. I had been worried about my father when Millie Farber moved away, afraid that he would end up like Uncle William. But opening the laundry gave my father a sense of purpose again. "Ah, Reesa," he said to my mother one night. "Together, we will start again. We'll make a new future."

"We will try," she said. For a moment, she gazed at him with tenderness.

I didn't know why my parents had made life so difficult, created their own hell, as Simon had said. But things seemed to be changing. Maybe the fire had reminded my parents of their love for one another. Or maybe they realized it took the strength of two to survive the afflictions of the world, to make a home. I knew I would never understand what had passed between them, or brought them together again. This was *their* secret. But I noticed a new quality of attention in them. My mother sometimes rested her hand on my father's arm, or brushed back a coil of red-gray hair that had fallen onto his forehead. She did her sewing repairs at the new laundry now.

Max and I met in his room whenever we could. I was less nervous, and I hadn't become pregnant. I didn't know who or what to thank—God or luck. We were more careful now. Sometimes I drew pictures in Max's living room while he played the piano. He and I went to movies together and always to the lake, as if the stretch of water and broad, bright sky were our true home. And sometimes Simon and Mary Hall walked along the sand with us. We went to the museum, too, the one Mrs. Paulina had mentioned, the Art Institute of Chicago. I was amazed by the colors and shapes in the paintings there, the swirling texture of the paint. I hadn't known such beauty existed.

My father used some of the money to buy me books about Rembrandt and art, and ones for Simon on basketball and baseball. My mother hid the rest of the money in pouches she sewed to the bottoms of mattresses and to the back of the living room curtains.

"We must bring the money to a bank, Reesa," my father said.

"I do not believe in banks," she replied. "This is our future. If we are forced to run away again like we had to do in Russia, if we need something for William or the children, the money will stay here. Where we can always find it. Where the money will be safe."

And so the money was hidden.

The family club started to meet again, too. The snap of pinochle cards and hum of conversation rose noisily in the living room. I didn't mind this so much now. I remembered how my father had once said the purpose of the club was to enjoy life. I decided we should try to seize as much joy as we could. The club didn't meet often. My parents were busy at the new laundry, and my mother was also occupied with studying and the synagogue. Sometimes people gathered when she was at her class. Our family was so small now that my father invited friends and customers from the laundry to join us. Mrs. Komansky stopped by with her husband. Mr. Abe Shusterman and his wife came over, and so did Mr. Boris Schneider and his wife, and Mr. Mort Seligman. On occasion, Mr. and Mrs. Sloan joined us, too. My mother even invited three students from her class.

One afternoon at the new laundry, I asked my father, "Are you happy now, Papa?" We stood side by side at the front counter. No one else was there except Hadie, and she was pressing shirts in the back.

"There are many kinds of happiness," he said. "We've had luck. From the bad has come the good. We've survived many things, my Lena, as a family. I *am* happy. And your mother…you and Simon are her jewels." His face looked relaxed, for a moment free of worries. His dimples appeared in his cheeks as he smiled. "Even you have survived that terrible teacher. And the future? We can only hope." He looked at me. "And you? Are you happy?"

"Yes. Even happy to be in the laundry," I laughed.

My father and I didn't discuss Uncle Maurice again. I didn't tell him how surviving my uncle was harder than surviving Miss Marshall. I decided some actions in the world could never be forgiven. My grandfather's murder and what my uncle did. I didn't know whether I would have forgiven Uncle Maurice if I had seen him again. Maybe if I'd known he had truly tried to repair his past sins, this might have been possible, but now I would never find out.

I often thought, with astonishment, how both good and evil had come from Uncle Maurice. He taught me ugly secrets. He destroyed my father's business. Yet he left us money— soiled, secret money— and this money saved us, pulled us into the future.

"Sadness and happiness are brothers," my mother had said to me. "They walk hand in hand."

My whole life so far had been laced with sadness and happiness. When we left our white wooden house in Belilovka, I never believed I'd know happiness again. But then I discovered I could draw. I met

Max. Simon and I became friends. My mother was right. Sadness and happiness did walk hand in hand. I thought about Uncle Maurice again; perhaps, on occasion, evil and goodness walked together, too.

On a breezy Saturday in April, I visited Uncle William. For all these months, I had kept the pages with the musical notations I'd found at the Diversey Avenue apartment. I put them in my wooden box beneath my bed along with my drawings and Millie Farber's letter. Once, I had brought the sheets of music to Max's house. He laid them on the piano, then tilted his head to one side, studying the small black marks on the pages. After a few minutes, he placed his hands on the keys and began to play. The music was beautiful.

I didn't tell my mother or father what I was doing. I was afraid they would forbid me from going to see Uncle William, and I wanted to give my uncle his music. Maybe the music would help him. He had saved me long ago in the wagon in the Russian forest; this was the least I could do in return.

Max walked me to the streetcar stop. "Let me come with you," he said.

"I have to see Uncle William myself. And he doesn't know you, Max. It doesn't seem right to introduce you now." I grasped Max's hand. "You won't be upset if I go without you?"

"No. I just thought you might like company. Tell your uncle that I played his music on the piano, and that it's very, very good."

Max kissed me, and then I rode the streetcar alone, clutching Uncle William's music. The hospital was in a neighborhood I'd never been to before. I got off the streetcar at the closest stop and walked five long blocks until I reached a tall iron fence with beige brick buildings behind it. This felt like a brave act, to go to this strange place myself. The buildings looked like a prison, and the land around them like a Russian forest, thick with shrubs and trees, patches of tall weeds, like the dark, damp pine forest Simon and I had once run through. Behind that fence was a separate country, a separate world.

I unlatched the gate, walked up a path, and entered the first building I came to. A stocky nurse sat at a metal desk in the entryway. She wore a drab white uniform and had short, coarse gray hair. I explained who I was and who I wanted to see. The hospital wasn't called Dunning, as my mother had said. That was the old name, the nurse informed me impatiently. This was the Chicago State Hospital, she told me. This name seemed more chilling to me.

The woman searched for my uncle's name in a thick black notebook. She frowned. "If you wish to see Mr. William Rubolsky, follow me," she said curtly.

We climbed a steep flight of cement stairs, which led to a drafty room. A torn red sofa and three wooden chairs stood in the small space. The nurse left me alone to wait. I sat on the sofa and placed the pages of music on my lap. I wanted to draw this bare, lonely place so I would remember it always, but I hadn't brought a pencil.

After a few minutes, the woman returned. Uncle William shuffled beside her, his back hunched forward, his pale face pinched into a frown. She held his hand.

"Uncle William," I said. I stood up.

He was still so terribly thin. His dark hair had turned completely white, like the clouds that hung over the lake in summer. He wore baggy, wrinkled black trousers and a white shirt that swallowed his chest and arms. I smiled at him, although I understood, with a heaviness, that this was how he would live until the end of his days—bereft from a broken heart. I winced and vowed to myself this would never happen to me.

"Oh, Lena." He sat in a chair across from me. "Is that you? Have you come to see me?"

"Yes, it's me," I said. I sat down again.

"How nice. Only your mother comes to visit me." His voice pulsed with delight. "And now you are here."

"I've missed you," I said. "Your voice."

The nurse waited at the door. A scream echoed from somewhere in the building. This was from one of the other patients, I was sure, and the sounds made me shudder.

My uncle didn't seem to notice. "It was a beautiful voice I had," he said wistfully. His hands rested limply in his lap. "I am hoping it will return."

He hummed *Ochi Chyornye*.

"I found your music," I said when he finished. "I showed it to my friend, Max. I want to return it to you."

"Music?"

"What we found in Uncle Maurice's apartment," I went on hopefully. "Your name is written on all this music." I handed him the pages.

"Maurice." He shook his head. "I shouldn't have gone away with him. You went to California, too? Such a long journey for a young girl."

"No, I didn't." I explained nothing more. "Did you know that music is a creation for the ears, just like art is a creation for the eyes?"

"This, I didn't know." He shrugged his shoulders.

"It's true, I think. Maybe you can sing this music."

"This is something I do not know about either." He sighed, and his thin chest heaved up and down. He stared vacantly at the pages. "These are not mine. These belong to someone I do not know. You must find the owner and return them. That is the right thing to do." His hands trembling, he reached to give the papers back to me.

"Do you remember when you used to sing? My friend Max played your music on the piano. He said it was very, very good. I heard it, and your music is beautiful." I had listened as Max played these songs. They were tender melodies, love songs, I imagined, written for the woman who had broken my uncle's heart.

"Then you're lucky to have such a friend. One who plays music for you."

"Yes, I wish you knew him. Maybe someday I'll introduce you."

He didn't reply.

We sat in silence for a few minutes. I didn't know what else to say. "I need to leave now," I told him. I stood up and bent to kiss my uncle's pale cheek. "Be sure they take good care of you here. Please. Goodbye, Uncle William."

"Will you come to see me again?" He clutched my hand in his

bony fingers. "And tell me when you've found the owner of these songs. I hope he will be happy to have them back."

If only I could make Uncle William become the man he used to be. I wanted him to stand in our kitchen and sing with his beautiful voice. I wanted him to sing in nightclubs and on the radio, just like he'd once hoped. I held his hand and pushed away my sadness for him. "Of course, I'll visit you again," I said.

Time had also brought a change in my luck. I hadn't decided yet if luck was just a stupid superstition or if it was something real, but I was happy for the change in my own luck. Mrs. Paulina hadn't failed me last year. I had passed seventh grade, and this year she was my teacher again. I was only in eighth grade now, still far behind where I should have been as a sixteen-year-old, but at least this was better than what Miss Marshall would have done. And this whole year at school had been a pleasure, so different from last year.

Except for Philip Schloss. He was in my class again, and he continued to taunt me, but not as often as before. Some of his friends had shunned him after the incident with the blackboard last year. Mary Hall and I had confronted him again and told him he was prejudiced and wrong. I knew we couldn't change him, but I didn't let his comments bother me so much now. I didn't think anyone could solve the problem of prejudice in the world. All you could do was fight against it, I decided, say what you believed, and hope other people would, too. And if life became too difficult or dangerous, like it had in Russia, all you could do then was leave. Philip Schloss had learned to make people into scapegoats, I thought, learned to hate. I wondered about his life and what had made him so cruel, but I didn't care enough about him to try to find out.

Time had brought a change in the world, too. Again my father read aloud articles to us from the *Chicago Tribune*. He'd stopped talking about the newspaper and the world after the laundry fire. My mother often listened now. "There will soon be a new president of America. The election is in November," my father told us at dinner one night. "We'll have to wait to see who the president will be. Mr. Coolidge will not run for office again."

Simon and I nodded. We knew this from school.

My father also said an ambitious man, Joseph Stalin, was the leader of the Union of Soviet Socialist Republics, and nothing good would come of it. And last year a man named Charles Lindbergh piloted an airplane across the ocean. "This is the most exciting news," my father said. "The President has just given Mr. Lindbergh an important medal. And now there are others piloting airplanes. One day we may all be able to fly across the ocean. We'll visit Abie and Ida then. Or they will travel here to see us."

"You are a dreamer, Chaim," my mother said. She paused. "If only this dream could come true."

The week after my visit with Uncle William, Mrs. Paulina stopped me on my way out of the classroom. I was in a hurry to meet Max, but I always enjoyed talking to her. She had been wonderfully kind to me. She had saved me last year, just as Uncle William had saved me in the Russian forest.

"Lena, I have such good news," she said. "First, I've decided to promote you this year, two grades."

"You will?" I said, thrilled. "Thank you so much."

"Yes!" She looked almost as happy as I felt. "You'll be in the second year of high school with children who are almost your age. Of course, I can't promote you until June, but I wanted to tell you now, so you wouldn't worry like you did last year. But the best news is: You've won."

"Won?" I didn't know what she was talking about.

"You've won a prize." Her voice swelled with excitement. "I submitted your drawings to the school competition in the fall. I shouldn't have done this without asking you, but I thought you might say no, so I went ahead."

"You did?"

"I still had the drawings you and your father gave me. I never returned them to you, remember? Since you won, they'll be sent to the state competition, and eventually they'll be displayed in the school here. They're excellent, Lena. Truly."

"Thank you." I didn't know what to say. I could barely think. "What should I do now?"

"Nothing. Enjoy it." She rested her hand on my arm. "I knew Miss Marshall was wrong about you. Not because you've won a prize, but because of who you are."

I threw my arms around Mrs. Paulina and hugged her. I didn't know how to thank her. She smelled of jasmine soap and chalk. I stepped back quickly, embarrassed by my rush of emotion.

She smiled. "Enjoy every moment of this."

"Oh, I will. Thank you for everything, for all you've done for me."

I ran through the hall in a daze, as if I were running through a dream, out the door, down the steps, through the schoolyard, block after block until I made my way to Bittersweet Place. I couldn't believe I'd won a prize. My drawings had always brought me such happiness. In a way, they had saved me, too.

At home, I found my mother huddled over an English grammar book at the kitchen table. I couldn't wait to tell her, to tell my father and Max. Simon, too. I might even write to Millie Farber about this, I thought. But standing in the doorway of the kitchen, I realized I was afraid to tell my mother. Afraid of her opinions, her impatience, of her anger.

She closed her book and glanced up. "So you are home after school, no wandering about today."

"Yes."

She smiled. A new softness flooded her face whenever she studied. Her books pulled her out of the past.

"Look at this, Lena," she said. "Here, another letter from Abie and Ida. Soon I will be able to read it myself." She handed me the thin white paper so I could read it aloud:

My darling family, I write in English so I do
not forget the language. We are still grateful for
your unexpected gift, Reesa. We have used the
money to buy a table, a piano, a new stove. Poland
is everything we hoped! There is air, food, God,
naches. Our life is full of blessings, except we miss
the love we left behind, we miss all of you.

Your loving brother,

Abie

"So," my mother said. "They are happy there."

"That's nice for them," I said. I gave her back the letter and sat
at the kitchen table. "But I have something to tell you. Something
wonderful." I paused and studied her upturned face. "I've won a
prize for my drawings. They were the best in the whole school, and
now they'll be sent to a state competition. Mama, can you believe
that?"

"The school? Lena. This *is* wonderful! The most wonderful." Her
voice chimed with pride, not anger at all. "I have yet to see those
drawings. Your father once showed me some, but how I've waited
for you to show me yourself. I've waited, Lena, such a long time. In
such silence."

"I'll show you now, Mama."

In my room, I dug the drawings from the wooden box, sketches
of the fire, the lake, of my father's hands, a portrait of Leah Grace. I
left Millie Farber's letter safely at the bottom. The package with the
broken glass cup and blue porcelain ballerina wrapped in pages of
the *Chicago Tribune* still lay beneath my bed, a shadow pushed to the
furthest corner.

I took the drawings and carefully placed them on the kitchen
table, as if I were sharing a secret, giving my mother something
fragile, telling her what was in my heart. What if she didn't like
them? What if she found fault?

She lifted up each drawing and studied it. "I didn't know you
could…" she said softly. "And here is Leah Grace. Just like her. That

smile. And these are your father's hands. I can see that. They are beautiful."

"Next time I'll draw a picture of you," I promised. "I'll make many drawings for you."

"I would like that so. Perhaps after all of this, you may want to study art."

"After all of *what*?" I asked. Oh, I wanted to study art, but what did she know of my struggles and problems?

"After all the lessons you have learned." She stood up. "After so many changes in our lives, the good, the bad…" She placed her hands on my shoulders and gazed into my eyes. "You are a young woman, Lena. Strong and beautiful. I didn't understand this before. But these last months and after the fire, I can see it. You are on your way to only good places, I know. May God will it for you."

"I hope so," I said, trying to calm myself. My mother understood, and she was right.

"I know this will be," she said.

She had noticed me, as if a fog had lifted around her and there I was—not the frightened girl who had fled Russia, who was bursting with wanting and shame—but the grown-up me, with all my strength and my hope.

She wrapped her arms around me and I melted into the warmth of her housedress, her skin, her big, bony body.

"Our luck is changing," she whispered. "May it always be good for you."

I lingered in her arms. I didn't want to let go.

Finally, she released me and stepped back. "You're ready to leave us. I can see."

"But I'll be back soon," I promised. I hugged her again and left the drawings on the table. As I hurried down the hallway in our apartment, I could feel her watching me. At the door, I turned. She smiled, and I smiled back. Then I bounded down the stairs and outside. The new leaves on the trees shimmered in the sunlight like a canopy of glittering golden coins, arching over the street. Max and I were going to walk along the lake in the warm April breeze. He and I had made plans for the weekend, too—to go to his house, and then visit the art museum.

As I waited for him, I thought of my mother's words, about the fire and all the changes, good and bad, that had happened these last years. Time *was* a whisper.

Max turned the corner, coming into view. He raced down Bittersweet Place, as if he were late to catch a train. Was this how the world moved—in increments of happiness? Max hurried toward me and reached for my hand. The springtime air had never smelled so sweet.

Acknowledgments

I wish to thank those who have encouraged my work. The Ragdale Foundation gave me the gift of uninterrupted time during the writing of this book. My gratitude as well to the Bread Loaf Writers' Conference, New Rivers Press, The Writers Room in Manhattan, and especially the New York Foundation for the Arts for awarding me a fellowship in Fiction.

I've been fortunate to have wonderful friends and colleagues in my life. I am deeply grateful to David Milofsky. Without his friendship and extraordinary teaching, I would still only be thinking about writing a novel.

Thank you to Walter Cummins, Donna Baeir Stein, Mary Mitchell, and Lois Winston for their unwavering support. Appreciation to Susan Malus, Eva Mekler, Anne Korkeakivi, Louise Farmer Smith, and Mina Samuels for advice and camaraderie. My thanks to Sarah Twombly, Jules Hucke, the Two Bridges Writers' Group, Margot Livesey, Anne LeClaire, Lois Nixon, and Danielle Ofri. Thank you to Martin Blaser for his support when I began to write short stories. I'm grateful to Besty Werthan, Monica Glickman, Nancy Elkind, Dale Stephenson, Frank O. Smith, S. K. Levin, Victor Brener, Stephanie Hiram, Diane Pincus, the Uslans, and Robert Roth for friendship and encouragement.

On Bittersweet Place is a work of the imagination and not a scholarly account of the 1920s, although history plays a role in the story. I have taken an occasional fictional liberty with descriptions and locations in Chicago, Russia, and Ukraine. Various sources provided me with historic information for the book: *Jewish Chicago: A Pictorial History*; *Chicago's Jewish West Side*; and *The Jews of Chicago*,

all by Irving Cutler; *The Encyclopedia of Chicago*, edited by James R. Grossman, Ann Durkin Keating, and Janice L. Reiff; *Streetwise Chicago* by Don Hayner, Tom McNamee, and John Callaway; and *Chicago Street Nomenclature* by William H. Martin. Thank you to Martha Acosta at Harold Washington Library Center, Chicago Public Library; to Johanna Russ at Special Collections, Chicago Public Library; and to Ellen Keith at the Chicago History Museum Research Center.

Immense appreciation goes to my sprawling family. They have provided me with shelter and wrapped me in warmth. My late grandparents and other relatives were persecuted in Russia and parts of Europe, left their homes, and arrived as impoverished immigrants at Ellis Island. They inspired me, and taught me about survival and building new lives. My gratitude particularly to Nancy Levine, Sol Davis, Connie Rubin, Lisa Rubin, Doris Schechter, and my cousins.

A special thank you to Steven Bauer, a gifted editor, for his superb suggestions and insights.

I am grateful to Dallas Hudgens and Lauren Cerand for their belief in my work, for their generosity, and for giving me the opportunity to transform these pages into a book.

Above all, my greatest debt of gratitude is expressed in the dedication.

4.29.14

CPSIA information can be obtained at www.ICGtesting.com
Printed in the USA
LVOW12s0104021214

416595LV00003B/190/P